ONE DOWN, SIX TO GO!

Slocum stood. "Hold it right there, mister!" he called.

The big man started at the unexpected sound, then whirled toward Slocum, the rifle muzzle coming up. Slocum fired. The .44-40 slug slammed into the big man's gut and drove him a half step backward. Slocum saw the flash from the rifle muzzle, heard the angry whack and buzz as lead hit the sandstone beside him. The slug whirred away as Slocum worked the action of the Winchester. He took a split second to be sure of his aim and drove a second shot into the big man's belly. . . . But the big man wouldn't quit.

Slocum shot him in the chest, then quickly levered a fresh round and fired again. . . .

Special Preview!

Turn to the back of this book for a sneak-peek excerpt from the exciting, brand-new Western series . . .

FURY

. . . the blazing story of a gunfighting legend.

OTHER BOOKS BY JAKE LOGAN

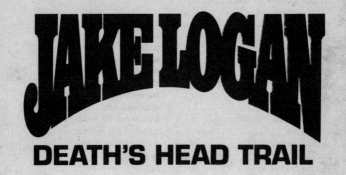

JAKE LOGAN

DEATH'S HEAD TRAIL

BERKLEY BOOKS, NEW YORK

DEATH'S HEAD TRAIL

A Berkley Book / published by arrangement with
the author

PRINTING HISTORY
Berkley edition / July 1992

ISBN: 0-425-13335-4

A BERKLEY BOOK ® TM 757,375
Berkley Books are published by The Berkley Publishing Group,
200 Madison Avenue, New York, New York 10016.
The name "BERKLEY" and the "B" logo
are trademarks belonging to Berkley Publishing Corporation.

PRINTED IN THE UNITED STATES OF AMERICA

10 9 8 7 6 5 4 3 2 1

1

Slocum eased the big Kansas-bred bay to a stop on a wind-swept knoll on the banks of Sweetwater Creek and studied the town below. It was a habit born of caution and honed in brawling frontier towns throughout the West. A man who knew what lay ahead could ride around danger or straight into it, depending on his mood and his intentions. Slocum was in no mood for trouble.

The streets of Mobeetie were crowded, as befitted a Texas Panhandle cow town growing faster than a yearling colt. Wagons of all sizes from spring buggies to big Studebaker freighters jockeyed for space along the dusty main street. Pedestrians shouldered past one other on the crude plank walks. Others lazed against porch railings or the walls of adobe, native stone, or imported lumber buildings.

The crowd was a blend of cowboys, merchants, and ranchers, with a smattering of blue-clad soldiers from Fort Elliott, which was less than a mile to the north. Here and there women battled the wind as it tried to lift skirts or turn parasols inside out. *Must be a Saturday, and after payday at that,* Slocum thought. He didn't know what day it was and didn't particularly care. Freedom was not being tied to a clock or even a calendar. The changing seasons were enough of a calendar for Slocum.

There had been a time when Slocum avoided Texas in general and Texas lawmen in particular. But now the wanted posters and flyers were gone; the governor of the state was a fair man. He had totaled up the good Slocum had done, subtracted the bad, and decided the balance was enough to justify a full pardon. Slocum was now free to ride into Texas without having to look over his shoulder for the law.

The bay between Slocum's knees snorted the dust from his nostrils and shook his head, jangling the bit. The shudder spread down the animal's neck and through the muscled body until the bay's hide shook like a wet dog slinging water from its fur. The saddle jiggled under Slocum, drawing a frown and a jerk on the reins. Slocum would put up with a lot from a horse, but that shaking was one thing that grated on him. Slocum was sure the bay knew it. The horse seemed to take some perverse delight in finding ways to aggravate Slocum. Basically, the bay was a good horse, gentle until the notion to buck got hold of him. Slocum dreaded those sessions. So far he and the horse were about even in those pitching contests.

The gelding was big—almost sixteen hands tall—and weighed a good eleven hundred pounds. He was strong as a young bull buffalo, and he had stamina. But when it came to speed, a ten-year-old Kiowa boy with a thorn in his foot could give the Kansas bay a fifty-yard head start and still catch up with him in a half mile. The horse was half Morgan, and he had feet as big as a dinner plate. Slocum had taken one look at those hooves and renamed the big beast Jugfoot. Mostly, he just called him Jug. Sometimes he called Jug by other names, but he tried not to use those names around women and children. The price had been right, though. Jug was a bonus from a Kansas cowman who needed help with a rustling problem. Slocum helped. The rustling stopped.

Slocum touched spurs to the bay's side. "Have your fun while you can, Jug," Slocum muttered, "because I'll have myself a decent horse soon."

Slocum's gaze swept the Mobeetie street as Jug trotted along, behaving himself. The saloons didn't need any signs on them. The hitchracks in front of Mobeetie's drinking establishments were crowded with cow horses. There were a lot of different brands on the ranch ponies' hips, but none was the one Slocum sought—the ES brand of Major Edward Storm.

Slocum reined the bay to a stop before the Hidetown Saloon, named for the original settlement of buffalo hunters and hiders whose camp on Sweetwater Creek eventually grew into the town of Mobeetie. Two young boys played an intense game of mumblety-peg with an oversized pocket knife on the boardwalk. One of the youths had blood on a finger. Slocum smiled to himself. He had played the game as a boy in Calhoun County, Georgia, and remembered that the sight of blood most often marked the loser. Hc had spilled a few drops of his own blood before he mastered the complexities of the knife.

He stopped alongside the boys and waited until the freckled red-haired one, a lad of about nine, had finished his turn. Slocum fished a dime from his pocket. "Would one of you gentlemen watch my horse for a few minutes?" He held the dime aloft between thumb and forefinger. "Sure would hate for someone to make off with old Jug here, or some of my equipment."

The red-haired boy's face lit up at the prospect of making a whole dime for doing not much of anything. "Sure, mister."

"Anybody touches my horse or equipment, just stick your head in the door and yell, 'Slocum.' I won't be in there long." He handed the treasure to the red-haired boy. He had picked him for the assignment because he was the one with the bloody finger.

Slocum stepped inside the saloon door, paused for a moment to let his eyes adjust from the bright sunlight outside, then strode to the bar. The Hidetown watering hole was like many Slocum had frequented in his travels. Its centerpiece was a long pine bar tended by a middle-aged man who seemed to be mostly nose and belly. A double row of bottles sat on the backbar, above which hung a painting of a nude with enormous tits. She reclined on a red couch, a knowing leer on her full lips. A long, narrow mirror filmed with tobacco and lantern smoke ran above the backbar and below the impossibly endowed woman. Card games were in progress at two of the larger tables. At one end of the bar stood a doorway curtained in red velvet drapes, obviously leading to the bedrooms where the girls of the house plied their trade. The place was crowded, considering that it was not yet noon. Later, Slocum knew, the crush of drinkers would be four deep. He decided he would try to find a less popular spot when he returned to Mobeetie tonight. He wasn't fond of crowds.

Slocum caught the bartender's attention and ordered a beer and a shot of Old Overholt. The combination cost thirty cents, but it was worth it. The beer was cool and wet, with just enough head to arouse the flavor of malt and hops. Slocum quickly downed a third of the mug, washing the trail dust from his throat.

He lowered the beer and let his gaze drift around the saloon. He saw no familiar faces, but two men caught his attention.

One was seated at a table near the bar, a tall man with dark eyes, wearing an expensive suit. A bowler hat rested on the table beside a bottle of Irish whiskey. The man in the suit stared with obvious interest at Slocum and nodded and smiled cordially when their gaze met.

The other attention-getter was a young man in range clothes fifteen feet down the bar. His main features were an obnoxiously loud voice and a Colt .45 Peacemaker in a new hand-tooled leather holster tied low on his left hip. Slocum doubted the kid was over seventeen, but he sure as hell was trying to act the man. Every few seconds he would slip his fingers around the butt of the Colt and slide it up and down in the holster. He stroked the walnut grips the way a grown man would caress a woman's thigh. Slocum fought back a touch of irritation. The kid couldn't seem to make a whole sentence without half a dozen cusswords in it. Slocum admired creative swearing, but he hated to see the art form tarnished by a rank amateur.

Slocum sipped at his whiskey and tried to ignore the kid. The liquor went down smooth and touched off a warm glow in his belly. He glanced in the backbar mirror as he lowered his glass. The kid was staring straight at him. Slocum had seen that look in other men's eyes. *Christ,* he thought, *here we go again.*

The kid moved toward Slocum, followed by two other men he hadn't noticed before. They were tough-looking men, faces lined by wind and weather. Where the kid's gun belt was new, his companions' rigs were worn from use and well oiled. Slocum knew their kind. They were shooters, and that made them dangerous men. But the kid was an unknown quantity, and that made him the bigger threat. Young men had quick reflexes—you never knew how fast they could be—and they had no concept of their own mortality, of the fact that they would die one day. That made them even more dangerous than the professionals.

The kid pushed two drinkers aside and stopped ten feet from Slocum. His two companions fanned out an arm's length apart and a step behind the youngster.

"Hey, you!"

Slocum slowly turned to face the kid. Up close, he could see the angry red pimples on the youngster's chin. "Are you talking to me?" Slocum kept his voice level and calm.

"Damn right I am. I know you, mister." The kid's fingers drummed against the grips of the Colt. "You're Slocum. A stud hoss gunfighter, I hear."

At the edge of his vision Slocum saw the two other gunmen exchange wary glances at the mention of Slocum's name.

"You got the advantage on me, son. I don't know you."

"Name's Wes Calhoun. That's a name you ought to know, Slocum."

Slocum studied the kid's face. The eyes glittered with the confidence of youth polished by a generous dollop of whiskey. "Sorry, Calhoun. No offense intended, but I never heard of you." Slocum heard the shuffle of feet and the clatter of chairs as the saloon crowd pushed away from the bar, smelling a showdown and not anxious to be caught in the line of fire.

"I killed four men."

"Congratulations," Slocum said. He deliberately turned away from the kid and picked up his shot glass with his left hand. He kept his right near his belt buckle, within quick reach of the handgun that rested against his left hip, butt forward, cross-draw style.

"Don't turn your back on me, Slocum!"

Slocum downed the last of his whiskey. "Calhoun," he said softly, "I have no quarrel with you. I just stopped off for a drink. I'm not looking for trouble."

"Well, by God, you've found it, Slocum. I'm going to take you down." Calhoun's sudden giggle was high-pitched, like that of a young girl. "Look at the stud gunfighter, boys," he said to his companions. "Don't even know how to wear a pistol. Hell, he's got the damn thing on backward!"

Calhoun's companions didn't laugh.

Slocum turned to the young gunman, fighting the cold anger that churned in his gut. He was facing a stacked deck and he knew it. Slocum was fast with a gun, but nobody could take out three men in a close-quarter shoot-out. If it came to a gunfight with these odds, Slocum knew, he was almost sure to catch some lead.

"Tell you what, Calhoun," Slocum said amiably, "why don't I just buy you a drink and we'll let it drop. Hell, you can tell your friends you backed down Slocum. No sense in anyone getting hurt."

Calhoun's eyes gleamed in brash arrogance. "You scared of me, Slocum?"

Slocum shrugged. "Smart man's always scared of somebody with a gun." *This kid's getting to be a pain in the ass,* he thought, *and it doesn't look like he's going to listen to reason.* Slocum felt the anger drain from his body. His muscles went loose and relaxed, his senses alert. He picked his targets: the kid first; the sandy-haired gunman at Calhoun's left next; then hope the third man didn't hit anything that wouldn't heal before Slocum got lead into him.

"You talk too damn much, Slocum." Calhoun flexed his knees, fingers curled above the butt of the Colt in the fancy holster. Slocum supposed the kid thought he was in a gunslinger's crouch. "You're a dead man, you son of a bitch! You just ain't fell down yet. Now, go for that gun!"

Slocum sighed. He knew there was no way out now. *Just take one at a time, Slocum,* he cautioned himself. His right hand whipped across his body, slapped around the familiar grips of his .44-40.

The kid was fast; his pistol was clear of the holster and rising before Slocum's first shot slammed into Calhoun's chest. The kid staggered back, the slug from his .45 tearing harmlessly into the bar at Slocum's side.

Slocum thumbed back the hammer at the top of the recoil, squeezed the trigger back, and swung the muzzle toward the sandy-haired man. The gunman had his pistol clear of leather, the bore coming into line, when Slocum let his thumb slip from the hammer. The soft lead .44 slug hammered into the gunman's shoulder. The impact spun him around, knocked him off balance.

Through the dense haze of gray-white powder smoke, Slocum saw himself looking at death, the round hole in the muzzle of the pistol in the third man's hand. Slocum knew his own shot would be too late, but the gunman suddenly stumbled to the side with a grunt of surprise. His shot flew wild past Slocum's head. Slocum took a partial heartbeat to center his aim and shot the man in the chest. He went down hard.

Slocum risked a quick glance toward the table a few feet away. The man in the suit held a short-barreled .38 Colt in his fist. A wisp of smoke curled from the gun.

Slocum stepped quickly toward the fallen Calhoun and kicked the pistol out of his reach. The kid's eyes were open, but already beginning to glaze. Slocum's slug had shattered his breastbone. "Jesus, I—" Calhoun coughed, spraying pink spittle, and died. The sandy-haired man slumped against the bar. His breath came in quick gasps as the red stain spread over his shirt. Slocum knew at a glance that the man was out of the fight. The third gunman twitched, a stain spread over his crotch, and his boot heels clattered against the rough pine flooring in a chittering death dance.

Slocum turned from the trio and gazed through the thick, acrid swirl of spent black powder at the man in the suit. "Much obliged, friend," he said. "That man had me dead in his sights."

The man in the suit shrugged and grinned. "My pleasure. Didn't like the odds." He waved toward a man standing against the wall. "Pete, fetch the doctor. Might as well bring the sheriff, too." The pale-faced Pete all but sprinted for the door. The man in the suit tucked the little .38 into a shoulder holster beneath his left armpit and gestured toward a chair. "Sit down, Slocum. I'll buy you a drink." He waved for the bartender to bring a fresh glass.

Slocum worked the ejector rod of his Colt, kicked the empty cartridges from the cylinder, thumbed in fresh loads, and holstered the weapon before easing himself into the chair. His ears rang from the muzzle blasts. The crowd in the saloon began to recover from the shock of the quick battle. A low mutter started, grew louder as the drinkers and gamblers gathered around the two dead men, already rehashing the fight. Two cowboys eased the moaning, half conscious sandy-haired man into a chair.

The man in the suit offered a hand. "Name's Houston," he said. "Temple Houston. District attorney in this neck of the woods."

Slocum took Houston's hand. The grip was dry and firm. "Reckon I owe you one, Mr. Houston," he said.

Houston chuckled. "You don't owe me a thing, Slocum. Those three have been nothing but trouble around here." He took the new glass from the trembling bartender and poured a shot for Slocum. "Damn fine shooting," Houston said. "I reckon you're as good as they say you are."

Slocum studied Temple Houston's face for a moment. The man bore a strong resemblance to his father, the man most people considered the savior of the state of Texas. Young Houston had intense dark eyes that held a hint of laughter, a thick shock of curly brown hair, a strong jaw, and high cheekbones.

Slocum sipped at his drink. "I wish to hell nobody knew about me, Mr. Houston. It seems everywhere I go there's some kid who wants to take a pop at me. Plays hell with a man's nervous system."

"Goes with the reputation, Mr. Slocum," Houston said. "Some youngster's always trying to make a name." He sighed. "I know. Been there a few times myself. Not easy being the son of a legend. I've been trying to move out of Dad's shadow for years. Had to learn to use a handgun to protect myself a long time ago. Now the kids look at me and see a man with his own rep as a gunhand. Complicates life considerably."

Slocum nodded. He liked the tall and slender Temple Houston, and felt a kinship with him. The kinship of the gun. It was a powerful tie.

The conversation stopped for a moment as two men strode into the saloon. One was a short, slender man with flowing handlebar mustache and beard. A badge was pinned on his shirt and he carried a Smith & Wesson .44 New American in a worn gun belt which rode high on his right hip. The other was of medium height with half-moon spectacles perched on a narrow nose. He carried a black bag in hands that seemed overly large for his frame.

"The one with the badge is Sheriff G. W. Arrington," Houston said. "Good man. Also, a good man not to fool around with. He hollers 'frog,' people jump. Other one's Dr. Emil Crabtree. We're lucky to have him. Educated back East. Top-flight surgeon and good all around doctor. His specialty is gunshot wounds. Didn't start out that way, but he specialized quick out here. Folks say Doc Crabtree can cure the warts off a toad."

Slocum watched the two men work. It took only a few minutes to see they were good at their respective jobs.

"I suppose Arrington will want a word with me," Slocum said. The sheriff was talking with a group of excited saloon customers. Slocum idly wondered how many different versions of the gunfight Arrington would hear in the next twenty minutes.

Temple Houston shrugged, nonchalant. "When he's ready. Arrington's a fair man. He's not jail-happy. And," Houston added with a grin, "you do have a fairly reputable witness to back your story—the district attorney. There'll have to be an inquest, a formality. You did everything you could to avoid trouble."

Slocum sighed. "I should have just walked out."

"And Wes Calhoun might very well have shot you in the back." Houston raised his glass and peered over the rim at Slocum. "You just passing through?" There was no challenge in the question, just honest curiosity.

Slocum nodded. "Looking to buy some horses. Saw a story in the Dodge City paper that Major Edward Storm was breeding some of those spotted Nez Percé ponies. Always been partial to them, but they're not easy to find. Thought I'd drop in on the major and see if he'd part with a couple of good ones. Stopped off here for a drink and directions to the ES outfit." He sighed. "Looks like now I should have stopped someplace else."

Houston poured two more drinks. "What's done is done. Can't change that." He leaned back in his chair. "When you leave here, Mr. Slocum," he said, "follow the main street to the west end. There's a wagon road leads off to the south. Follow it three miles, you'll come across a fork. Take the west fork road. The major's place is two miles up that road. Can't miss it. You serve with Storm in the war?"

"We were in the same outfit for a time. Jackson's Brigade. Storm was a lieutenant when the Shenandoah Campaign started, made brevet major at Second Manassas. We went separate ways after that."

Houston nodded. "Heard you wound up with Quantrill."

"Everybody's done something in his life he's not too proud of, Mr. Houston," Slocum said.

Arrington appeared at Houston's side, his steady gaze locked on Slocum's face. "Want to tell me what happened here, gents?"

The sheriff nodded as Slocum finished his account of the fight and Houston backed up his story. "I'll need a statement from you, Slocum. Inquest'll be tonight, after supper, Judge Frank Willis's place. That'll give you time to go buy your horses." Arrington didn't wait for a reply. He turned on a heel and strode for the door.

Slocum pushed back his chair and stood. "Sounds like I best get on with my business. Thanks again, Mr. Houston."

"De nada." Houston returned Slocum's handshake. "One more thing, Slocum. I'd watch my back if I were you. That kid was Silas Calhoun's youngest. The dead one is the kid's cousin and the wounded man is Silas's top hand. Old Silas is going to be as pissed as a stepped-on rattler. And he's got some good guns on his payroll."

Slocum sighed. "Dammit, why do the young ones always have fifteen relatives? Once in a while you'd think one of these fool kids would be an only child. See you at the inquest."

Slocum strode from the saloon, nodded his thanks to the the red-haired boy for watching his horse, and swung into the saddle. He stopped at the livery and paid in advance for a stall for Jug for the night, then at the Grand Central Hotel to book a room for himself.

The southwest wind was hotter and stronger as he reined Jug toward the wagon road at the end of town. It was going to be a sweaty ride to the ES outfit.

2

Major Edward Storm lowered the Winchester and let a wide grin crease his weathered face as the man on the big bay rode into the front yard of the ES Ranch.

"Well, I'll be double damned for a pregnant possum," Storm said as he propped the rifle against a support post and stepped from the broad front porch. "Slocum. Of all the whirlwinds that whip down this valley, you're about the last piece of Confederate trash I expected to blow in."

Slocum stepped from the saddle, his own grin wide enough to make his jaws ache. "Major, you sully the fine name of the South," he said. "Such an affront must be settled on the field of honor. I suggest whiskies at two paces. Preferably your whiskey."

Storm took Slocum's hand in a grip that seemed strong enough to crush a billiard ball. "Challenge accepted, Captain. God, Slocum, it's good to see you again. We heard you got killed. Several times."

Slocum chuckled. "Good rebel takes a lot of killing before it finally sticks, Ed."

"Don't I know it. We had some close calls, you and I." Storm released Slocum's hand. "Bring that oversized plow horse around to the corrals and we'll get some water in him." Storm stepped back onto the porch and retrieved his Winchester. The rifle was a big bore model, probably a .45-90 Express, Slocum thought. Storm's gaze continually swept the horizon as they walked to the pens behind the house.

11

Slocum nodded toward the Winchester. "What's with the heavy artillery?"

The smile faded from Storm's face. His jaw tightened. "Ounce of prevention. Line rider from the RO outfit came by a few days ago. Said they'd lost fifteen head of horses. Diamond F lost ten. Looks like we've got some horse thieves around. Rumor is that a couple of Blue McCorley's gang showed up in Tascosa a week or so back."

Slocum's eyes narrowed as he led Jug through the corral gate. "I've heard of McCorley," he said. "Tough bunch. Mostly Jayhawkers, according to the stories I picked up. They'd as soon kill a man as look at him." He stripped the saddle from Jug, laid the blanket on a fence rail to dry, and let the big bay drink.

"That's for damn sure," Storm said. "At least Blue McCorley won't be hard to spot. Picked up the name Blue when a point-blank pistol shot peppered the side of his face with gunpowder. Left a blue-black mark on his jaw that he'll wear to the grave. If there's any justice, that'll be damn soon."

"Maybe they've already got what they wanted and moved on," Slocum said.

"Maybes don't keep the coyote out of the henhouse. I worked damned hard to build this place. I don't intend to lose it now." Storm's smile abruptly returned. "My dugout awaits. Come in and meet the family."

"My pleasure, Major." Slocum glanced around as they strode back toward the house. Edward Storm had done well. The ES Ranch nestled in a broad valley watered by a spring-fed stream. Sleek, fat horses grazed in the rich green grass, obviously blooded stock from Tennessee and Kentucky. Foals a few weeks old ran, bucked, and kicked at each other in some game older than man. The sport toned young muscles and sharpened reflexes. On the far slopes of the valley a few cattle grazed. The cows looked to be mostly red Shorthorns, the bulls mulitcolored Texas Longhorns.

The house was part native stone, topped by shiplap framing of sturdy hardwood planks that must have cost a small fortune, Slocum thought. Good lumber was all but unheard of in the Texas Panhandle. It had to be hauled by rail to Dodge City or Fort Worth and then freighted into the plains, where only a smattering of cottonwoods or elms along rivers and springs broke the treeless expanse of horizon. A wooden windmill stood beside the house, its blades whirling in the stiff breeze as it pulled sweet water from beneath the valley floor. The barn was expansive, well built, and flanked by corrals made of cedar posts and cottonwood logs as thick as a man's leg.

"Nice place, Ed," Slocum said, making no attempt to hide the admiration in his voice.

"Lot of work, but worth it," Ed said as he held the door open. "Hey, girl," he called, "we got a visitor. Lock the chicken coop and hide the whiskey."

Slocum laughed aloud and shook his head. On the field of battle, there was no man more serious than Major Edward Storm. But when the firing stopped, his natural bent toward joshing bubbled over before the echoes faded. And he was fair about it; Ed Storm would joke with a general or a private, often with both at the same time. Sometimes it pissed off the generals. Storm didn't care. The privates loved it, and they were the ones who did the fighting. It was accepted among his peers and his men that as long as Major Storm was cracking jokes about you or with you, all was well. When he ignored you or leveled that hard stare from those pale blue eyes in your direction, it was best to hunt a hole and not come out for a spell.

They were an unlikely pair, Slocum realized. The two former Confederate officers were outwardly opposites: Slocum was six foot one, with jet black hair and green eyes, built lean and quick like a mountain lion; Storm had the stocky, compact build of a badger, blue eyes, brown hair tending now toward gray at the temples, but he still had the erect and confident stance of a man accustomed to being in command. When push came to shove, though, neither man took a step back.

A lot of men who had tried to push had wound up as worm food over the years.

Slocum's musings ended when a tall, stately woman stepped into the room. She must have been in her forties, Slocum thought, but she had the slender, shapely form of a woman half her age. Blond hair tied back into a ponytail framed a pleasant face with gentle brown eyes. Slocum raised his already high opinion of Ed Storm another notch. The major could pick women as well as he picked horses.

"Eva, meet Slocum," Storm said with a wink in Slocum's direction. "Watch out for him, honey. He's a heller with the ladies."

Slocum felt his face flush. Eva Storm's smile was soft, but the hand she offered hinted at a solid strength. "A pleasure to meet you, Mr. Slocum," she said. "Ed's mentioned your name a number of times. Can I get you some coffee? Or something to eat?"

"We'll have something with a bit more bite to it," Storm said. "Would you please fetch that special bottle of prime old Kentucky bourbon from the cabinet?" He toed a couple of chairs from the dining room table as Eva strode from the room. "Wonderful woman," Storm said, a genuine tenderness in his tone. "How in the hell she tolerates an old soldier like me, I'll never understand." He sighed. "I'm a lucky man, Slocum."

"Major," Slocum said, "you've always had a disgusting habit of being right. It looks to me like you've done it again."

The two men expressed their thanks as Eva brought the bottle and two glasses, then retreated to the kitchen. Slocum raised his glass in response to Storm's silent toast and sipped at the bourbon. It was the best whiskey he had tasted in months.

Ed Storm sighed in appreciation and licked his lips. "So, Slocum. Is this a social call, or can I help you with something?"

"Bit of both, Ed. I understand you're raising some of those spotted Nez Percé ponies. Thought I'd see if I could buy one or two."

"I have a few. Interesting mounts. Mountain horses, sure-footed as a goat. Lots of bottom. They'll go two days on a cup of water and half a biscuit. Pretty to look at, too." He paused for another sip of whiskey. "I bought a seed herd up in Oregon a while back. Mostly I breed Kentucky and Tennessee racing stock. Cross the best ones on native mustangs to get good cow ponies. Cowboys don't care much for the spotted horses; not much cow sense bred into them."

Storm paused to fish a battered pipe from his pocket. "The Nez Percé ponies bring a good price from men who want a good trail horse. The grandees over in Santa Fe who want to look sharp and shiny on horseback will pay most any price for one of them." He finished stuffing the pipe from a sack in his pocket, fired a match, and puffed up a cloud of bluish smoke. "They're also big with the money men from back East and from Europe who are buying up some big ranches around here," Storm said. "Those greenhorns like to look good, even if they don't know their butts from a branding iron when it comes to range cattle."

The major refilled their glasses and grinned at Slocum. "From the looks of that big-footed beast you rode in on, I'd say you need a good trail horse. That one Montana bred?"

"Kansas. Probably Montana stock," Slocum said. "Ed, I've got a little over a hundred dollars in gold. I trust you not to horse-trade me out of all of it."

Storm nodded. "I won't skin you too bad, Slocum. I'll just take a couple of layers of hide. The spotted stock's on the south end of the ranch. We'll scout them out in an hour or so when Elaine and Martinez get back. They're putting some miles on a couple of broncs for me right now."

"Elaine?"

"My niece. Top hand with young horses. Martinez is my one and only hired hand, an old vaquero who speaks horse better than most Mexicans speak Spanish. Martinez and I take the rough edges off the young stock, then Elaine puts the polish on them for us. And she can shine one up pretty good in a hurry." Storm's tone reflected a solid pride in his niece's ability with horses. "Elaine's folks both died when she was just a baby. She doesn't have any other relatives, so she's lived most of her life with us. Eva and I never had any children of our own, unfortunately, but Elaine's been like a daughter to us."

Slocum wasn't prepared for Elaine Storm.

He had been expecting a tomboy type, a gangly young girl with freckles on her nose and hair in pigtails. What he found was a young woman just beginning to blossom.

Elaine was fifteen, with dark brown, shoulder-length hair that moved in the breeze like shimmering silk. Her deep blue eyes flecked with gold were set in an oval face with high cheekbones and there was a quick, contagious smile on startlingly full and sensual lips.

At first glance she seemed tiny, almost fragile. She stood barely five foot one in her riding boots. But a second look showed her to be anything but frail, and she wasn't all that small—in the right places, at least. She wore a plain man's style shirt, damp with the perspiration of hard riding on a hot afternoon. Levi's soiled with dust and streaked by horse sweat hugged a narrow waist and emphasized firm buttocks beginning to fill out in her rapid growth into womanhood. Her hands were slender, but with the small white scars and knuckle scrapes that marked any person who worked with horses, and the way she held the reins and sat a horse hinted at a strength and confidence beyond her physical size and her years.

Elaine rode at Slocum's right, the wind molding her sweat-damp shirt to the swell of surprisingly full and high, firm breasts. She was, Slocum thought, one of the most beautiful young girls he had ever seen. *Some lucky young stud's going to find a diamond one of these days,* Slocum thought. *Give her a couple of years and every man in the Panhandle will be trying to snort in her flanks.* Slocum felt a twinge of jealousy and even resentment toward that young man. It was a feeling that caught him by surprise. He had had girls barely Elaine's age—maybe even younger, for all he knew—but they were women in girls' bodies, wise beyond their years in the ways of the world, and tough. They plied their trade in the back rooms of bars and bawdy houses from Montana to the Rio Grande.

Elaine was a girl in a woman's body, and Slocum tried hard to keep from staring at her. She seemed trusting and vulnerable, open in her friendliness, unaware of the tension she triggered in a man's Levi's. The feeling brought a flush to Slocum's face, and he was a man who took a lot of embarrassing. In a way he couldn't explain he felt a strong protective urge toward the girl. He now understood the tender look in Edward Storm's eyes and the soft tone of his voice when he spoke to Elaine. It was obvious that the major saw the girl not as a niece, but as the daughter he'd never sired.

Her gentle nature also showed in the way she handled the young horse between her knees. She had a firm but affectionate touch, praised the sorrel gelding's good moves with a pat on the neck, and punished misbehavior with little more than a sharp word and an occasional quick yank on the hackamore reins. The sorrel seemed eager to please and was learning fast at her hands. Slocum considered himself adequate as a horseman, but soon conceded he was no match for the girl in that respect.

"There they are," Elaine said. She pointed toward a grove of cottonwoods along the winding creek.

Slocum's interest abruptly shifted from the girl as he studied the horses standing in the shade of the trees, head to rump so that the swish of one's tail brushed the flies from the other one's head. Storm had chosen his breeding herd well. The colorful horses with the speckled hindquarters were the equal of any Slocum had seen in his travels through the Northwest.

An hour later Slocum was in the horse business. He had selected a three-year-old mare, a flashy yearling stud colt that moved with the natural quickness and grace of a good athlete, and a gelding for a saddle horse.

Storm was true to his word. There wasn't a lot of the usual horse-trading bullshit that Slocum hated involved in the deal, and the price was fair. The three horses cost Slocum one hundred ten dollars. That left him just enough cash to get back to Dodge if he watched his expenses.

Slocum and the major closed the deal with a handshake. "The gelding's gentle enough, Slocum," Storm said, "but the mare and young stud aren't broke to halter. If you'd like, Martinez and Elaine can work with them a little tonight. You'll stay for supper and spend the night with us."

Slocum shook his head in regret. "Sorry, Ed. I do appreciate your offer, and I'd enjoy the company." He glanced at the sun halfway along its slide to the western horizon. "But I've got to get back to Mobeetie. Had a little trouble in town this morning and need to finish cleaning it up. I can ride out and pick them up tomorrow."

Ed Storm didn't push for details. He merely nodded, knowing that Slocum would have volunteered any information he thought important. "No problem," he said. "In fact, Elaine and I will bring them into town for you. I've some other business I've been putting off there. We'll have the horses to you by nine o'clock at the latest."

Elaine and Slocum reined in behind the Nez Percé ponies, edging them toward the ranch. The major rode point, leading the small band. The horses followed his mount without trying to break and run.

Martinez, a short, bandy-legged vaquero with a pistol in his worn leather holster and a Winchester in hand, swung the gate open as they edged the horses into the corral. Ed Storm had left Martinez behind with Eva. The major made it a point, he had told Slocum, never to leave the women without an armed escort as long as there were rumors of bandits about. Especially if the rumors mentioned Blue McCorley.

Elaine slipped the tie-down thong from her Manila hemp catch rope and dismounted. "Might as well get started now," she said. "I'll try to have them broken to halter by sundown."

Slocum watched in silent admiration as Elaine shook out a loop, waited until the yearling milled to the edge of the band, then whipped her rope in a backhand figure eight. Slocum had seldom seen such a smooth execution of the catch the Texans called the "hoolihan." The loop settled gently about the colt's neck. The colt fought the noose for a moment, then settled down to face Elaine, snorting and wide-eyed with fear. Slocum glanced at the major and saw the look of admiration in Storm's eyes.

"Well, Slocum," the major said, "we might as well leave them alone. With Elaine and Martinez working the horses, we'd just be in the way."

Slocum reached in his pocket and produced the small sack which held his gold coins.

The major waved a hand. "Pay me on delivery," he said.

Slocum counted out a hundred and ten dollars, then grinned at Ed Storm. "Major, you better take it now," he said. "Mobeetie looks to be a town that could eat a man's poke fast. If I don't have it, I won't waste it on"— he caught himself before he said the word "whores," in case Elaine were still in hearing distance— "things I need less than horses," he finished lamely.

Storm chuckled. "I understand, Slocum." He pocketed the coins. Slocum swung back aboard Jug, leaned down, and offered a hand to the major.

"See you in Mobeetie tomorrow morning, Captain Slocum," Storm said.

Slocum reined the horse toward town. He glanced over his shoulder once. Elaine Storm had already slipped a hackamore over the colt's head. "By sundown, Jug," he said aloud to the big horse under him, "that colt will be leading like he was born in a hackamore." He lifted his gaze and glanced briefly at the sun, then nudged Jug into a steady trot. "We best get a move on. Don't want to keep an inquest waiting."

• • •

Slocum leaned against the bar of the cantina in Mobeetie's Mexican section, nursing a shot of passable whiskey and twirling a cigarillo in his fingers. His belly was comfortably stuffed with a supper of steak, fried potatoes, beans, hot biscuits, and gravy, and he was at peace.

The inquest had been, as Temple Houston predicted, a formality. Justifiable homicide in defense of life, the judge ruled. Slocum had Jug rubbed down, watered, and grained at the livery, and all he had to do now was settle into his room at the Grand Central Hotel and wait for his horses to be delivered tomorrow morning.

He felt a hand on his forearm and turned to face the woman who had stepped to his side. She was dark-skinned with shining brown eyes, her long black hair swept over one shoulder and tied in place with a red ribbon. She had the seductive, lithe carriage that many young Mexican women possessed before too many babies and too many tortillas caught up with them in later years. Her blue dress was cut low, and as she leaned against him Slocum saw the swell of a full breast tipped by an erect nipple. The glimpse of smooth dark skin set Slocum's loins glowing again.

"Eh, señor," the woman said, letting a firm hip rest against his, "you one *muy hombre.* For you I have much, a fine time. Only five dollars American."

Slocum smiled at the Mexican prostitute. She was one damn fine looking woman. He shook his head reluctantly. He had no extra money to spend on pleasures of the flesh tonight. "Sorry, señorita. Nothing personal, you understand. It's just that I'm a little short of cash." He patted her on the arm. Even whores needed a softening of rejection. "But tonight I will dream of you and wish that you were with me. Perhaps another time?"

She pushed a soft breast against his arm. "Another time." She glanced toward the stocky bartender, then back at Slocum. The bridge of her nose wrinkled as she smiled. "And then perhaps my patron Juan will not be here. Then for you it will be free. I think maybe you show a girl a better time than she show you."

Slocum watched as the woman strode away, full hips swaying beneath the gown, and sighed. *Good thing I already paid for the horses,* he thought; *that was one hot woman. Might just be worth riding hungry for a night with her.*

He finished his drink and strode from the bar before he changed his mind. He stood outside the cantina, breathing deep of the cool air. It always surprised Slocum how much the temperature dropped when the sun went down in the Texas Panhandle. He stared for a moment in the direction of the ES Ranch. By tomorrow afternoon, he would be on his way back to Dodge. A week from now he'd be riding toward the Rockies. He could almost smell the pines and hear the rustle of the aspens now.

3

Slocum leaned against the wall of the Grand Central Hotel and fought a losing battle with the feeling that something was wrong.

He had learned not to ignore that feeling. It was hard to define—a tingle on the hairs of his forearms, a slight twitch in the gut—and in the past it had saved his hide on the battlefields of war or in the dusty streets of some small frontier town in the middle of nowhere.

He studied the shortening shadow of the hitchrack. It told him the hour was nearing eleven. And it kept reminding him that Ed and Elaine Storm were two hours overdue with the horses. He had never known Major Ed Storm to be late for anything, whether it be battle, bottle, or brothel.

The worm in his gut tied itself in another knot. Slocum stared off toward the southwest, the Panhandle wind pushing stronger against his hat brim as it gained strength. There was no sign of movement along the wagon road which led to the ES Ranch except a solitary dust devil that kicked its narrow column of sand across the horizon.

Slocum muttered a tight curse, lifted his bedroll and saddlebags from the boardwalk beside him, and strode to the stable. He saddled the big bay, mounted, and set off at a steady trot toward the ranch. He fought down the impulse to put the spurs to Jug; a man on a worn-out horse was less than useless if any trouble was afoot.

The miles passed slowly and the knot in Slocum's gut grew

tighter. He slipped the .44-40 Winchester from its saddle boot and checked the loads, his gaze sweeping the landscape for signs of life. He saw nothing. And that wasn't good. His senses sharpened with each stride of the Kansas bay's hooves. A jackrabbit burst from the shade of a flowering bush cactus, startling Jug. Slocum had the rifle halfway to his shoulder before he realized the sudden movement was no threat. A meadowlark's five-note song pierced the windswept air as Slocum reined onto the road leading to the Storm place.

A mile farther Slocum abruptly pulled the bay to a halt and stared toward the low, ghostly gray smudge against the green hills of the valley. He blinked his eyes, hoping it was some kind of illusion, a trick of wind and heat waves. His heart sank as he realized the wisp for what it was.

Smoke.

And above the smoke, buzzards soared in lazy circles against the cloudless blue sky.

Slocum touched the spurs to Jug's ribs and covered the final mile in a high lope, his thumb hooked around the hammer of the Winchester.

He yanked the horse to a sliding stop in the front yard of the Storm ranch, the taste of bile bitter in the back of his throat. The remnants of the barn smoldered behind the main house. Charred streaks of blistered framing and scorched paint left obscene traces along one side of the house where the flames had tried and failed to find a foothold.

Major Edward Storm lay facedown in the yard just outside the door. His right temple was blown away, blood and brains spattered in a fan-shaped pattern in the dust. A large-caliber rifle bullet had struck him over the left ear; four more rounds had slammed into his body at point-blank range. The major's gun belt and rifle were missing.

Grief and dread slammed a painful fist into Slocum's belly as he swung down from the saddle. He sprinted to the side of the open door and stopped. He flattened his body against the side of the building, rifle at the ready.

"Eva? Elaine? Martinez?"

His call brought no response.

Slocum crouched and hurled himself through the doorway, rolled over a shoulder to come to his feet in a crouch, the muzzle of the rifle sweeping the living room. He found no targets. The acrid scent of scorched wood and the coppery smell of blood bit into his nostrils.

"Eva! Elaine!"

Still no response. The doorway to a bedroom stood ajar at his left. Slocum toed the door open.

Eva Storm's body lay across the bed. Slocum almost heaved his breakfast as he stared at what had once been a beautiful blond woman. Eva's dress had been ripped away. Blood and froth flecked the silky hair at her crotch. The skin of her breasts had been peeled away, stripped as if for pelting. Blood soaked the rumpled sheets beneath her mutilated torso. Slocum stood in sickened shock and stared at the carnage for several heartbeats before he noticed the round hole in her temple. The bullet wound had bled little. Eva Storm had suffered the torments of multiple agony. She probably had died before that slug hit her head.

Slocum was about to turn away when the glint of sunlight on metal caught his eye. He knelt beside the bed. His fingers touched metal. He lifted a little .32-caliber rimfire derringer, wiped a smear of blood from the grip and broke the action. The upper barrel had been fired. *At least she didn't go without a fight,* Slocum thought; *maybe she got a slug into one of them.* He slipped the double-barreled weapon under his belt and staggered from the room, stunned by the savagery. *Even a goddamn renegade Comanche wouldn't do that to a woman. Elaine—Christ, where is Elaine?*

Slocum searched the other rooms, afraid of what he might find. The rest of the house was empty except for the wreckage left by the raiders. Bureau drawers stood open, their contents dumped onto the floor. The major's desk had been rifled; a cash box lay empty amid a clutter of papers. The gun rack on the wall was stripped of weapons and ammunition. There was no sign of Elaine.

Slocum sprinted from the house toward the charred wreckage of the barn. The corrals were empty, rails down, all the horses gone. If Elaine had been in the barn—

He skidded to an abrupt stop as he glanced toward the small outhouse, its walls riddled by bullet holes. A worn boot protruded from the door. The boot moved.

Slocum sprinted to the outhouse and yanked the door open. Martinez sat on the floor, his head resting against the platform of the two-holer. Blood from half a dozen bullet wounds covered his body. The Mexican's eyes were closed. Slocum heard the vaquero's soft moan.

"Martinez?" He knelt beside the bullet-wracked body. The man's eyes fluttered open. Slocum saw at a glance the man was near death. "It's Slocum, Martinez. The horse buyer. What happened?"

"They—" Martinez coughed at the effort of talking. Spittle bubbled at the corners of his mouth. "They come at—at sunup. Eight, maybe ten—men. One with—blue face. Tried to fight—no chance. Too many—too quick. They took the girl." Martinez's fingers crabbed weakly at Slocum's arm. "Follow them—get Elaine—before—" Martinez's hand dropped away.

"I'll get her back, Martinez. Count on it."

The Mexican nodded weakly and coughed again. His head fell to the side, eyes glazed in death.

Slocum knelt at Martinez's side a moment longer, the pain of loss gradually giving way to outrage and the heat of growing fury. He slammed a fist into the outhouse wall in frustration. The impact seemed to partly ease the ache in his chest. He stood, let the rage in his gut feed on itself until it consumed his whole body. *The man with the blue face. McCorley.* Slocum felt the trembling, white-hot rage slowly fade until an icy calm relaxed his muscles. *You're a dead man, McCorley,* he silently vowed, *and I don't give an unholy damn how many men you've got. And if you've harmed that girl, you've never seen a Comanche at work until I get hold of you—*

Slocum stepped from the outhouse, pushed Martinez's foot inside, closed the door, and dropped the latch into place. He strode to the house, picked up Major Storm's body and carried it inside. He didn't look at Eva Storm again. Slocum closed and secured the doors and windows. At least the coyotes and buzzards couldn't get at them now.

He stepped outside and drew a deep breath, trying to cleanse the stench of blood and death from his nostrils. He pulled a cigarillo from his shirt pocket and fired the smoke as he calculated his tactics. McCorley and his bunch had better than a half-day start. Horses naturally trailed at a faster clip than cattle, so they would be miles away by now. He was outgunned at least eight to one, maybe more. He had few traveling supplies, but did have a hundred rounds of .44-40 ammunition, a spare pistol in his bedroll, and one hell of a mad on. It didn't even the odds, but it was a start.

He swung aboard the bay and made a slow circle of the ranch house. The tracks were easy to find. Blue McCorley's raiders had butchered three people, ransacked the house, and then taken Ed Storm's entire herd of horses—about fifty head, according to the signs. The trail led northwest from the ranch toward the rugged Canadian River breaks a day's ride away.

Slocum nudged Jug into an easy lope along the trail left by the bandits and the stolen stock. It would be simple to follow. Fifty horses left a lot of tracks. McCorley did have one thing slowing him down. He had taken Storm's breeding stallions along, and moving a herd of mixed mares, geldings, and foals, with two studs along, while riding strange horses, was a big order. The studs would fight anything—including each other—that threatened their harems. They would cause all sorts of headaches for the rustlers until they finally settled down.

After a mile he pulled the bay to a walk. He would lope a mile, then walk two, so that he could close steadily on the gang without killing his horse in the process. Slocum knew he wasn't likely to catch McCorley before sunset. He tried not to think what might happen to Elaine, but the vision of Eva Storm's mutilated body was burned into his brain. Slocum could only hope he could catch up with them in time. *One thing's for damn sure,* he promised himself; *the man who used that knife on Eva Storm is going to be a long time dying.*

"You've got to hang on, Elaine," he muttered aloud. "Stay alive, no matter what they do to you. The bastards will pay, I promise you."

Elaine Storm huddled in a corner of the small tent and battled to hold back the tears. *They won't see me cry, damn them,* she vowed silently. *They won't see me cry.*

She struggled against the ropes that bound her wrists and ankles. The bonds held firm. She had lost the feeling in her hands as the tight bindings cut into her wrists. It seemed that the more she struggled, the tighter the ropes became.

Elaine stopped fighting her bonds for a moment to rest tired arms and shoulders. She tried to force back the images that swirled in her brain: the sudden attack, the rattle of gunfire, Eva Storm's screams of agony. Her own near escape. But she had been unable to reach the horses, and the big man with the blue mark on his face had run her down barely fifty yards from the house.

The long ride from home to here was a blur in her memory, filled with shock and raw terror. She had emerged from the daze a couple of hours before the raiders turned the stolen horses into this small box canyon a mile from the river. Elaine knew the canyon well. It had been one of Ed's favorite hunting spots. There was one way in and one way out for a horseman. She knew her only hope of escape was to somehow slip her bonds, clamber afoot up one of the deer trails that wound along the sheer canyon walls, and find a hiding place.

She lay still, gathering her strength, and listened to the voices outside. Occasionally she caught a glimpse of the main camp as the tent flap fluttered open in the wind. It was nearly sundown. The outlaws were laughing and joking, passing around bottles taken from Ed's liquor cabinet. Elaine knew her time for escape was rapidly running out.

When she had finally emerged from her trance of stunned disbelief into the harsh light of reality, Elaine concentrated on learning the faces of the men responsible, names to go with the faces when mentioned, the horses they rode. If and when she escaped, she could give names and descriptions. Then she would watch and laugh aloud as these men were hanged one by one or shot down like the mad dogs they were.

She resumed her futile struggle against the ropes. Elaine knew what lay ahead for her. A girl didn't grow up on a horse ranch around stallions and mares and not know why these men had bothered to keep her alive.

The high-pitched, almost girlish giggle of the tall, thin man the others called Arkansas triggered a fresh wave of despair in Elaine. She could see him through the slit of the tent flap. He held the skin he had carved from Eva's breasts close to his narrow-set eyes. "Make a couple damn fine tobacco pouches, man cures 'em out right," he said. "Ever time I has myself a smoke, I'll remember them tits and that blonde bitch who shot old Smokey with that little popgun." Arkansas giggled again. "Smokey, you don't look so good. Hell, that ain't nothin' but a little derringer slug in your shoulder." He pulled a long, thin-bladed knife from his belt. "Be glad to dig her out for you, Smokey."

The broad-shouldered and bearded man called Smokey sat with his back to the tent, hunched over in pain, his left arm in a dirty sling. "Go fuck yourself, Arkansas."

The man with the knife giggled again and rose to his feet. "Hell, I know where there's somethin' better'n that," he said, staring toward the tent.

"Sit down, damn your soul!" The low, rumbling voice of the man called Blue cut through the mutter of drunken conversation. "I got first call on that filly. Nobody touches her until I'm finished. And, by God, I might as well get started. Been gettin' me a hard-on since I grabbed her the first time."

The words sent a shudder through Elaine's body, the cold icy grip of dread and despair. She struggled harder against the ropes.

She heard footsteps approach. The tent flap whipped aside and Blue McCorley squatted in the opening. His leering grin exposed chipped teeth stained yellow-brown by tobacco juice. The blue mark slashed across a third of his stubbled face from cheekbone to earlobe. He held a blanket under one arm.

"Well, hello there, sweet thing," McCorley said, his tone mocking. "Keepin' it warm for old Blue, are you?"

Elaine made no reply. All hope of escape drained from her, leaving only an aching emptiness. She made up her mind. This man would see no emotion from her. No tears, no whimpers. *Let him take you,* she told herself, *but don't give him the pleasure of showing fear or hate. Then one day you can kill the bastard. If you live.*

McCorley stripped off his gun belt and put it beside the tent flap, then tossed the soiled blanket into the tent. The man's rank, unwashed scent quickly filled the small space. Elaine fought back the urge to vomit at the smell. "Our marriage bed, sweetie," McCorley said. "Now, let's see what you've got to offer old Blue."

McCorley pulled a folding knife from his pocket, leaned over Elaine, and sliced the ropes from her wrists. She almost choked at the vile touch of the man's hands against her skin, the sight of the bulge in the crotch of his dirty trousers. McCorley grabbed her shirt, the knife still in his fist, and yanked. The cloth parted with a quick, rasping tear. McCorley's breathing quickened as he stared for a few heartbeats at Elaine's exposed breasts, his lips pursed in a soundless whistle.

"Damn fine tits for such a young filly," McCorley said. He ran a callused palm over Elaine's left breast. His thumb and forefinger closed over her nipple, then brutally pinched and twisted the tender flesh. Elaine almost gasped aloud at the quick stab of pain. "Fight me, you little bitch, and I'll twist 'em smooth off." McCorley's breath came in rapid gasps now. He cut the ropes from her ankles and yanked off her boots. Then Elaine felt the cold touch of the knife blade against her waist, heard the rip as the keen edge sliced through her belt and the heavy denim of her Levi's.

McCorley stripped away her ruined pants, leaving her naked except for the tatters of torn shirt. She felt his big hands stroke the side of her legs, then slide up her inner thighs to her crotch. "Jesus," McCorley half whispered, "that's quite a bush for such a little gal." His rough fingers drove into the patch of dark hair between her legs. Despite her resolve, Elaine winced as a finger rammed inside her, triggering a spasm of pain. The finger moved, in and out, the pain sharper with each stroke. "How you like that, girl? Feel good?"

Elaine made no reply.

"Can't recall the last time I had me a virgin," McCorley said, "but I got me one now." Sweat beaded his forehead. He closed the knife, slipped it back into his pocket, and reached for his belt buckle. "By God, girl, you're gonna remember your first man. A real man."

Elaine gritted her teeth and stared at the seam along the ridgepole of the tent, unwilling to watch as McCorley stripped off his trousers. She felt her knees pulled up by scratchy hands, her legs forced apart, and she gasped in pain as McCorley tried and failed to penetrate her. Coarse fingers roughly parted her labia. Elaine almost screamed aloud as McCorley shoved himself brutally into her. A sharp, stinging pain spread through her pelvis; she felt the blood flow as tender tissue tore. McCorley's hips backed away, then slammed into her crotch, each thrust deeper and harder until tears of agony threatened to break Elaine's will not to let him see her cry. The thrusts came quicker, more violently for what seemed to be an eternity, until McCorley's gasps reached a peak; he shuddered, rammed himself to his full length inside her. His body convulsed. Elaine felt him throbbing, became aware of the gush of fluid into her body.

McCorley suddenly collapsed on her, the weight of his big body pressing the breath from her chest. She struggled to pull air into squeezed lungs. Then, abruptly, McCorley lifted himself above her. He supported his weight on his elbows and leered at her. "Bet you liked that, didn't you, girl? By God, I think I'll keep you around a spell. Maybe you don't know nothin' about fuckin' yet, but you'll learn."

McCorley rolled off Elaine, lay breathing hard for a moment, then pulled up his dirty trousers. Elaine felt the smear of blood and fluid along her thighs and in the dark hair of her crotch. The pain persisted, and with it her humiliation deepened. She fought back the urge to spit in McCorley's face. She kept her gaze locked onto the seam at the top of the tent. *You dirty bastard,* she thought through barely contained tears of hate and disgust, *I'll kill you for this one day.*

Elaine slowly became aware that McCorley had stepped outside the tent. She caught a glimpse of the sky through the tent flap. The sunlight was fading fast. *If they let me live a few hours longer,* she thought, *I might have a chance—*

"Hey, Blue," a voice from outside called, "how was it?"

"Best pussy I've ever had, Arkansas. Never used before, tight and hot. And now it's wetter'n hell."

Laughter rippled through the gathering of men outside.

"Reckon I'm next." The words sent a fresh chill of terror through Elaine. It was the voice of the sadistic one called Arkansas.

"All right, Arkie," she heard McCorley say, "but I warn you—keep that damn pig-sticker of yours in the sheath. You ain't gonna carve this one up. You cut her, I'll tear your balls off and stuff 'em down your throat."

"Aw, shit, Blue." Arkansas made no attempt to hide his disappointment. "What the hell difference does it make? We're gonna kill her anyway."

"The hell we are!" McCorley's tone turned hard and sharp. "We'll keep her a few days to play with. After that, I know a rich Mexican out by Taos who'd part with a helluva lot of money for a prime young mare like that. So you keep your goddamn knife to yourself or answer to me!"

"Whatever you say, Blue. You're the boss. Just so long as I get my piece."

"Everybody gets some, Arkansas." McCorley unexpectedly

laughed in genuine amusement. "But pore ol' Doby's standin' first watch. It's gonna be sloppier'n a hog trough when he gets his turn."

The comment brought a roar of drunken laughter from the men outside.

Elaine clenched her fists and dug her fingernails into her palms until she felt the sting through the smoldering pain in her pelvis. The seam at the top of the tent blurred through welling tears. She blinked them away. *God, I've never asked you for a thing,* she prayed, *but please—give me the strength to live through this nightmare.* Her silent prayer faded as the tent flap swung open. The man called Arkansas stood there, his hand on his belt buckle, the long thin knife in a sheath at his hip.

Elaine forced her concentration back to the tent seam as the tall man unbuttoned his trousers.

4

Slocum lay beneath the branches of a stunted cedar tree on the edge of the steep canyon wall and studied the outlaw camp below.

He cursed silently as a short, stocky gunman emerged from the small tent at the edge of the camp, buttoning his pants. The stocky one was the fourth who had gone into that tent in the last hour. It didn't take any mental giant to figure out why. He had found Elaine.

Slocum clenched his fist in helpless frustration. The image of Elaine beneath those sweaty bodies would not leave his brain. But at least she was still alive—for now—or there would be no men going into the tent. Rage boiled cold in Slocum's gut, screaming at him to charge into the camp, guns blazing. Common sense damped the fury. Not even the Tenth Cavalry could ride into that gang of gunmen and expect to come out without heavy losses, and a dead Slocum wouldn't help Elaine. This had to be a silent action, a campaign of stealth. Get the girl out first, to a safe place. Then he would start thinning out this bunch one man at a time. He owed that to the major, to Eva, to Elaine, and to himself. No one butchered Slocum's friends and lived to brag about it.

Slocum forced himself to concentrate. There was, with luck, a way to get Elaine out of there alive. At least now he knew the layout of the canyon and the odds he faced.

The south end of the canyon was a bell-shaped meadow framed on three sides by sheer, rocky walls. The stolen horses, including Slocum's Nez Percé ponies, grazed there and drank

31

from the deep pool formed by a natural spring. At its north end the canyon narrowed into a deep notch before opening onto the rugged sandstone outcrops and broken badlands along the Canadian River.

The outlaw camp was a third of the way into the canyon. The tent was pitched on the north side of the camp; at least that could work in his favor. He wouldn't have to go through ten men to reach her.

If he could manage to slip into the camp and free her, there was still the matter of escape. The herd of stolen horses might as well have been on the moon for the good they would do. There was no way to steal a mount without riding a gauntlet of guns twice—once on the way in and once on the way out. The outlaw's picket horses were on the far side of the camp, also out of reach. Two people afoot wouldn't live long with mounted riders on their trail.

That left Jug as their only means of escape. Slocum had tethered the big bay in a willow thicket two hundred yards away on the banks of the Canadian. The big horse was strong enough to carry two people with ease, even if he couldn't run fast enough to scatter his own biscuits. They wouldn't survive a chase. It all came down to a few simple, hard facts. He had to wait until the time was right, the gunmen asleep or drunk, then move in like a Comanche on the stalk. Get the girl and go on the dodge until they were safe from pursuit.

He glanced over his shoulder. The moon was a pale crescent resting on the eastern horizon. It would give light enough to aid their escape but not enough to help trackers. Slocum knew a thing or two about hiding a trail.

Darkness fell on the camp as Slocum waited. Two of the gunmen passed out fully clothed on their bedrolls, courtesy of stolen whiskey. Others began to shake out blankets and settle in for the night. The campfire gradually died until only small flickers of flame licked among the coals. And mercifully, the parade of men into and from the tent stopped. Slocum could only hope Elaine still lived—and that she still had control of her mind. He had seen women who had been through what Elaine had endured. The strongest survived, but they never forgot. The weakest retreated behind vacant, staring eyes and never returned. Some simply lost their will to go on and died.

Slocum twisted to study the jumbled rocks, stunted juniper, and scattered cottonwood trees that marked the opening of the canyon. No commander worth his salt would camp without putting out at least one picket, and to give the devil his due Blue McCorley had to be a competent leader or he wouldn't have survived this long in a dangerous business. A few minutes later Slocum saw the flare of a match at the base of a cottonwood tree at one side of the canyon mouth. He grunted in grim satisfaction. He knew where the lookout was.

Slocum eased his way from beneath the cedar and began a long, circular stalk that brought him within a few yards of the cottonwood. He stopped in a clutter of sandstone rocks, waiting and watching. He heard the squeak of a cork on glass, the slosh of liquid, a pause, and a long sigh. The lookout had brought a bottle from camp to help him pass the time. The liquor would dull his senses, give Slocum even more of an edge.

Slocum slipped the heavy skinning knife with its razor-sharp edge from its sheath at his belt and began the final few steps of the stalk, his movements fluid and relaxed. He was within an arm's length when the sentry scratched a match against a stone and lit another cigarette. The flare of light would leave him half blind for a few seconds. The man yawned and stretched, broke wind noisily, and stepped away from the tree as he reached for the buttons on his fly. His rifle leaned against the cottonwood and his pistol was still in its holster.

Slocum's left hand clamped over the sentry's mouth and chin. He yanked the head back and swiped the keen blade across the man's throat. Blood spurted from severed neck arteries. Slocum tightened his grip against the man's weakening struggles. He knew it took a few seconds for a man to die from a slit throat.

"That's for Major Storm, you miserable son of a bitch," Slocum whispered into the man's ear. The sentry's muscles went limp. The odor of excrement filled Slocum's nostrils as the man's sphincter let go at the moment of death.

Slocum propped the body against the tree in a sitting position. In the pale moonlight the pool of blood on the sand of the canyon floor was as black as death itself. Slocum wiped the warm, sticky fluid from his knife on the back of the dead man's shirt and stood. He slipped into the inky shadows cast by juniper and cedar trees and worked his way silently to the edge of the camp.

Slocum paused ten yards from the tent and once more studied the campsite. He was in luck; the tent was unguarded. He heard the ragged snores from the outlaws in their bedrolls. *For Christ's sake, don't let any of them get up to take a piss,* he thought. He stayed low, moving in a half crouch, until he reached the back of the tent. He thought he heard a faint whimper from inside. The tent was a standard U.S. Army issue of coarse, tough canvas. Slocum knew he couldn't risk cutting through the tent. Even such a slight sound could get them both killed. He tugged at the bottom of the tent. The canvas lifted easily. They hadn't bothered to stake it down.

Slocum slithered inside, into a darkness that seemed endless, the stench of numerous unwashed bodies and the musky smell of sex heavy in the small enclosure. Slocum waited, holding his breath, until he heard the faint sigh of Elaine's breathing. He crept toward the sound on hands and knees until he could sense her nearness. Finally, his eyes adapted to the blackness enough that he could see her huddled into a ball in a far corner of the tent.

Slocum reached out and put his hand over Elaine's face. She came awake with a start and a soft, muffled cry. She cringed from his touch, tried to fight his hand. He realized then that her hands and feet were bound.

"Elaine, it's Slocum," he whispered, his face near her ear. "I've come to get you out. Do you understand?"

The girl stopped struggling. Slocum felt her nod of agreement. He moved his hand from her mouth.

"We've got to keep quiet, Elaine," Slocum said. "Just nod when you can, whisper if you have to talk. Are you all right? Can you walk, run if we have to?"

She nodded twice. Slocum slipped the big knife from its sheath, ran his hands over her arms, and cut the ropes from her wrists by feel. He slid his hand across her hips, felt her involuntary recoil from his touch. His hand moved down her legs until his fingers touched hemp. He sliced the final bonds away. "Let's go now," he whispered. "Someone could come in here any minute. Are you ready?"

"Yes." Her reply was barely audible. "My clothes—"

"No time for that. Come on. Slow and quiet."

Slocum held the canvas up as Elaine crawled through. His heart skipped a beat as one of the men in the sleeping bags awoke with a snort and stirred in his blankets. Then the man's breathing settled again into a steady, deep pattern.

Slocum held Elaine's hand as they crept toward the safety of the deep shadows. He hardly dared breathe until they were fifty yards past the dead sentry. He released Elaine's hand and quickened his pace.

A few minutes later they reached Slocum's tethered bay. He spent a precious few moments to pull a blanket from the roll behind the saddle and wrap it about Elaine. She shivered in the chill of the night air, or perhaps it was the memory of her experience in the camp. Slocum couldn't be sure which.

Slocum swung aboard Jug, reached down, and boosted Elaine onto the saddle skirts behind him. The bay fidgeted for a moment, then settled down to accept the idea of a second rider on his back.

Slocum didn't bother to caution Elaine again of the need for silence. She hadn't spoken since those three whispered words in the tent. He wished he could see her face, and at the same time felt relief that he couldn't. He was afraid he would see madness there. He reined Jug to the east, laying the first loop in a convoluted trail that even the best of trackers would have trouble sorting out.

They rode silently through the night, doubled back on their own tracks, left false trails, gradually worked back toward the west. That was the one direction, Slocum figured, that Blue McCorley wouldn't expect them to ride. At one time they passed within a mile of the bandit camp in the canyon, but it was a chance Slocum knew they had to take. They threaded their way through the river badlands, crossed and recrossed the treacherous red quicksands of the Canadian.

Slocum stopped frequently to study their back trail. The wide landscape remained empty in the faint moonlight. He tuned his senses to the slight southwesterly breeze, heard nothing, and was reassurred. Sounds carried a considerable distance in the dry air. He could have heard a sharp curse or the clink of a horseshoe against stone a quarter mile away.

The deep blue-violet of dawn found them twenty miles from the camp in the canyon, at the edge of a sprawling salt cedar thicket on the north side of the Canadian. Slocum eased Jug deep into the dense thicket, following a narrow cattle trail, and pulled the horse to a stop in a small clearing.

"We'll be safe here for a while, Elaine," he said. He reached back with his left arm and helped Elaine dismount. He sat in the saddle for a moment, studying her face for the first time since her ordeal. The sight unnerved him.

The laughter that had waited just below the surface of her blue eyes was gone; her gaze was dull and unseeing. She stared straight ahead and seemed not to blink. Tangles matted her shoulder-length hair, now speckled with dirt and twigs. Her shoulders sagged as she leaned against the bay's side. Scratches and welts showed on the skin not covered by the blanket. But it was the eyes that bothered Slocum most.

"Elaine?"

There was no response. Slocum realized the girl was still in a state of shock and disbelief. He touched her arm. She tried instinctively to pull away. Slocum took both her shoulders and twisted her about to face him.

"Elaine, I know what you've been through. But dammit, girl, you've got to help me!"

For the first time a spark of life appeared in Elaine's eyes. A sudden flare of grief and hurt and a glimmer of hate swirled to the surface in a storm of emotion. The brief expression faded into the mist of welling tears. Her shoulders trembled and silent sobs wracked her body. Slocum pulled her to him. She tensed, her hands raised to push against his chest as she fought his embrace.

"It's all right now, Elaine," Slocum said softly. "They won't hurt you anymore." She struggled against his grip for a few seconds more. Then her resistance weakened and gradually faded. She leaned against his chest. Slocum tried to comfort her, tried to feed her strength from his own tired muscles, and stroked her tangled hair tenderly.

He held her for a long time, until she had cried out at least a part of her inner agony. Slocum welcomed the tears that soaked his shirt. They were a release, like the easing of tension on a trigger spring when the hammer was lowered. Slocum wasn't sure yet, but he thought Elaine's mind would survive. She would never be the same young girl he had first met. But maybe she would live in the real world now, not pull back into some dark and distant corner where there was no reality, no hurt, no pain to touch her.

Slocum finally released Elaine. He helped her sit and tucked the blanket around her so that most of her body was covered. He lifted the canteen from the saddle and handed it to her, then turned to care for his horse as she drank. He loosened the cinches, rubbed the bay down as best he could without unsaddling, and wished he had some grain. Jug had earned a good feed with his night's work.

Slocum pulled his possibles pouch from a saddlebag, found a strip of beef jerky, and offered it to Elaine. She shook her head silently. Slocum slipped his Winchester from the boot and sat beside Elaine, the weapon cradled in his arms.

He waited in silence for several minutes, listening to the sounds of the cedar thicket. A blue quail called, summoning other members of its covey. A beetle scuttled across the sand. Overhead a circling red-tailed hawk sounded its shrill hunting call. The wind began to pick up, quaking the thin, narrow leaves of the salt cedars.

"We'll rest here a while longer," Slocum finally said. "Then we need to get you to a safe place and let the law know what happened."

He became aware of the cold expression in Elaine's eyes as she stared at him.

"No."

The flat tone of the word surprised Slocum.

"Mr. Slocum, I owe you my life. Those men would have killed me—or worse. I want them dead. I want to stand over their bodies and laugh. I want to rub my hands in their blood." Elaine's voice was now calm and steady, as though she were discussing the weather, and it left Slocum chilled. "McCorley's gang took everything. They murdered Uncle Ed in cold blood. They tortured and shot Aunt Eva, stole all our money and our horses, and then they—they took the only thing I had left."

Elaine raised her gaze to Slocum. "I want you to help me track them down and kill them all, Mr. Slocum. They've got to pay for what they've done."

The cold, detached tone of her voice cut into Slocum's gut. He wasn't sure if he heard the beginning of madness there, or a tightly controlled rage. Still, he understood. Or at least he thought he did.

"Elaine, there's no man alive wants those bastards dead more than I do," Slocum said. "But there's nine of them and only two of us. We have only one horse, no food, no supplies, and I've got less than thirty dollars. Those are not good odds."

"We can make our own chances, Mr. Slocum. Those animals took every dime Uncle Ed had, more than eight hundred dollars. It's yours if you'll help me."

"My gun's not for hire." Slocum raised a hand as she started to protest. "Now, wait. I didn't say I wouldn't help. After all, I have a stake in this, too. Not as much of a stake as you do, but enough. Ed was a friend of mine. The men who killed him also took three horses that belonged to me. I just want you to know what we're up against. McCorley and his men are hard cases, gunfighters, tough and ruthless. Half the lawmen in four states have tried to take them at one time or another—"

"And they didn't have the reason I have, Mr. Slocum," Elaine interrupted. "All they wanted was justice. By God, *I* want revenge! Look at this!" She whipped the blanket aside.

Slocum's gut crawled in disgust and rage as he stared at Elaine Storm's body. Her skin was scratched and bloody. Deep bruises showed an angry purplish red on her stomach, thighs, and breasts. The dark swatch of her pubic hair was caked with dried blood and semen. Slocum noticed for the first time the trickle of fresh blood down her side. Elaine lifted her left breast to expose the tender flesh of its underside. A puncture wound a half inch wide seeped scarlet just above the fold where the skin of the breast met her rib cage.

"There." Elaine touched a finger to the cut. "That son of a bitch called Arkansas did that. He wanted me to move while he was—was taking me. He said he would cut it off if I didn't cooperate. I knew he wasn't bluffing. He has my aunt's breasts. I heard him say he was going to tan them out for tobacco pouches." Her hand dropped to her crotch, fingers trying to wipe away the crusted fluids. "And here," she said. "They dirtied me. I feel like I'm full of lice and other crawly things."

Eline slowly wrapped the blanket back around her body. Her gaze bored steadily into Slocum's face. "I want that bastard with the knife myself, Mr. Slocum. I want him to know what pain is before he dies."

The rage that had been churning in Slocum's gut for more than a day flared fresh and hot. "You'll have him, Elaine. God knows you've earned the right."

"There's one more thing, Mr. Slocum. I want no one other than you to know what those men did to me." Her voice was heavy with humiliation and pain. "Law-abiding people can be just as brutal, in their own way, as those outlaws," she said. "I couldn't stand the way the women would look at me, like I was some barroom whore. The way men would look at me, wondering if I enjoyed it. Looking at me and seeing me naked, my legs spread and my crotch stuck up in the air and welcome to any and all. I couldn't stand that."

Slocum nodded. "I'll tell no one, Elaine. You've suffered enough."

An uncomfortable silence fell on the clearing for a few moments before Elaine finally spoke. Her voice trembled in anger and self-loathing. "Mr. Slocum, when that man stuck that knife in my breast, I should have thrown myself on the blade, to end my own life. I didn't do it. I wasn't strong enough."

"Elaine Storm," Slocum said softly, "I think you may be the strongest young woman I've ever met in my life." He sighed. "Now, if we're going to join forces to wipe out Blue McCorley's gang, you might as well drop the 'Mister.' I answer to Slocum just fine."

"Thank you, Slocum. For everything."

"Thank me later. If we both live." Slocum stood and strode to the bedroll tied to his saddle. He rummaged in the roll, brought out his spare shirt and pants, and handed them to Elaine. "They're way too big for you, but they'll keep you covered until we can find some decent clothes." He turned his back, the show of respect more instinct than anything else. He had already seen all there was to see of Elaine Storm. He listened to the rustle of clothing as she dressed.

"There's a plaza—a small settlement of Mexican shepherds—about five miles downriver from here," Elaine said. "Martinez was from there. I know his people well. They will go back to the ranch and bury my folks. One day I'll return and put markers over them." Her voice trailed away for a moment. Slocum didn't speak. There wasn't much to say.

Finally, Elaine sighed. "The Martinez family will loan me a horse and clothes. And let me have a bath. I'm filthy, Slocum, especially inside. From the plaza it's about four hours' ride into Tascosa. When we get to town I want you to buy me a gun. I'll repay you when we recover Uncle Ed's money and the horses."

Elaine stepped to Slocum's side and handed him the carefully rolled blanket. She looked like a vagabond waif in the oversized clothing, with her hair tousled and dirty, bruises and smudges of grime on her face. Slocum fought back the urge to take her in his arms and give her a reassuring hug.

"I have a spare pistol," he said. "It's too big for your hands, but—"

"No pistol or rifle," Elaine said, her voice calm. "I want a double shotgun. Sawed-off. With double-ought buckshot shells. I'm a lousy shot, Slocum, but not with a weapon like that. And I want to see guts splatter when I pull those triggers."

Slocum winced inwardly at the matter-of-fact tone of the girl's voice. "Elaine, I'll get you the smoothbore. But you have to promise me you won't let your hate for these men cause you to do something foolish. Hunting men is a dangerous game."

"And you're my guide, Slocum. Don't worry. I'll do as you say. I won't be stupid or reckless. Now, can we move on to the plaza? I've got to get rid of this filth."

Slocum tightened the cinches, swung aboard Jug, and offered Elaine a hand up. *You can wash that filth off your body, Elaine,* he thought. *I just hope that someday you can wash it from your memory.*

Slocum reined the bay along the narrow game trail to the edge of the thicket, waited for a moment to make sure no one was about, then kneed Jug in the direction Elaine pointed. He kept the rifle crooked in one arm as they rode toward the plaza.

Ten miles southeast of the salt cedar thicket, Blue McCorley shifted his chew to the other cheek and spat in disgust.

"Sorry, Blue," a short, wiry man kneeling on a stretch of sandstone shale said. "We've lost 'em. I don't know who this jasper is, but he can damn well hide a trail with the best of 'em."

"Ah, shit." McCorley's voice was thick with sarcasm. "I've got me a tracker who can't track a grown man and a girl on one horse. I've got a man who followed his pecker right into a slug from a peashooter pistol. I've got a man dead with his throat cut because he had his mind on a jug instead of his job." He spat again. "Idiots. I'm surrounded by fools and idiots."

"Blue, I give it my best try," the wiry man said with a shrug. "This guy's good."

Blue McCorley snorted. "Let 'em go, Bill. We got horses to move, anyway. Best clear this country before some posse gets on our tail. The damn girl wasn't worth nowhere near what them horses are." He twisted in the saddle to face the tall man at his right. "Arkansas, you're new in this part of Texas. People won't know you on sight like they would most of us. You get that damn stupid Smokey into Tascosa. Take him to Hogtown. There's a sawbones there name of Dutchy Meuhler who don't ask many questions. Get Dutchy to carve that slug out of Smokey. He ain't no good to us with one arm. Besides, I'm gettin' damn tired of his whinin'."

"Sure thing, boss," Arkansas said. "Need anything else from town?"

McCorley worried the chew for a moment. "Yeah. Take a packhorse along. We need whiskey, a dozen or so bottles. A side of bacon, sack of flour, three pounds of Arbuckle's, a couple pounds apiece of salt and sugar. Ain't very damn many stores between Tascosa and Santa Fe, and we got a hell of a long ride ahead of us." He probed in a pocket, pulled out a couple of gold pieces, and handed them to the thin man.

"A couple more things, Arkansas. Keep your goddamn pecker in your pants, that knife in the sheath, and don't get drunk on me. We need them supplies and we need Smokey back. Screw it up and I'll have your nuts for breakfast."

"Savvy that, boss," Arkansas said with a chuckle. "Where do we meet up?"

"Know the Death's Head Trail?"

"Nope."

"Old trace runs from south of Tascosa to Santa Fe. Stay on the south side of the river, top out of the breaks for a quick look every hour or so. Twenty, twenty-five miles upriver from Tascosa you'll see a big flat-top mesa, sort of a little mountain in the middle of nowhere. It's called Torrejo Peak. Death's Head Trail runs right beside it. We'll hold the horses in the breaks on the north side of the peak till you two get back."

Arkansas touched the brim of his hat in a salute and reined his mount back toward the camp.

"Blue," the tracker said, "do you trust Arkie to stay out of trouble like you said?"

"Hell, no. He's a dumb bastard. But him and Smokey's the only two of us might not meet up with somebody we know in Tascosa, and word might of got around about them horse ranchers. 'Sides, Arkansas knows I wasn't kiddin' about cuttin' his nuts out if he don't do like he's told." McCorley spat out the wad of tobacco. It sat like a single horse apple on the hardpan. "You boys head on back, get ready to move camp," McCorley said. "I got me some thinkin' to do. I be along shortly."

Blue McCorley fumbled his tobacco twist from his pocket and gnawed off a fresh chew as he watched the four men ride away. He hadn't felt right since they'd found the girl gone and the sentry dead, his head cut half off. He hadn't felt right about splitting his forces, taking four to hunt the girl and this jasper on the big-footed horse while leaving the others behind to guard the stolen remuda. With those damn stud horses raising hell every step, four men weren't enough. They might spill the whole herd.

McCorley had an instinct for trouble. He didn't know and didn't care where it came from, but he knew to pay attention when his asshole puckered. He studied the horizon as he worked the fresh chew. *One thing's for damn sure,* he thought. *That man out there ain't no greenhorn. And what the hell's his tie with the girl? Boyfriend? Relative? Lawman?* McCorley snorted. He didn't like questions, didn't like the unknown. *And if the man on old bigfoot wants more than the girl, he could give us more bloody hell than a whole posse of soft-ass townfolk.*

One man could move stealthily and be hard to spot, like a Comanche. A posse raised a dust cloud and made a ruckus a man could hear a mile off. One man could sneak in at night, cut another throat. Maybe run off a few horses. If he was good enough and if he wanted to, he could be a real pain in the ass.

"I don't know who you are or what you want, you son of a bitch," he muttered, "but I got a feelin' you're out there somewhere. If it was just the girl you're after, take her and welcome. Somethin' tells me you want more than that." He picked up the slack in the reins and turned his horse toward camp. "You want us, we ain't gonna be all that hard to find, trailin' fifty horses. So just come on. Let's see what kind of balls you got."

5

Slocum stood in the small courtyard of the plaza and watched as Elaine Storm swung the heavy vaquero saddle onto the back of a wiry Spanish mustang, adjusted the saddle pad, and pulled the single cinch tight.

"Elaine, for the last time," he said, "please stay. You'll be safe here. These people will take care of you—"

"No. Slocum, you promised." She turned to face him. "I'm going with you. And if you try to ride away without me, I'll follow."

"Do you realize what we're going to be riding into? The two of us against nine gunmen? It's just too dangerous for you."

Elaine's features twisted in a scowl. "And what are they going to do to me that they haven't already done, Slocum? Kill me? Somehow that doesn't scare me a hell of a lot." Her tone was tight and bitter. "I won't slow you down. And when we catch them, I'll be in on the kill." She fixed a steady, cold gaze on Slocum's face. "You don't owe me a thing, Slocum," she said, "but I'll hold you to your promise."

Slocum sighed in resignation. "All right. But I had to try." He tried not to show his impatience as Elaine said her good-byes to the three families who lived in the plaza. The day-long delay chafed at Slocum like a salt-crusted saddle blanket. It meant Blue McCorley and his bunch had gained a few more hours. Every hour put McCorley that much farther away.

Slocum already had lost a day on the trail, and now he faced the loss of at least one, possibly two, more. Yet the stay at the plaza had been good for Elaine, Slocum had to admit.

The Mexicans had taken Elaine in as one of their own, shared her grief, tended her injuries, fed her, and let her sleep for most of a day. Slocum noted that the color had returned to her cheeks. The gold-flecked blue eyes had regained some luster. They now glittered cold, reflecting the hate and bitterness that burned within her. It was the look of a rattler poised to strike. Elaine had not smiled or laughed since Slocum had pulled her from the tent in McCorley's camp.

A hot bath and several hours of rest had restored some of her strength. Borrowed clothing now covered the scratches and bruises on her body. The Mexicans had pooled their meager resources and outfitted Elaine as best they could. She wore plain black trousers tucked into calf-high leather boots, a white shirt, a vest decorated in silver stitching and a wide-brimmed sombrero that would shield her from the scorching sun. At a casual glance Elaine could be mistaken for a young Mexican cowboy in that outfit, Slocum thought, and that might not be such a bad thing.

They had also loaned her the mustang. The wiry little gray gelding wouldn't weigh nine hundred pounds soaking wet, Slocum thought, but he seemed to have plenty of spirit, speed, and a lot of staying power. The mustang could run all day if need be. And that time might well come.

Martinez's family had no money or food to spare, but they had helped the would-be hunters as much as they could. An old but useable coffeepot and skillet and a couple of extra blankets now rested behind the borrowed saddle. They still needed more supplies, but every little bit helped, Slocum thought. The money pouch in his shirt pocket was painfully light. It would be all but empty after he bought the minimum supplies they needed in Tascosa and returned to the hunt.

Three men from the plaza already were on their way to the Storm ranch, a small cart laden with the tools needed to carve graves into the hard soil. After the burials, the men would take turns watching over the place, tending to the small herd of cattle, until Slocum and Elaine returned. The ES Ranch would be in good hands.

Elaine swung into the saddle. The mustang humped his back, but soon gave up the inclination to buck under her firm hand. Slocum mounted his own horse, touched his hat brim in salute to the Mexicans gathered about, and reined Jug toward Tascosa.

The sun was near its midpoint when Slocum kneed Jug onto the sandy, well-traveled thoroughfare of Tascosa's Main Street. His gaze swept the buildings and alleyways for any signs of danger as they rode.

Tascosa was quiet despite its reputation as a wide-open town, the only settlement of any size between Mobeetie, one hundred thirty miles southeast, and Santa Fe. Tascosa was a settlement of some four hundred permanent residents nestled amid cottonwood groves on the north bank of the Canadian. The town overlooked the only reliable ford of the treacherous riverbed and its deep quicksand pools for miles around.

The buildings were primarily stuccoed adobe, with a native stone structure here and there and an occasional building made of imported lumber. The townsite, if not the community itself, was old; Spanish explorers had crossed the Canadian here in the mid-1500s, and before them Indian tribes for centuries had camped among the trees where fresh springs fed two small creeks winding toward the river. The site had sheltered buffalo hunters, Comancheros, and Mexican shepherds. Now it was the trading center for vast cattle empires that had grown throughout the Panhandle, its stores, saloons, and dance halls catering to cowboys looking for a good time after days or weeks of drudgery and danger on the treeless plains.

Tascosa's most prominent landmark bore silent testimony to the occasional violence of the times. Boot Hill Cemetery sat atop a rocky hill on the west side of town, a few of its stone or wooden markers visible from almost anywhere in the community.

"Slocum, he's here!" Elaine's call was soft but urgent.

Slocum checked his horse, let his hand drop to the stock of the Winchester booted beneath his right leg. "Who?"

"The one with the knife. Arkansas, they call him." Elaine's voice trembled, not from fear but from hate and fury. "That's his horse. The sorrel with the Walking T brand on the left hip." She pointed down the street to a building where several horses stood hipshot at a hitching rack. A weathered sign proclaimed the building to be the Equity Saloon.

Elaine started to spur the mustang toward the saloon. Slocum stabbed out a hand and grabbed the reins. "Wait a minute. You can't just go charging in there like the Seventh Cavalry. There may be more than one of them here. This is a war, Elaine. We don't ride into any fight without a plan—"

Elaine Storm strode toward the Equity Saloon, battling the whirlwind of emotions that swirled through her body. But through the revulsion, dread, and pure raw fear, her hate for the man with the knife kept her feet moving. The little .32 rimfire derringer stuck into the top of her boot chafed her calf. Even though it still held only one cartridge Slocum had insisted she carry it, "just in case something goes wrong."

She paused at the wooden door that sagged on well-used hinges outside the saloon. *Courage, Elaine,* she admonished herself, *you can do it; just remember it's your turn at that skinny son of a bitch with the knife.* She stepped inside.

A moment later her vision had adjusted to the dim light in the saloon. She suppressed a shudder as she recognized the tall man standing at the end of the bar, a bottle before him, the skinning knife sheathed at his belt. She took a deep breath to calm her nerves and stepped to the man's side. She forced a smile.

"Hello, cowboy," she said. "Remember me?"

The man called Arkansas stared at her for a moment through a whiskey haze. Then he stiffened in surprise and shock at seeing her there. His hand drifted toward his holstered pistol, his eyes narrowed in suspicion.

Elaine put a hand casually on his forearm and let her unbuttoned shirt fall open, exposing a firm young breast. She kept her back to the other drinkers. The exposed breast was for Arkansas's eyes only. "I was hoping it was you," Elaine said. For a moment she felt an almost overpowering urge to turn and run, but the impulse faded under the heat of hate. Her flesh crawled at the feel of his forearm beneath her hand, the look in his eyes as he stared at her breast. "You were the only good one of the bunch," she whispered. She hoped the breathless rasp in her voice sounded like a seductress, not like a woman who wanted a man dead. "I want more, cowboy. More of you."

The suspicion in Arkansas's eyes gave way to a glimmer of lust. "If you want some more, too, just come with me," Elaine said.

Arkansas pushed away from the bar, his eyes now bright with anticipation. He let her lead him outside.

"Where are your friends, cowboy? We don't want anybody else around this time. God, you were good, sugar. I never expected a man could be so much fun."

She heard the tall man's breathing quicken. "Ain't but one other of 'em around," he said. "Old Smokey, the one got shot. He's down to Hogtown at the doc's. Won't be no bother to us, honey."

Elaine forced herself to tighten her grip on his forearm and tried not to cringe as she let her hip brush against his. "Where are the others?"

"Rode on. Smokey and me is to meet up with 'em later."

Elaine glanced around. "Not here, I hope?"

"Naw." He put a hand on her rump. She felt her face flush in humiliation as his fingers worked against the flesh of her buttock. "Where we headed?"

"Just a little farther. Be patient, cowboy. And I promise this time you won't need to encourage me with that knife."

She led Arkansas down a small side street to an alley behind a livery stable. "Found an empty tool shed back here," she said. "We'll have plenty of privacy and no need to hurry this time. I want to feel you in me." She forced her free hand to caress his crotch. He was aready swollen.

Elaine pushed open the door of the tool shed, stepped inside, and turned to face her one-time tormenter. She flipped her shirt open. "Come on in, honey," she said, smiling. "I've got something special in mind for you."

Arkansas stepped into the tool shed and reached for his belt buckle. He never saw Slocum waiting at the side of the door, an ax handle in his hand. The hard hickory slammed into Arkansas's forehead. The thin man dropped like a poleaxed steer.

"Good work, Elaine," Slocum said as he reached for a length of sturdy rope. "That must have been pure hell for you."

"It could have been worse," she said as she rebuttoned her shirt. "It was worse the first time."

Slocum worked quickly. Within seconds he had stripped the gun belt from Arkansas's unconscious body and tossed it aside. He forced the man's mouth open, crammed a dirty rag between his teeth and bound the gag in place with a sleeve torn from Arkansas's shirt. He fashioned a noose with a slipknot in one end of the rope and dropped it over the man's neck.

"He say anything about the others?"

"Only that there was one more in town. The one Eva shot, a man called Smokey. This one said Smokey was at the doctor's in Hogtown. I couldn't get much out of him about the others," Elaine said.

Slocum tugged the final knot into place. The ropes bound Arkansas's feet beneath him, legs bent sharply at the knees, and secured his elbows and wrists behind his back. The slipknot around his throat tied into the bonds around his feet and arms; any attempt to struggle free would tighten the noose.

"Well, he's not going anywhere for a while," Slocum said. "When he comes around, we'll find out about the others." He noticed for the first time that Elaine's fingers were trembling. "Are you all right?"

She swallowed and nodded. "I'm all right. Just a little— scared, I guess. That awful man—"

"He won't bother you. In fact, I expect he'll be out for quite a while. I'm going after this friend of his." He handed Elaine the ax handle. "If this one comes to before I get back, give him another clout." He smiled at her. "I don't expect you'd find that too difficult to do."

"It would be my pleasure."

Slocum pulled his Peacemaker, checked the loads, and dropped the weapon back into its holster. "I'll be back soon, Elaine. Going to pay a call on old Smokey." He nodded toward the trussed-up Arkansas. "Don't worry about this one. He can't hurt you now. When I get back and we get all the information we can out of him, I promise you he'll never hurt another woman again."

Elaine watched Slocum step through the door into the bright wash of sun outside. When the door closed behind him she reached for the long, slender knife in Arkansas's belt. "No, Slocum," she whispered, her voice like ice, "this son of a bitch will never hurt another woman again—"

• • •

Slocum strode across the footbridge leading to Lower Tascosa, also known as Hogtown. It had cost him a quarter for a quick drink at the Cattle Exchange Saloon, but now he knew where a man wanting a bullet hole patched on the quiet would go.

He walked a hundred yards to a small adobe on the edge of town and tapped on the doorjamb, since the door was open to catch the breeze. A stout woman stuck her head through the doorway, her eyebrows arched in an unspoken question.

"Looking for a friend of mine. Fellow named Smokey. Stocky, broad shoulders, beard. He had a hole in him."

The woman frowned, then called out something in what seemed to be German. Moments later a short, rotund man with a thin blond mustache appeared at the door.

"Your friend isn't here," the doctor said. "It wasn't a serious wound. He's probably taking the edge off the pain in one of the cantinas."

"Much obliged," Slocum said, touching fingers to his hat brim. "I'll find him." He started to turn away, then almost as an afterthought, winked at the physician. "Old Smokey's a randy sort," Slocum said softly. "Always has a hard-on. Know where a man could get a drink and get his milk drained at the same place? Bet I'd find him there."

The doctor stepped away from the porch, glanced around to make sure the heavyset woman was out of earshot, and grinned. "Margarita's. Third building up the path toward the spring." He nodded toward a narrow, winding trail. "Margarita's got two daughters. They're sort of, well, in business, you might say. With their mother." He winked at Slocum. "Ask for the young one, Rosa. Three dollars well spent, friend."

"Thanks." Slocum strode up the path, not bothering to look back.

The third house was a three-room, low-roofed adobe. The door was open to catch the breeze, the interior thick with the scent of tobacco smoke and stale liquor. A Mexican woman with a broad smile and haunches wider than a singletree greeted Slocum with a nod from behind a crude bar, a pine plank stretched between two flour kegs.

"*Cerveza, por favor,*" Slocum said. He paid the nickel and sipped at the beer. It was lukewarm and not especially good. He held up a fifty-cent piece. "Friend of mine might have come in. Just had a patch put on a bullet hole by the doc. I don't see him around." He dropped the four bits on the bar.

"Ah, the one called Smokey." The coin disappeared between two enormous breasts. "*Sí*, he is here. In the back room with one of my girls. He be out in a minute. Rosa, she good— and quick." The big woman leered at Slocum. "I got another daughter—"

Slocum finished his beer and shook his head. "Maybe I better go check on old Smokey."

"No, señor! You cannot—"

Slocum ignored the woman, pulled his Colt from its holster, and pushed past her toward the back room. There was no door, but he heard soft moans of pleasure from behind a drawn curtain. He shoved the material aside.

The girl's back was to him. She was on her knees at the side of a cot, her head bobbing up and down at a man's crotch. The man had a small bandage on one shoulder. His eyes were closed. A pistol lay on a bedside table.

Slocum stepped forward silently and tapped the woman on the shoulder. She glanced up, startled, but made no sound as Slocum placed his finger on his lips in the signal for silence and nodded toward the curtain. The woman stood and strode from the room.

"What the hell you quit for, Rosa? I was just about—" Smokey's eyes fluttered open, then went wide in shock and surprise at the sight of the big man standing by the bed, pistol in hand. "Who the hell—"

"Hello, Smokey. Hate to interrupt a good time," Slocum cocked the .44-40, "but I need some information. Where's old Blue headed?"

Smokey swallowed hard, his gaze locked on the impressive bore of the pistol. "Who wants to know?"

Slocum shrugged. "Doesn't matter. Old Blue's got some of my horses. I want 'em back, and I haven't got time to play games with you. Now," he leveled the pistol at Smokey's left eye, "where's Blue headed?"

"Santa—Santa Fe." Once Smokey got the first couple of words out, the rest came in a rush. "We're supposed to meet up with him at Torrejo Peak on the old Death's Head Trail. For God's sake, mister, get that cannon out of my face."

Slocum grinned. "Thanks, Smokey. By the way, I've got a message for you. From a pretty young girl. Her name's Elaine Storm. She tells me you boys had some fun at her expense. She asked me to send you her regards. Forty-four caliber regards."

Smokey's face went chalk white. He stared at Slocum for several heartbeats, then made a desperate grab for the gun on the table. Slocum shot Smokey in the head. The heavy slug spattered blood and brains on the adobe wall behind the bed.

Slocum holstered the Colt and sprinted for the door. "Smokey's shot himself," he yelled, "somebody get a doctor!"

By the time the excited yammering started, Slocum was through the door and sprinting for the cover of a stand of cottonwoods a hundred feet away. He reached the trees without drawing fire—or for that matter, any notice at all—and paused for breath. He worked the ejector rod, kicked the spent shell from the Colt, and thumbed in a fresh cartridge.

"Well, Elaine," he said with a smile of satisfaction, "we're cutting down the odds a little."

Elaine Storm waited patiently as the tall man called Arkansas fought his way back to consciousness.

He moaned in pain, the sound barely audible through the gag stuffed into his mouth. His eyes fluttered open. They were glazed from the wallop of the ax handle against his head. He stared vacantly toward the ceiling at first. As his senses returned he struggled against the ropes, weakly at first and then with more vigor. The bonds held firm.

After a few seconds he noticed Elaine. He had trouble focusing glassy eyes; then reality returned with the impact of a sledgehammer. His eyes widened, first in surprise, then in growing fear, as the girl stood before him, his thin-bladed knife gripped in a small hand.

"Welcome back, Arkansas." Elaine's tone was pleasant, almost cheerful. "I was afraid Slocum might have killed you. But I guess your head is harder than that. I'm glad you're still alive."

Elaine tested the point, then the cutting edge of the knife against a thumb. "Real sharp, Arkansas." Her voice went cold and hard. "I was hoping you hadn't let it get dull since you used it on Eva and then on me."

Arkansas struggled frantically against the ropes, his whimpering cries muffled by the gag. He lay on his back, feet curled beneath his buttocks, his pelvis thrust upward and exposed. Elaine knelt at his side. Light filtered through a crack in the tool shed and glinted from the keen edge of the blade.

"You're so fond of knives, Arkansas." Elaine clucked her tongue in mock disapproval. "Little boys shouldn't play with knives." The tall man's eyes widened in terror as she slipped the sharp blade beneath his belt. The leather gave way with a soft rip.

Elaine heard her own breathing quicken as her hate boiled to the surface. "You remember Eva? She's the one whose tits you skinned out, you son of a bitch." She slipped the knife beneath the waistband of his trousers and ripped the cloth all the way to the crotch. "Well, damn your soul, you'll never rape or carve up a woman again." Her fingers closed around his exposed penis and testicles. She touched the knife blade to the skin at the base of his shaft and smiled at Arkansas. She swept the blade down.

The tall man's screams of agony gurgled against the gag. Crimson spurted from his crotch. Elaine lifted the gory parts carved from his groin and shoved them close to his face. "See what I mean, Arkansas? No more pussy for you." Elaine's voice began to tremble in fury. "Not as much fun when you're on the other end of the knife, is it?"

Arkansas kept screaming, unheard, his eyes wide in shock and horror. Elaine listened to the gurgle for a few seconds, savoring the man's agony. Then she dropped the severed organs onto Arkansas's chest. She plunged the knife deep into his gut, ripped the blade upward, and stepped back as Arkansas's intestines tumbled free.

Elaine casually wiped the knife blade on the tall man's shirt, stared into his eyes, and waited. She felt no queasiness, no remorse, only a deep sense of satisfaction.

The man called Arkansas died hard. Blowflies buzzed around the gore.

Elaine's blood lust had subsided when the door swung open and Slocum stepped into the room. He stopped dead in his tracks and stared in shocked silence at the mutilated body.

"My God, Elaine—" Slocum heard the disbelief in his own voice.

"Close the door, Slocum," Elaine said calmly. "You might let some of the flies out."

6

Twenty miles and almost five hours had passed before Slocum was finally able to relax.

The troubles in Tascosa had added more wood to the already hot fire under Slocum, but they had managed to get supplies, a pack mule, and still get out of town before the law started nipping at their heels. Now, in a secluded side canyon studded with wind-twisted juniper and cedar trees south of the Canadian, he squatted on his heels, sipped coffee from a tin cup, and studied the girl seated across the small campfire.

He still hadn't completely recovered from the jolt over the way Elaine had carved up the man called Arkansas. That the bastard deserved it was beside the point. Slocum would have done the same thing himself. But Elaine?

In the twilight Elaine Storm looked more like a young kitten than anything else. Curled against the seat of her saddle, she seemed little bigger than a mite. *This kitten,* Slocum thought, *has turned into a real hellcat.*

Elaine had spoken little on the ride from Tascosa, but he had heard her soft humming from time to time. She seemed more relaxed and content than she had since Slocum's first day at the ranch. Once she had even flashed a quick smile. It was the first time he had seen her smile since he had pulled her from the outlaw camp.

Elaine had proved she could drive a bargain as well as she could wield a knife. Slocum had to stay out of sight, since he had been seen by several people at Margarita's place. That left most of the shopping to Elaine, and she had to work fast before somebody stumbled onto Arkansas's body. They couldn't risk taking Arkansas's horse—that might be hard to explain to any lawman who happened by—but she had haggled a livery owner out of a stout, compact mule complete with pack saddle for less than thirty dollars. And she had stocked well. The packs held enough supplies to see them to Santa Fe if they rode on less than full rations. More important, she had bought grain for the animals and morrals for feeding them. She had picked up a change of clothing for herself, and the most wicked-looking scattergun Slocum had ever seen.

The shotgun rested within Elaine's reach. It was a twelve-bore coach gun with the barrels nubbed to less than eighteen inches and the stock cut down to fit her smaller frame. The weapon showed signs of heavy use. The stock was scratched and gouged, receiver pitted with rust from sweaty hands, and the graceful metal swirls of the twist-steel Damascas barrels was almost worn away. That thing, Slocum thought, would make hamburger out of a good mule team. God only knew what it could do to a man.

Elaine had also bought a box of .32 rimfire cartridges for the little derringer, which she now carried in a spring clip holster under her waistband at the small of her back. She hadn't scrimped on ammunition. She had two boxes of double-ought buck for the smoothbore and another box of .44-40 cartridges. The .44-40s fit Slocum's rifle as well as his handguns.

The girl's only extravagance was one Slocum greatly appreciated—a quart of Old Overholt. He held back the urge to uncork the bottle. He might feel the need for it a lot worse in the days ahead. Slocum tapped the coin pouch in his shirt pocket. The late and unlamented Arkansas had contributed a blood-stained double eagle to the cause, but outfitting for a long ride in a town where goods were so expensive had left Slocum with the grand total of two dollars and eight cents in his poke.

The shortage of funds was a concern. But of more importance to Slocum, they were finally on the trail. He wasn't sure where Blue McCorley's bunch might be by now, but he knew where they were going and the road they would travel to get there. The only problem was to catch up with them before they reached Santa Fe. It was their only chance to reclaim the stolen horses.

He became aware of Elaine's gaze. "Something bothering you, Slocum?" she asked.

Something was. A well-carved body in an empty tool shed back in Tascosa. But he shook his head. "Not really."

Elaine rose in a smooth, catlike motion, wrapped a bandanna around her hand and reached for the coffeepot at the edge of the fire.

"Slocum," she said as she refilled his cup, "I've just now realized I don't know much about you. I don't mean to pry, and God knows I'm in your debt." She filled her own cup and sat. "Uncle Ed mentioned you from time to time. Fondly, I might add. I guess I've just now had the time to wonder."

Slocum shrugged. "Not much to tell. When I came home to the farm back in Georgia after the war, I hung up my guns and swore I'd never again use them to kill another man. It didn't work out that way."

"What happened?"

"One day a federal judge rode out to the farm. He wanted the land. Claimed my dad hadn't paid the taxes on it during the war. That was a damned lie. William Slocum never left a bill unpaid. The judge came back a few days later with a man he called a sheriff but who was really just a hired gun. I killed them both, burned the house and barn to the ground, saddled up, and headed west. Been drifting ever since." He drained the last of his coffee.

"Don't you worry about them coming after you? For killing the judge and the other man?"

Slocum shook his head. "Not as long as I stay west of the Mississippi. Lawmen out here don't care much about Georgia's problems. They probably take any wanted notices from that part of the country to the outhouse with them. I stopped worrying about it a long time back." He raised an eyebrow at the girl. "How about you, Elaine? If we're trading life stories, it's your turn."

Elaine dropped her gaze to the dying fire. "I was born in Tennessee. I never really knew my real parents. I couldn't have been more than four when they died."

"What were they like?"

"Big. That's about all I remember. But at that age all grownups are big." She sighed. "I had no other family. Spent a few weeks in an orphanage before Ed and Eva Storm came for me and brought me to Texas to live with them. I always knew they weren't my real parents, but I wouldn't let myself admit that. They were good to me, Slocum. We had a good life until—" Her voice trailed away. Slocum detected a hint of moisture in the corners of her eyes.

"So what will you do after we settle this mess, get your horses and money back?"

Elaine stared into the fire for a moment. "I don't know. I'd always planned on staying with the horse ranch, someday meeting a nice young man, maybe raise some kids." Her sigh bordered on despair. "Now, I'm not sure I'll ever be able to stand the touch of a man's hand again."

Slocum gazed at her in silence. There was nothing he could say. He realized for the first time the extent of the tragedy Blue McCorley and his gang had dealt this young girl. They hadn't just taken her family. They had taken her future. Slocum's own rage began to stir anew in his gut. *My God, what a waste,* he thought bitterly. *McCorley, you bastard, you're going to pay for that.*

Darkness had descended on the canyon as they spoke. Slocum rose, smothered the fire with a few handfuls of sand, and stretched. "Better get some rest, Elaine," he said. "We'll be pulling out at first light. We've a lot of miles to make up."

Elaine shook out her bedroll, pulled off her hat and boots, and slid into the blankets. Slocum sat for a moment, staring at the growing brilliance of a blanket of stars in the blue-black sky above the canyon.

"Slocum? What's this Death's Head Trail? Do you know it?"

Slocum reached for a cigarillo. He had only two left, and then it would be back to cigarettes until he got his hands on some more money. He scratched a match on the sole of his boot and fired the smoke. "I know of it, and generally where it runs." He settled back on his blankets, savoring the rich flavor of the tobacco. "Years ago, during the days of the California gold rush, Josiah Gregg opened a wagon road that ran south of Tascosa and west to Santa Fe. He was hoping to find a more southern route than the old Santa Fe Trail. One that would give people a couple more months of good traveling weather before winter hit. The trail generally follows the Canadian, but it swings out onto the Staked Plains where the river breaks are too rough for travel."

"Why do they call it Death's Head Trail?"

"At the time this was Indian country. Comanche, Kiowa, and Kiowa-Apache. The Indians didn't take kindly to white men moving across their hunting grounds." Slocum paused, blew a smoke ring, and watched the gray-white circle drift away. "The Kiowa ambushed a number of travelers along the trail. They cut their heads off and stuck them on stakes as a warning to others who might be tempted to follow the river trail. A few of the skulls stood for years after travelers quit using the trace. That's where the name came from. The grinning skulls on stakes. Death's Head Trail."

"It's a scary story," Elaine said.

Slocum took a long drag from the cigarillo. "It's a scary country, Elaine. Full of scary people."

Elaine was quiet for a moment. "Slocum," she said at length, "I've no reason to be scared."

Slocum finished his smoke as Elaine's breathing settled into the regular pattern of sleep. *No, girl,* he thought, *after what you've been through, I guess you don't.* He stared at the small form huddled beneath the blankets against the growing chill of the plains night. *It's our job now to make it scary for some other folks. And I think we just might be the team to do it.*

The thought startled Slocum a bit. He hadn't thought of Elaine and himself as a team before. But Elaine wasn't a helpless young girl. A week ago she might have been. Now she was tough, determined, carrying a load of hate and willing to be as ruthless as any grown man. *You'll do to ride the river with, Elaine,* he thought, *and someday maybe you'll learn to live with this, find your young man, and settle down to raise a few horses and a few kids.*

The midmorning sun broiled the rolling hills of the sweeping grasslands along the southern edge of the Canadian River breaks. The still air compounded the heat; sweat trickled steadily down Slocum's back. He had spent most of his time in the Texas Panhandle cursing the infernal wind that seemed to constantly rake the region. Now, he would have paid his last two bucks and change for a breath of that cooling breeze.

In the distance the hazy mass of Torrejo Peak, the only near-mountain for scores of miles in any direction, shimmered behind the heat waves that danced from the tall grama grasses. The peak was the major landmark along Death's Head Trail. In another two hours, they would reach the trail. Then they would know if and when McCorley's gang had passed this way. Fifty horses left a wide track, one that would tell Slocum how much of a lead McCorley had on them.

Slocum stared toward the peak. It seemed only a short ride away, but in this country distances were deceiving. He knew it was almost a day's travel to the base of the tall flat-topped mesa.

The peak had served as a lookout point for centuries to nomadic Indian tribes, and it was a formidable fortress. The problem Slocum faced was finding a way to approach the peak without being seen by a lookout near or on the top. It seemed an impossible task, but there was always a way to get the job done. Especially when a man wanted to do it badly enough, and Slocum wanted Blue McCorley's bunch so much that he could almost taste their blood.

He wondered if McCorley and his gang were camped at the peak, awaiting the return of their two men from Tascosa, or if they had given up the watch and moved on. Slocum decided that for the moment it didn't matter. He would wade that creek when he reached it.

Elaine rode behind him, leading the pack mule, her shotgun slung over her shoulder in a makeshift carry rig. She had spoken little today. The dark fire was back in her eyes this morning. Slocum knew she was even more impatient than he to catch up with McCorley, but she had the common sense and self-control to curb the urge to charge ahead. Slocum's admiration for Elaine grew by the hour. There were even times when he forgot she was a young woman, thought of her only as a reliable—and deadly—companion on the hunt.

The trail they followed rose in a slow grade before dipping down into a shallow arroyo ahead.

Slocum topped the grade and abruptly reined in.

In the bottom of the arroyo sat a fringed surrey. It listed sharply to the left, a shattered rear wheel lying beside the rig. A sleek sorrel mare tethered by a picket rope grazed at the edge of a spring-fed stream little more than an arm's length wide.

And a woman stood beside the crippled coach.

She was a tall woman, her back straight and bearing erect. She was dressed in a full-length dark green gown complete with layer upon layer of petticoats with what appeared to be a whalebone corset underneath. A floppy green hat with big feather plumes sat atop her head. Slocum thought she looked like she was waiting for the first dance at a ball in an expensive hotel.

Elaine reined up beside Slocum and stared toward the woman. "What the hell is she doing out here, Slocum?"

"Damned if I know." He slipped the Winchester from its saddle boot and let his gaze sweep the rocks and brush of the crossing. He saw no other signs of life, heard nothing out of the ordinary. A blue quail called an alarm to its covey as a hunting hawk soared overhead. "Could be a trap. Any women with McCorley's bunch?"

"Not as far as I know. I don't like the looks of this." Elaine's tone was cold. "Let's just ride around—"

The sorrel mare suddenly looked up and whickered a greeting to the horses on the ridge. The woman turned, saw the two riders, and waved.

"Let's go, Slocum," Elaine said, the irritation plain in her voice. "We've got some hard riding to do if we're going to catch McCorley."

Slocum lifted a hand. "Hold on a minute. We can't just ride on. She might be in trouble."

"Who gives a shit?"

The acid tone of the expletive startled Slocum. He turned to Elaine. "Dammit, girl," he said, "suppose I had just ridden on when you were in trouble? Where would you be now? Besides, it can't hurt to spend a few minutes checking on her." Slocum didn't wait for a reply. He kneed Jug toward the surrey.

The woman stood with long, delicate fingers clasped demurely at her waist as Slocum reined in before her. Up close she was quite a package. She looked to be in her mid-to late-thirties. Sunlight laced flecks of gold over auburn hair pulled back in a bun below the green hat. Her eyes were a deep violet, a startling contrast to the pale, smooth skin of her face. Full lips lifted in a smile that dimpled her cheeks and crinkled laugh lines around the expressive eyes. The corset struggled to contain lush, full breasts and a narrow waist that flowed smoothly into swelling hips and a flat stomach.

"Praise be." The woman's voice was husky, and somehow almost liquid. It reminded Slocum of the murmur of water over boulders in a trout stream high in the Rocky Mountains. It seemed to hold a slight accent. Some place back East, Slocum figured. "Mr. Mabry sent you, I trust?"

"Mabry?"

"Oh, my, yes. Mr. Tuttle Mabry, my escort. Is he not with you?"

Slocum shook his head. "Lady, I never heard of this Tuttle Mabry. Now, why don't you just tell us who you are and how you happen to be alone out here."

"My name is Mrs. Iris Funderburk. My calling brought me from Boston to this wild and untamed country. I employed Mr. Mabry to escort me to my husband in Santa Fe. When the wheel of our conveyance broke, he took fifty dollars, saddled his horse, and promised to return with a new wheel or send help." She glanced past Slocum toward the pack mule. "Did you bring the wheel?"

"We weren't exactly expecting to need a surrey wheel, Mrs. Funderburk," he said. "How long have you been here?"

"Four days, sir. And four nights."

Slocum sighed. "Then you won't see this Tuttle Mabry again, I'm afraid. It's only a day's ride to Tascosa. Buggy wheels don't cost over six, seven dollars. To be charitable, maybe he ran into some thief and got killed. Most likely, he just took your money and kept going."

"The money doesn't matter, sir. But I am sorely disappointed in Mr. Mabry if your suspicions are correct." Her brows narrowed in a frown of disapproval. "He seemed like a basically good man, despite his filthy habits." The frown faded and a bright smile lifted the corners of her full lips. "At any rate, you and your young companion have arrived. My ordeal is ended. The Lord provides those who trust. Sometimes it just takes Him a little longer. May I inquire as to your identity, sir?"

"What?"

"Your name."

"Oh. I'm Slocum." He nodded toward Elaine, who sat in brooding silence aboard the wiry little mustang. "This is Elaine Storm."

Iris Funderburk's violet eyes widened in surprise. "Elaine? But that's a girl's name. I thought your companion was a young man, riding astride and all." Her lips pursed in disapproval.

Slocum glanced at Elaine and saw the cold, silent anger in her eyes. Elaine glared at the older woman for a moment, then snorted in ill-concealed contempt. "We're wasting time, Slocum. Let's ride."

Iris Funderburk turned her attention back to Slocum. "Mr. Slocum, I have a proposition to put before you."

"I'll bet," Slocum heard Elaine mutter.

"I am prepared," Iris Funderburk said, "to offer you a rather nice sum of money to repair my wagon and escort me to Santa Fe. I have some cash. My husband will pay handsomely upon my safe arrival in New Mexico; he is a rather wealthy and influential man. I will pay you one hundred dollars now and another four hundred when we arrive in Santa Fe."

Slocum raised a hand. "Pull the reins in a minute, Mrs. Funderburk. Elaine and I have other business."

"Mr. Slocum, I can't *believe* you would even *consider* abandoning a lady in this—this wilderness! You don't seem to be so heartless and cruel as to do such a thing."

Slocum fought back a quick surge of irritation. "Mrs. Funderburk, I did not say we wouldn't help. I didn't say we would, either. Now, Elaine and I are going to ride off a ways and talk this over. We'll let you know what we decide."

He reined Jug upstream. Elaine followed, a deepening scowl furrowing her face. When they were out of hearing range Slocum pulled the bay to a halt and reined about to face Elaine.

"Dammit, Slocum," Elaine groused, "it's not our fault that woman is out here alone. Every minute we dawdle around, Blue McCorley's getting farther ahead of us."

"I know, Elaine," Slocum said with a sigh, "but she's right. I can't—we can't—just ride on and leave her here to starve to death. Or worse. McCorley's gang isn't the only bunch of cutthroats and bandits along this river. What if someone like him should come across her? Would you like having that on your conscience?"

"Conscience, my ass! I saw the way you were looking at her tits!"

Slocum threw his hands in the air in disgust. "Jesus Christ, Elaine! Do you really think that's the only reason I've got for helping her?"

Elaine didn't answer. Her lower lip protruded in a pout. It made her look like a sullen schoolgirl.

"Look at it this way," Slocum said. "We have no money. It takes money to run down outlaws. Suppose we can't get the horses and your money back before McCorley gets to Santa Fe? Without money, we'd have to give up. We'd be stranded in New Mexico with less than three dollars to live on. Then we'd never recover the horses and you'd never get to settle the score for what they did to you and your family. This woman's offered us enough cash that we can follow McCorley to Mexico or Canada if we have to."

"She'll get in the way. Slow us down."

"Elaine, if she gets in the way, she'll probably get killed, just like you or me. And if she slows us down too much we'll just ride on without her. Maybe we'll get lucky and run across a ranch house where we can leave her until we catch up with McCorley." Slocum sighed. "I know how you feel. But I just can't leave her out here alone."

"I don't like her."

"You don't have to like her."

Elaine shrugged. "All right. We'll do it your way. What you say makes sense, about the money and all." She paused for a few heartbeats, then gathered the reins. "Slocum, do me a favor? Promise me you won't pick up any other stray pups we run across?"

Slocum half smiled. "One of my many faults, Elaine. I'm like that guy in the story who tried to spear windmills, I guess. I'll probably live to regret Iris Funderburk. But there's one stray pup that I'm glad I picked up. Her name is Elaine Storm."

He reined Jug back to the broken-down surrey and sat in the saddle for a moment. "Mrs. Funderburk, we'll take you to Santa Fe. But I want you to understand something right now. Elaine and I are trailing a gang of dangerous men, thieves and killers. We'll be riding long miles and hard hours on short rations with little rest. Elaine and I may both be killed in the process. In fact, *you* may be killed in the process." He glared at her for a moment, letting the cold expression in his green eyes drive the point home. "To give us all some chance of staying alive," he continued, "you will stay out of our way when I say so, you will be quiet when I say shut up, and if you can't keep up we leave you behind to fend for yourself. Agreed?"

"Mr. Slocum, I don't see that I have a choice." She glanced again at Elaine. "But I must tell you I do not approve of your traveling in the company of such a young and innocent girl. It just isn't proper."

"Mrs. Funderburk, I don't give a rip what you consider proper. In addition to which it is none of your business. Now, let's get down to basics. The wheel can't be fixed. Is that sorrel mare broken to ride?"

"Yes."

"Can you ride?"

"I have no habit."

"Habit?"

"A riding outfit," Iris Funderburk said.

Slocum frowned in exasperation. "Mrs. Funderburk, I didn't ask the state of your wardrobe. I asked if you can ride."

Iris Funderburk's nose wrinkled in distaste. "Mr. Slocum, I detest horses. They are sweaty, slobbery beasts, and they smell terrible. Besides, I don't have a proper sidesaddle. It's indecent for a woman to ride astride a horse with—with her legs all splayed out for the world to see." She glared in obvious disapproval at Elaine, who sat silently aboard her mustang several yards away.

Slocum fought to control his growing aggravation. "Mrs. Funderburk, your sense of modesty doesn't mean spit out here. It's your life we're talking about. Now, answer my question: *Can you ride a horse?*"

She thrust her chin out in defiance. "I have ridden to the hunt, sir. Of course, that was in proper costume, with the correct equipment. I did not enjoy the chase or the senseless, brutal violence of the killing of the poor little fox, but one must participate in certain social events in the circles from whence I came."

Slocum stared at Iris Funderburk in disbelief. A society woman who hated horses and bled blue blood for a fox that would kill half the chickens in Boston, given the chance. *We are not,* he thought, *off to a good start here, Mrs. Funderburk.*

"So you can ride. At least you finally got around to answering the question," he said. He tried to keep the sarcasm from his tone but wasn't sure he had succeeded.

Slocum dismounted and took a quick inventory of the surrey. There was no saddle of any sort, standard or side. "We can make an Indian-style rig from the surrey top, a couple of blankets, and some pieces of harness leather. It won't be all that comfortable, but it'll be better than riding bareback. How are you fixed for supplies?"

"I have no food, Mr. Slocum. I ate the last of it for dinner yesterday."

Slocum's frown deepened. *Now we've got to stretch thin rations a third thinner,* he thought. "I don't see a gun here, Mrs. Funderburk."

"I do not approve of those instruments of death, Mr. Slocum." Iris Funderburk's jaw was set, her mouth drawn into a thin slit of disapproval. Slocum didn't like that expression. It gouged vertical wrinkles in her upper lip, aged her twenty years, and made her look like a setting hen bowing up to protect a clutch of nested eggs.

Slocum stared at her for a few seconds, suddenly not sure whether to curse or laugh. "Okay," he finally said, "you don't like horses and guns and violence. That's a personal problem you'll have to handle on your own, because if you ride with us you're likely to see plenty of all three." He reached into the surrey, retrieved a Gladstone bag and handed it to her. "Put your absolute necessities in here. It's all you will be able to take along."

"But—my things! I've some very expensive gowns—"

"Take your choice, Mrs. Funderburk. Say good-bye to your gowns and take a chance on living through this, or stay with them and die." Slocum shrugged. "That, madam, is the way the jackass ate the crabapples."

Iris Funderburk sniffed in outrage. "You don't have to be snippy about it, Mr. Slocum."

An hour later Slocum boosted Iris Funderburk onto the makeshift saddle. He tried without success to ignore the flash of an impressive amount of shapely white leg as the heavy skirt and petticoats rode up past her knees. Slocum tied a roll of blankets wrapped in a canvas groundsheet behind her, then handed up the Gladstone bag. It was heavy, and it made a curious sloshing sound.

Slocum mounted and reined his big bay toward the south, cursing himself inwardly for losing time and getting himself saddled with another female at a time and place when it was going to be hard enough for a man alone to stay alive. But he hadn't had much choice in the matter. Iris Funderburk had all the qualities to be a pain in the butt, but she didn't deserve to be left out here to starve to death. *Elaine, I solemnly swear I will pick up no more stray puppies,* he thought.

Slocum glanced back after a half mile. Iris Funderburk fidgeted and squirmed on the blankets of the crude saddle, fighting a losing battle to keep her skirts down. Elaine rode well off to one side, leading the pack mule. She ignored the other woman's presence.

"Slocum," he muttered under his breath, "you've stepped in it up to the hocks this time. Two women to watch out for, two hundred miles to go, and seven gunhands up ahead waiting to kill you. Just a little Sunday afternoon ride in the park."

He studied the massive gray-hazed peak towering in the distance and wondered if Blue McCorley was on its top looking back at him.

7

Blue McCorley sat on his bedroll in the camp at the base of Torrejo Peak and waited impatiently as the wiry tracker gasped for breath after the long climb down from the lookout point atop the mesa. One of the nice things about being boss, McCorley mused, was that a man didn't have to bust his own butt climbing two hundred feet almost straight up and then back down again. It was a damn sight easier to tell somebody else to do it.

"See anything, Bill?"

Bill Duggan sat at McCorley's side, trying to massage the quiver from his leg muscles after the hard climb down through scrub brush, loose shale, and rocks. "No sign of 'em yet, Blue."

McCorley grumbled a curse and spat a stream of tobacco juice at a dung beetle four feet away. The spittle knocked the bug end over end.

"Looks to me," Duggan said, "like Arkie and Smokey found themselves some whore to hole up with. They ought to of been back by now."

McCorley gazed toward the northeast for a moment, a worried frown on his face. "Somethin' tells me those two won't be comin' back."

Duggan's eyebrows lifted. "Reckon the law caught up with 'em?"

"Somethin' or somebody did. I don't reckon it was the law, or there'd be a posse on our tail sure by now." McCorley wiped a dirty sleeve across his sweaty face. "I still got that crawly feelin', Bill. Like there's a rattler layin' in my bedroll. Somethin' out there ain't right." McCorley abruptly stood. "Tell the boys we're movin' out. We can still make Coldwater Spring by dark."

"What'll we do for supplies, Blue? We're short on near everything. Down to our last bottle of whiskey, and that's the main thing this bunch lives on. We got plenty of ammunition, but eatin' bullets is damn hard on a man's digestion."

McCorley stared off into the distance for a moment, then shrugged. "Maybe we'll find us a ranch house or Mexican squatter's place somewheres and take what they got. Meantime, we make do. Tell Turk Cannon I want to see him. I'll leave Turk here to watch in case Arkansas and Smokey happen to show up in the next day or so. Or anybody else."

Duggan nodded and strode away on legs still unsteady from the climb. McCorley grimaced in self-disgust. He didn't snort at shadows and he didn't see ghosts, but he still was about half spooked over something he couldn't see and didn't even know for sure was out there. His asshole was puckered up tighter than ever.

He reached for his saddle. He wouldn't mind saying good-bye to this camp, even if they would be traveling without much grub and no liquor. Torrejo Peak wasn't McCorley's favorite spot. The water had a touch of alkali to it, enough to loosen up the crew's guts so they couldn't ride more than two hours without having to bail off and drop their drawers. McCorley had his own canteen of fresh water, and he wasn't about to share. Besides the bad water, it seemed like there was a scorpion or a rattler under damn near every rock.

Worst of all was trying to hold the stolen horses in the breaks around the peak. A herd of mustangs claimed this range, and the little black stud that ran the band was as good a horse thief as ever drew a breath. Twice in a day and a half the black had tried to run off some of the mares. He'd nearly done it, too. It took some hard riding to get them back. The black had tangled with the big bay Tennessee Walker stud, and the bay came mighty near losing the scrap. He was missing several chunks of hide. It would cut the bay's value with the horse buyers.

"Should have shot that black son of a bitch," McCorley muttered. At the same time he knew he couldn't. He admired a scrapper, and the mustang was a first-class fighter, pound for pound a better horse than the bay. Besides, a good stallion fight was something to watch. Those two had torn up a quarter section before the bay's advantage in height and weight had overcome the black's guts and quickness.

The mustang band was still nearby. Their tracks would help cover the trail of stolen stock.

At least the two studs with the ES brand had finally settled down and stopped scrapping all the time. A man still had to keep a close watch on them or wind up spilling the whole remuda or getting his own saddle horse gnawed out from under him. McCorley had considered shooting the two studs, but they were worth too much money. That Nez Percé stud in particular would fetch maybe two-fifty or three hundred from the buyer. Mexicans liked their studs with big testicles, and that Nez Percé stallion had cojones like cantaloupes.

McCorley saddled his roan and was securing his gear when Turk Cannon strode up, a big man with broad shoulders and hips, scarred knuckles. He wore a blue and green checked shirt he hadn't washed all year. Turk carried a .38-40 Winchester in a ham-sized fist and a gutta-percha gripped Colt .45 in a worn holster. "Bill said you wanted to see me, Blue."

"Yeah. I want you to stay here a day, day and a half. Keep a sharp lookout. Arkansas may still get here with the grub, but don't count on it. You see anybody else trackin' us, don't try to fight 'em yourself. Light a shuck after us and let me know. You know Coldwater Spring?"

Cannon nodded. "Held some rustled cattle there a while back. Reckon I can find it again."

"One more thing, Turk. If nobody comes along, see if you can shoot one of the mustang mares. Bring a hindquarter along with you." McCorley's nose wrinkled in distaste. "Don't like horsemeat, but we can eat it if need be."

McCorley watched until Cannon had gathered his canteen and started the long climb to the top of the peak, then pitched in to help the men break camp. There wasn't as much grousing and cussing as usual, he noticed. It was like the thing that gnawed at Blue had sunk a tooth in them all. McCorley wished he could talk out his antsy feelings with his mother. She would have had the answer. She was half Sioux and had a nose for medicine sign and spirits.

McCorley reined his roan toward the stolen herd. In the distance he heard the shrill whinny of the black mustang stud. He shivered despite the heat. This place didn't belong to the white man. Never had and never would.

He paused on a rocky outcrop and stared along their back trail. Nothing moved except the flash of an antelope's tail, the shimmer of heat waves, and a couple of buzzards circling overhead. McCorley touched spurs to the roan. Whoever or whatever is out there can have Torrejo Peak and welcome to it, he thought.

Slocum pulled Jug to a stop near the lip of the narrow arroyo he had been following and studied the peak, its features more sharply defined now that they had moved to within a couple hours' ride.

The butte stood in stark relief, backlighted by the lowering sun. Slocum detected no movement, no campfire smoke, no dust lingering on the horizon. Still, he couldn't take a chance that McCorley's bunch was not there, waiting. Riding into a nest of rifles was not Slocum's idea of a good time.

The tracks along Death's Head Trail told him the stolen horses and seven mounted men had passed this way, headed toward the peak, less than two days ago.

"Mr. Slocum?"

Slocum glanced over his shoulder at Iris Funderburk, irritated that she had interrupted his train of thought.

"Mr. Slocum, my—my bottom—is so chafed it feels positively raw." She squirmed in the makeshift saddle. "We simply must stop and rest—"

"Mrs. Funderburk," Slocum interrupted, "the condition of your bottom is no concern of mine." He glanced at Elaine and saw the glimmer of satisfied amusement in her eyes. "We've got an hour of riding left before we run out of daylight and have to make camp. Until then, you will ride, sore bottom and all, and you won't complain again."

He turned his attention back to the peak. There were at least a dozen ways to approach the butte, but he could see none where a man might ride up unseen by a sentry on top of the mesa. He would have to go in alone, at night, in unfamiliar terrain. Slocum had done it many times before. He had never learned to like it.

The arroyo they followed twisted and turned, gradually snaking back toward the peak. It was choked with wild plum thickets, an occasional stunted juniper or two, and flowering bush cactus dotted the bed of the dry creek. Previous flash floods had littered the few open stretches with rocks ranging in size from pebbles to hefty boulders. It would be tough going. Mrs. Funderburk's tender bottom was going to feel like somebody had taken a blacksmith's hoof rasp to it by sundown.

Slocum knelt by a small seep on a bend in the arroyo in the lowering dusk, dipped a finger into the water, and touched it to his tongue. The chalky taste of alkali sat sour in his mouth.

"We'll camp here," he said to the women. "Don't drink the water. It'll give a human the trots, but it'll do for the horses." He started stripping the saddle from Jug, listening to the rustle and creak of leather as Elaine pulled gear from the pack mule and her horse. After a few moments he became aware that Iris Funderburk was still sitting astride her mare.

"Problem, Mrs. Funderburk?"

She looked down at Slocum, her nostrils flared in disdain. "I was waiting, sir, for you to assist me in dismounting from this beast."

Slocum pinned a steely gaze on her violet eyes. "Mrs. Funderburk," he said, "you are going to learn to mount and dismount on your own. Getting off is simple. You swing the right leg over and just step down."

Iris Funderburk returned his stare for a moment, then sniffed. "I expect those in my employ to treat me as a lady, Mr. Slocum."

"Mrs. Funderburk, in the first place I am not in your employ. I am providing a service. I do not take orders. In the second place, out here you learn to fend for yourself. Now, you can stay on that horse all night if you want, or you can get down. It's that simple."

Iris Funderburk sniffed again, then dismounted. It wasn't a classic dismount; she all but fell from the mare's back, flashing an interesting amount of skin, then staggered as legs unaccustomed to riding almost collapsed beneath her. Slocum thought he heard Elaine snicker.

The auburn-haired woman quickly straightened her disheveled skirts and drew herself to her full height. She extended the reins toward Slocum. He glanced at the hand holding the reins, then at her face.

"Now what?" he asked.

"Why, I expect you to take care of this animal, Mr. Slocum."

Slocum snorted in disgust. "Mrs. Funderburk, I am not a stable hand. Tend to your own horse."

"But I haven't the slightest idea what to do."

"Then watch and learn, dammit!"

Iris Funderburk's upper lip pinched into vertical lines. "I don't approve of cursing, Mr. Slocum. Please mind your tongue in my presence." She abruptly turned from Slocum to Elaine. "Miss Storm, dear," she said, "would you be so kind as to prepare a cup of tea? It has been such a long and tiring day."

Slocum's frown of irritation quickly dissolved into a wry smile. *This,* he told himself, *is going to be worth watching.*

Elaine turned to Iris Funderburk, her eyebrows raised, the pack saddle she had just removed from the mule's back in her hand. Slocum waited for the thunderclap to break. To his surprise Elaine smiled sweetly and curtsied. "Of course, madame. And would madame prefer the Irish lace table cover, or would a simple oilcloth do?" The sarcasm lay thick on her tone. "I fear we have no biscuits, sugar, milk, or tea, but perhaps a cup of strong coffee, a strip of rancid beef jerky, and a can of cold beans would suffice? And perhaps madame would be so kind as to get off her scalded butt and fix her own damned supper?"

An expression of complete shock spread over Iris Funderburk's patrician features. "Well, of all the—the insolence," she sputtered. "And such foul language from a young woman—"

Slocum chuckled and raised a hand. "Ladies, please. Let's have no cat fights. Besides, Mrs. Funderburk, this wee slip of a servant lass here would tear you into small, bloody pieces should it come to blows. Now, ladies, let's finish with the horses and set up camp." He flashed a quick wink in Elaine's direction. The gleam in her eye was like an enraged panther's stare.

Silence fell on the campsite as the trio went about their work. Slocum watched Iris Funderburk from the corner of his vision. At least she was making an effort. She watched what he was doing and tried to duplicate the moves, rubbing the salt-crusted sweat from the mare and leading the animal to drink at the alkali seep. Slocum put a double handful of grain in the morrals and placed the feed bags over the heads of the mule, Elaine's mustang, and Jug. Iris Funderburk looked about in confusion for a moment. There were no more feed bags available. Then, with a quiet sigh, she removed her plumed hat, dropped grain into it, and held the hat while the mare ate. *What the hell,* Slocum thought, *she's handling it reasonably well for a greenhorn.* He had to help her hobble the mare. She had no grasp of the simple nature of hobbles or how they worked, but she did watch carefully as he buckled the leather strap into place above the horse's fetlocks.

Slocum decided they could chance a small fire for coffee. He gathered dry twigs and pieces of driftwood from the arroyo and soon had a smokeless blaze not much bigger than his own hand going. He poured the pot half full of water from a canteen and dumped in a partial handful of coffee grounds. While they waited for the coffee to boil Elaine retrieved their possibles sack from the pack, lifted out a few strips of beef jerky and two tin cups. She handed a cup to Slocum. Iris Funderburk strode to her Gladstone bag, rummaged a moment, and brought out a small blue-tinted bottle. She lifted it to her lips, downed two substantial swallows, then thrust the bottle back into the bag. She returned to the camp with her own cup, a fragile china container wrapped with care in a linen petticoat.

Slocum reached into his saddlebag, uncorked the bottle of Old Overholt, and poured a shot into his tin cup. He raised the bottle and an eyebrow in Elaine's direction. At her nod, he splashed a dollop of whiskey into her cup.

He became aware of Iris Funderburk's cold stare.

"Something bothering you again, Mrs. Funderburk?"

Her gaze was unblinking. "Liquor, Mr. Slocum. The devil's handiwork."

Slocum sighed. "I suppose you're against liquor, too?"

"I am, sir. That is my mission in life. It is what brought me to this—this wilderness of the spirit called Texas. It is my calling to deliver the souls of men from the effects of demon rum."

Slocum stared at her in disgust. He needed the drink worse than ever now.

"So whiskey is another one of your crusades?"

"It is, sir. And I find it absolutely repulsive that you provide this innocent young lady with the poison of the devil. It is obviously your intent to completely corrupt the poor child."

Elaine bristled. "I sure as hell don't need your protection from the evils of the world," she snapped.

Slocum tossed down his drink at a single gulp and poured another, even though he had planned to have only the one. It had suddenly become a matter of principle. "If good whiskey is the devil's handiwork, Mrs. Funderburk, I personally hope he hires more help and turns out a few more barrels a week." He glanced at Elaine. The girl stared at the older woman, her gaze cold as a February norther, as she sipped at her own cup.

Iris Funderburk ignored Slocum's challenge. "I am, sir, a founding member of an active chapter of the Ladies' Temperance Union of Boston." Her back was straight and stiff in obvious pride. "When my husband elected to move to Santa Fe to expand his business empire, my decision was to take a brief sabbatical and spread the message of temperance on the western frontier. I returned East, consulted with my sisters in the union, then traveled to Dodge City by rail to begin my work there. I then bought the surrey to follow my calling to the wicked cattle towns of Kansas and Texas."

Slocum couldn't help but chuckle. A woman who would try to banish whiskey from Dodge City, Mobeetie, and Tascosa was a bigger chaser of windmills than he was. "And the results?"

She sighed. "A start, Mr. Slocum. A few converts among the ruffians. More importantly, among their women. That, sir, is where the future of the temperance movement rests."

"So you wind up stranded in the middle of nowhere. Seems to be the long way around to spread a message to the poor and unwashed drunkards of the American West." Slocum made no attempt to hide the amusement in his voice.

"After Tascosa, my mission was complete for the time being. So I hired Mr. Tuttle to escort me to Santa Fe. It seemed the most logical way to return home."

Slocum became aware that the coffeepot was boiling. He flipped the lid open and added a little cold water to settle the grounds. As he did so, Iris Funderburk moved to his side and sat down. Elaine pointedly moved a few feet away.

Slocum wondered how he was going to keep these two from a knock-down-drag-out worthy of any saloon brawl. *I told Elaine I might live to regret Iris Funderburk,* he thought, *and it looks like we're getting there a damn sight sooner than I expected.*

"Mrs. Funderburk," he said, "we've established that you hate horses, guns, violence, cursing, and liquor. Maybe we ought to take the short road. Is there anything you *do* like?"

"Yes, Mr. Slocum. I believe in the human body as a temple of the spirit, a vessel not to be poisoned, but celebrated."

Sure, Slocum thought, *and just what the hell is left to celebrate with?* He studied Iris Funderburk's face for a moment. Her skin seemed to be flushed, the expression in her eyes more alive than when they first made camp.

Slocum wrapped the handle of the pot in his bandanna, filled all three cups, and sipped at the bitter liquid. In the future he would ask Elaine to handle the coffee detail. She was better at it.

"By the way, Mrs. Funderburk," he said casually, "I noticed you taking a nip from a bottle in that Gladstone bag. Mind telling me what it is?"

"Certainly. It is Lady Lydia's Elixir for Women, Mr. Slocum. A medicinal preparation which prevents chills, the vapors, and—and certain female problems."

Maybe I better get myself a gallon of it somewhere, Slocum thought. *God knows I've got female problems. Two of them.*

The campsite was in near darkness when they finished their coffee. Slocum scooped sand over the fire; there was no need to advertise their whereabouts to anyone who might be looking on. Iris Funderburk stood and glanced around. "If you will excuse me, I must attend my toilette."

"What?"

"The lady needs to pee, Slocum," Elaine said coldly.

"Oh. Pick a bush anywhere within twenty yards. Elaine, go with her and take your scattergun along."

Elaine's mouth twisted in a frown, but she reached for the shotgun. "Let's go, madame," she said.

"Watch out for rattlers," Slocum said. "Squat on one and we'll have the devil's own time trying to figure out where to put the tourniquet."

Despite the fading light, Slocum saw Iris Funderburk's face turn bright red.

Slocum chuckled at his own joke and watched as the two disappeared behind a cluster of low bushes. The chuckle soon faded. How in hell, he wondered, does a man get saddled with two women like these? One hurt, bitter, maybe not quite right in the head, and just plain mad at the world. The other a bluenose temperance biddy who hates everything a man needs in the world. Life could get damn complicated at times.

He forced the problem from his mind. There was still the matter of seven gunmen with horses and money that belonged to two people named Slocum and Storm. They were out there somewhere.

He glanced at the sky. The night would be as black as the inside of a bull's gut in another hour. Then he would saddle up and check out Torrejo Peak.

When the women returned Slocum took Elaine aside. "I'll be leaving soon on scout," he said. "Probably won't be back for several hours, maybe even after sunup. There's a lot of country around that peak. If I'm not back by daylight, saddle up anyway and be ready to move. If I don't come back at all, forget Blue McCorley and the horses and ride out of here as fast as you can." He worked the action of his Winchester, made sure there was a cartridge in the chamber, and lowered the hammer.

"One more thing, Elaine," Slocum said. "Do me a favor. Don't shoot Iris Funderburk while I'm gone. We need the money."

The Torrejo Peak breaks were even bigger and rougher than Slocum had anticipated. The sky had begun to pale in the east, and he still had not completed his cautious circuit of the base of the towering mesa. And so far, no sign of McCorley's bunch.

He felt the big bay weakening between his knees. Even such a stout horse with a lot of bottom could take only so many hours of driving through sand, loose shale, and rocks, up and down the treacherous walls of one barranca after another, without tiring. Slocum knew he had to rest the bay or risk winding up afoot.

He reined Jug around a jumble of sandstone rocks studded with junipers. A small meadow came into view. The bay's ears suddenly came up, alert. Slocum saw the other horse at about the same time. A leggy but deep-chested sorrel dozed on a stake rope at the far side of the clearing. The horse wore the Walking T brand, the same as the one on Arkansas's mount. Probably stolen from the same herd at the same time, Slocum figured. Whoever rode this horse would be one of McCorley's men. A saddle and other tack lay near the sorrel. A blackened tin can rested at the edge of a now-dead fire. That meant there was at least one of the gang somewhere close by.

Slocum clamped a hand across Jug's withers in a signal for quiet. He didn't want the horse to nicker a greeting and alert the man who belonged to the sorrel. He reined Jug about, rode well into the tangled boulders, and dismounted. He tied the reins with a slipknot to a juniper limb, pulled his rifle from its boot, and worked his way over the sandstone until he had a clear view of the camp below. He settled in to wait. Sometimes it was better to let the prey come to the hunter.

The faint gray light of first dawn gave way to a brightening sky as Slocum waited. He was satisfied with his position. The sun would be at his back, in the eyes of the man who rode the sorrel.

He heard the man before he saw him, the scuff of a boot on loose shale, a low curse, the panting and wheezing of someone trying to pull air into tortured lungs. The sounds came from Slocum's left. He shifted his position slightly and pulled the Winchester hammer to full cock.

The footsteps drew closer. Across the way the sorrel's ears came up. Then a big, powerfully built man with a tangled reddish beard stepped into the clearing. He carried a rifle in his hand. Slocum held the man in his sights until he was a good ten steps into the clearing, with no cover to duck behind.

Slocum stood. "Hold it right there, mister!" he called.

The big man started at the unexpected sound, then whirled toward Slocum, the rifle muzzle coming up. Slocum fired. The .44-40 slug slammed into the big man's gut and drove him a half step backward. Slocum saw the flash from the rifle muzzle, heard the angry whack and buzz as lead hit the sandstone beside him. The slug whirred away as Slocum worked the action of the Winchester. He took a split second to be sure of his aim and drove a second shot into the big man's belly. The impact staggered the outlaw again. His boot slipped on the loose sand and he went down, the rifle dropping from numbed fingers. But the big man wouldn't quit. His right hand clawed at the pistol at his gun belt.

Slocum shot him in the chest, then quickly levered a fresh round and fired again. He waited a couple of minutes, listening to the scuff of the man's boots on the sand, the moans of shock and pain. Slocum was in no hurry. He had seen men shot through the heart manage to get off two rounds and still run twenty yards before going down to stay.

After a few minutes Slocum approached the downed man warily, circling to come up on the big man's left, away from his gun hand. Slocum stopped ten feet away, rifle muzzle trained on the man's head. The big man's eyes were glazed in shock and growing agony, but he was still alive.

"Who—the hell—are you?"

"Name's Slocum. Where's Blue McCorley?"

"Left—yesterday afternoon." A shudder wracked the huge chest.

"Where's he headed?"

The big man stared, hate flashing in brown eyes. "Go to hell."

Slocum half smiled. "Likely I will one day. I'll hand you one thing, mister. You are one tough son of a bitch." He stepped forward and drove the muzzle of the Winchester into the bloody patch above the man's belt. The big man's breath whistled in a fresh wave of agony. "Now, one more time. You don't owe McCorley a damn thing, mister, but you owe a lot to a young girl and three other people you and McCorley butchered. Now, where's McCorley?" Slocum rammed the rifle muzzle into the man's ravaged gut again.

The bearded man screamed in agony. Slocum waited until the big man caught his breath again. The brown eyes were glassy with pain, but the defiant expression was gone from them. "Cold—Coldwater Spring," the outlaw gasped. "Two days—upriver. For Christ's sake, Slocum. You done killed me—ain't that—enough?"

"Maybe. I'm still a little pissed over what you did to the girl. Maybe I'll just poke around on those belly wounds a while."

Tears formed at the edge of the man's eyes. "God, Slocum— gimme—gimme water—canteen—on saddle."

Slocum shrugged. "Guess it won't hurt." He turned away from the dying man. He had taken two steps when he heard the click of a hammer being drawn to full cock. Slocum hurled himself to the sand, heard the air buzz as a slug went past his ear. He twisted on his belly, aimed, and shot the big man in the head. A Colt .45, the barrel sawed off and trigger wired back, tumbled from the big man's hand as the rifle slug took a big chunk of his head away.

Slocum levered a fresh round into the Winchester and stared at the body for a long moment. "One determined cuss," he finally muttered. "Four slugs from a rifle and he still goes for a belly gun."

A noise at his back brought Slocum around in a quick turn, rifle at the ready. The sorrel horse stood humped, its eyes edged white with pain and fear. The gelding's knees buckled slowly. The animal fell, hooves flailing. The bullet from the hideout gun had thumped into the horse's neck. Slocum sighed, raised the Winchester, and shot the sorrel in the forehead, saving it a slow death. It left a bad taste in his mouth. The Storm killings hadn't been the horse's fault.

Slocum frowned as he thumbed fresh cartridges into the Winchester's loading port. McCorley still had almost two days' lead on them.

At least Mrs. Iris Funderburk would have a saddle now. The thought reminded him of something else. He stripped the bloody shirt and trousers from the dead man. Maybe that would take some of the sting from her "bottom," as she called it. Slocum rummaged quickly through the dead man's belongings. Except for the clothes, saddle, blanket, and bridle, there was little of use. He picked up the man's rifle and gun belt and strode toward his horse. They could pick up the saddle later.

At the crest of the rockfall Slocum paused and stared at the body in the sand below.

"McCorley, you bastard," he muttered, "you're down to six guns now."

Slocum stowed the booty taken from the dead man and swung into the saddle. The odds were getting better all the time.

8

Slocum knelt by the ashes of Blue McCorley's abandoned campfire, a frown of disappointment deepening the lines of his sun-browned face.

The big man had been telling the truth. The signs around camp said McCorley's bunch had pulled out better than a day and a half ago. And now Slocum was going to lose more ground. He glanced up at Elaine, still astride the wiry little mustang.

"We'll have to make camp here for at least half a day," he said, aware of the exhaustion in his own voice. "Old Jug is worn down and I'm not in much better shape myself."

Elaine glanced at the big bay. Jug stood hipshot, his head drooping, salt-crusted streaks of dried lather mixed with fresh sweat on shoulders and flanks. She nodded silently. She had been around horses long enough to know when one was ridden down.

Slocum flexed his own aching shoulders. He had been without rest for more than a day and a night, and even the quarter-mile ride to the dead man's camp to retrieve the saddle and a few other items had left him feeling weak. He rubbed a hand across his stubbled face. He needed a shave as badly as he needed a rest. Slocum always felt grubby when the whiskers on his neck and chin got to itching length.

Elaine stepped down. "I'll take care of your horse, Slocum," she said. "You just take it easy for a while."

"I won't argue with you, Elaine." Slocum handed her a cloth-wrapped bundle. Blood was beginning to soak through in spots. "Dinner," he said. "Fresh meat will be a good change after beans and jerky. Would you mind cooking it, Elaine?"

Her smile was gentle. "Of course not. Now, get some rest. I'll wake you in four or five hours."

Slocum watched her move toward Jug, her strides long and lithe for so small a woman. When he told her of the gunfight she had quickly put a name to the dead man. Turk. She didn't know his last name, but she recognized him instantly from Slocum's description. A remarkable and confusing girl, he thought. He'd never had a woman actually thank him for killing a man before.

Iris Funderburk fretted and wrung her hands about the violent end of the man called Turk, but she had expressed no qualms about taking over a dead man's saddle. Apparently a raw bottom upstaged mere morality by at least one layer of skin. Slocum considered for a moment telling her to rub a little bacon grease on her butt. The thought even flashed through his mind that he'd offer to do it himself, just to see what sort of a snit she'd throw over that one. He quickly abandoned the idea. It was best, he decided, to let sleeping dogs lie and sore bottoms heal themselves.

She wasn't nearly as enthusiastic about wearing the dirty, blood-soaked clothing punctured with bullet holes, but she was coming around. She stood now at the edge of the campsite, the dead man's shirt and pants at her feet, as she loosened the bun at the back of her neck and shook her head. Long auburn hair tumbled down past her shoulders. Iris Funderburk had fine-looking hair, Slocum thought. It fell in gentle waves that shimmered in the sunlight. She picked up the dead man's clothing, her nose wrinkled in revulsion.

"I'll have to wash these in that little stream before I can wear them, Mr. Slocum," she said. "I just couldn't don them in this—this *awful* condition."

Slocum leaned back against a cottonwood tree trunk and blinked, trying to clear what felt like gravel from his eyelids. "Suit yourself, Mrs. Funderburk."

"And I must have a bath. My heavens, I'm simply filthy— and I just *reek* of horse. Smelly beasts, and so sweaty." She glanced down at the clothing. "That poor man. At least we should give him a decent Christian burial."

"The son of a bitch doesn't deserve it," Elaine snapped. "Let the coyotes and buzzards have him."

Iris Funderburk clapped a hand to her cheek in dismay. "Surely you can't be serious, Miss Storm! Just leave the body to the beasts, with no words said over him?"

"Mrs. Funderburk," Slocum interrupted, "Elaine is right. The son of a bitch *doesn't* deserve it. That may seem cold and heartless to you, but Elaine has her reasons."

"Yes, I do, madame," Elaine said bitterly, "and the buzzards and coyotes will probably get the shits after eating the filthy, stinking bastard."

"My land! Such foul language. And why such—such hatred and loathing—for a fellow human being?"

Slocum's anger bubbled to the surface. "Why, Mrs. Funderburk, is none of your business. Elaine will tell you when and if she wants to. In the meantime, I suggest you not be quite so quick to pass judgment without knowing the facts." Slocum heard the hard edge on his words and made no attempt to soften it. The woman could be a real pain in the ass. "Now, will you please be quiet?"

Slocum saw the upper lip wrinkle again. She pulled a small blue bottle from the bag, twisted off the top with an abrupt wrench and downed a hefty swallow. *Must be warding off another attack of the vapors,* Slocum thought. But at least she shut up. Slocum's eyelids were growing heavier by the moment. He heard the clink of the bit and the creak of leather as Elaine removed Jug's bridle and wrestled the heavy stock saddle from the big bay's back. *At least,* he thought as sleep came, *nothing's likely to go wrong for the next few hours.*

Slocum came awake to a light touch on his shoulder. The angle of shadows in the camp told him it was an hour past noon. The rich aroma of fresh coffee and the smell of frying meat set his mouth to watering.

"Dinner's ready, Slocum," Elaine said.

Slocum's belly growled. "Sounds like I'm ready, too," he said. He glanced around. "Where's your friend?"

Elaine's nostrils flared. "Your stray pup is getting dressed. She'll be along in a minute." Elaine sighed. "Slocum, that woman's driving me crazy. I'm going to bust her one right in the mouth soon."

Slocum grinned inwardly at the mental image of Elaine

popping a fist into Iris Funderburk's jaw. "Hold off until we get to Santa Fe," he said. "After we get our money you can bust her nose in four places if you want to. In the meantime, try not to fly off the handle. We're going to need our wits about us when we catch up with McCorley."

"I'll try. But one of these days she's going to push me too far. Oh, the hell with it. Let's eat." She turned back to the skillet and pots sizzling over the fire.

Lord, Slocum promised silently, *if I come out of this alive and even half sane, I swear I'm never going to have anything to do with another woman for more than thirty minutes and five dollars' worth.*

Iris Funderburk strode back into the clearing from behind a wild berry bush. Slocum stared at her for a moment in surprise. Without her ballroom finery, she didn't look like the same woman. To Slocum's eye she looked even better. The dead man's oversized shirt hung on her like a tent, but it didn't hide all that much. She had obviously discarded the whalebone corset; her full breasts jiggled slightly as she moved. She must have had a sewing kit in the Gladstone, Slocum thought. The bullet holes were mended, the cloth puckered where she had pulled the material together. Slocum noted with interest that one of the mended spots was directly over her left nipple. He noted with particular interest that the nipple was firmly erect. The dead man's trousers were bunched and wrinkled at the waist, but tantalizingly snug across lush, firm hips. She had managed to wash most of the blood from the clothes. Only a few dark smudges remained. She tossed her head, her long hair still damp, and sniffed.

"My, that smells delicious," she said, "and I'm simply *famished!*"

She rummaged in the Gladstone and came out with another cloth-wrapped bundle. It held a sturdy plate of stoneware and a separately wrapped knife and fork. She carried her plate to the fire and sat down cross-legged by Slocum. He noticed that she smelled of rose water and wondered what else she had in that one bag.

Elaine filled a tin plate and handed it to Slocum. She had done well. The meat was tender, well-done, covered in a crusty flour batter. Beans, wild onions, and skunk cabbage flavored with fatback, thin cornbread cakes baked Indian fashion on a flat rock beside the fire, and fresh, hot coffee rounded out the menu.

Iris Funderburk held her heavy plate toward Elaine. The younger woman glowered at her for a moment. "This," Elaine said, "is what those of us in Texas society circles call a buffet, Mrs. Funderburk." Her tone dripped venom. "In camp, you serve yourself or go without."

"Oh. I understand." Iris Funderburk's tone held a note of apology. "I'm sorry, Miss Storm. One gets accustomed to having servants, and I fear old habits are hard to break." She rose to her feet and set about filling her plate.

The three ate in ravenous silence for a few minutes.

"Miss Storm, this is absolutely delicious," Iris Funderburk said as she reached for another cornbread cake. "And where in the world did you find such a tender piece of beef? It just melts in the mouth."

Elaine smiled sweetly at her. "It isn't beef, Mrs. Funderburk. It's horsemeat."

Slocum watched Iris Funderburk's reaction with interest. He didn't add that he had carved the steaks from the dead sorrel McCorley's man had accidentally shot. He waited for the auburn-haired woman to turn pale, maybe even drop her plate. She surprised him. She reached out with a fork and speared another slab of horse steak.

"Well, I must say the smelly beasts are good for something after all," she said. "This is delicious. And I've never eaten anything with the delicate flavor of these greens. How in the world did you season them?"

Elaine glanced at Slocum, a puzzled expression on her face. Compliments from Iris Funderburk were obviously the last thing she expected. "They're seasoned with a bit of salted pork and a chunk of severe hunger," Elaine said.

Iris Funderburk smiled at Elaine. "Miss Storm, my compliments. You have the touch of a master chef."

Slocum speared two more pieces of raw meat, dusted them in the flour sack and dropped them into the skillet to fry. "We'd best eat all we can hold, ladies," he said. "It may be a long time before we see a hot meal again."

There wasn't a scrap left within a half hour.

Slocum leaned back against his saddle, sipped at his third cup of coffee, and wondered if his belt could take the strain.

He hadn't been so stuffed since his last visit to Kansas City. He reached into a pocket for his tobacco sack, rolled a smoke, and lit it. Iris Funderburk frowned at him briefly, but didn't protest.

Elaine dabbed the last speck of grease from her plate with a folded cornbread sliver, then stood and took Slocum's plate.

"Miss Storm, dear," Iris Funderburk said, "you sit down and rest. You prepared this meal. The least I can do is wash the dishes and utensils."

Elaine stood for a moment in confusion. It was the first time Iris Funderburk had volunteered to lend a hand at anything. "Thank you," she finally muttered, and returned to her seat at Slocum's side.

"You know, this feast reminds me of some of our outings back East," Iris Funderburk said as she worked. "We used to have the most glorious picnics at Cape Cod." Her voice turned wistful. "We had the most wonderful seafood. Lobster, clams, raw oysters, snails—"

"Snails? You ate snails?" Elaine's tone was incredulous.

"Certainly, dear. They're quite a delicacy."

"And raw oysters?" Elaine's face paled. "I've had mountain oysters, but never raw."

Slocum listened to the exchange with growing amusement.

"Mountain oysters?" Iris Funderburk picked up a plate, scoured it with sand, then stacked it for washing in the alkali creek. "I don't believe I've heard of mountain oysters."

"Calf testicles," Elaine said. "We have them at branding time. We castrate the bull calves and bake the testicles by the branding fire."

Iris Funderburk shuddered. "Oh, my. That's utterly revolting."

"No worse than snails, Mrs. Funderburk," Slocum broke in. "But you haven't had a treat yet. Wait until you taste my specialty. Fried rattlesnake."

Violet eyes went wide. "Surely you're joking, Mr. Slocum!"

Slocum chuckled. "Only a little bit. It's really tasty. A bit like chicken. And it's much better fried than raw. I've had it both ways. I don't suppose you want to hear my recipe for boiled scorpion?"

Iris Funderburk and Elaine Storm both winced. Slocum laughed aloud. He stubbed out his cigarette and stood. "I'm going to scout around some. See if I can pick up which way McCorley went from here. All I know is they're headed for Coldwater Spring upriver, and I don't have the foggiest idea—"

The piercing whinny of a horse sent Slocum's hand stabbing toward the Colt at his belt. He had the weapon out and cocked before he realized there was no target.

"There!"

Slocum's gaze followed Elaine's pointing finger. On a rocky ridge above the clearing, a small black mustang stallion stamped his front feet and whinnied again.

"It's him," Elaine said, suddenly excited. "The Midnight Stud! I've heard of him all my life. He's stolen mares from every ranch for miles around here."

Slocum lowered the hammer and holstered the Colt. The black tossed its head, snorted, then whirled and disappeared below the ridge in a clatter of hooves. "Someday," Elaine said wistfully, "I'm going to come out here mustanging and catch that horse. God, breed him on a tall Virginia-bred race mare—" Her voice trailed away in wonder.

Iris Funderburk stared toward the ridge where the black had stood. "Miss Storm, I've no wish to challenge your dream or your ability, but I do hope you fail to catch him. Such a beautiful animal, running wild and free like that."

Slocum glanced in renewed surprise at the auburn-haired woman. "I thought you hated horses," he said.

"Only when I have to ride them, Mr. Slocum. At a distance I find them a magnificent example of the Creator's handiwork."

Slocum shook his head. *I'll never understand this one,* he thought. "We've got more important things to do than admire one of nature's best mare thieves," he said. He reached for his saddle. "You two finish breaking camp and pack up. I'm going to see if I can cut the tracks of some horse thieves of the two-legged kind. We can still make twenty miles before sundown."

Slocum knelt in the gently rolling sea of wind-rippled grass on the plains south of the Canadian, where the Death's Head Trail veered away from the rugged badlands of the river breaks. He studied the hoofprints for a moment, then picked up a single ball of horse droppings at the edge of a pile. He broke the horse apple open and sniffed the dung.

"My God, Mr. Slocum!" Iris Funderburk's nose wrinkled in abhorrence. "That is the most disgusting thing I've ever seen!"

Slocum glanced at her, not sure whether to be amused or aggravated. He had lost an hour sorting out the tracks of the stolen stock from the hoofprints of the black stud's mustang band at Torrejo Peak, and every wasted moment gave McCorley's gang that much of a lead on him.

"Mrs. Funderburk," Elaine said, "cleanliness may be next to godliness in your book, but when it comes to tracking, Slocum can tell more from a single horse turd than most men can from a map."

Slocum managed to hold back a grin, but barely. He ignored Iris Funderburk's shocked gasp. "They're still a good eighteen hours up on us, Elaine," he said, "but at least they're not gaining much ground. We're running out of daylight. We'll have to find a spot to camp soon." He tossed the horse apple aside and mounted.

"Well, I certainly hope you intend to wash your hands before dinner, Mr. Slocum," Iris Funderburk sniffed.

Slocum smiled at her. "A touch of horse shit is good for the soul, Mrs. Funderburk. But don't fret. I'll wash. *If* we can find a campsite with water out here." He swung back aboard Jug and touched spurs to the bay.

The sun rested on the lip of the western horizon before Slocum found a passable campsite. It was little more than a shallow draw a quarter mile off the faint trace of Death's Head Trail, but it had everything they needed. Fresh water trickled from a low bluff on the west edge of what passed as a creek in the dry, rolling plains, and pooled in shallow depressions. Stunted juniper trees and a dense tangle of wild plum flanked a sandy U-shaped clearing. The site had adequate water and enough driftwood for a small fire. The trees and plum thicket would provide some cover if needed, and privacy for the women to answer nature's calls. The latter was a camp requirement Slocum didn't normally have to contend with. Modesty was no concern to a man traveling alone, or even with other men.

The campsite would do.

Elaine had anticipated his decision. She had already started stripping equipment from the mule, the shotgun slung over her shoulder as she worked. Iris Funderburk glanced at Slocum, then at Elaine, and stepped down from her mare. It was a more graceful dismount than her earlier near-flops; the Boston woman was learning. She had frowned, but didn't voice any objection when Slocum told her she'd have to carry the dead man's rifle. Slocum and Elaine already lugged so many guns and so much ammunition that they couldn't have squeezed a horned toad into their packs. The .38-40 rested in the late Turk's saddle scabbard, seven rounds in the tubular magazine but none in the chamber. A half-full box of ammunition for the gun was in Turk's saddlebag.

Slocum stripped the tack from his own horse, his movements mechanical, and watched over Jug's withers as Iris Funderburk uncinched the mare and pulled at the saddle horn. The weight of the big saddle staggered her when it slid from the mare's back. She grunted with the effort, but she didn't drop anything.

In fact, Slocum conceded as he watched her work, Iris Funderburk was showing signs of someday being a good hand on the trail. Without having to be told, she watered the mare, rubbed the animal down, fed it a bit of grain, then hobbled it within reach of what little grass was available. She spread the saddle pad on the plum thicket to dry. Only then did she see to her own comforts, the first of which was to pull one of the small bottles from the Gladstone and take a long drink. *Must be god-awful country for the vapors out here,* Slocum thought; *four times a day she has a solid belt of her Lady Lydia's Elixir.*

She sighed, replaced the bottle, and turned to Slocum.

"Mr. Slocum, I must admit you were quite correct. That poor man's saddle is much more comfortable than I expected. My— my bottom—feels much better today." She reached behind her head and loosened the string that held her auburn hair in a ponytail, shook her head, and let the hair fall free. "And it's more comfortable even than riding sidesaddle. I just hope none of my friends back East ever hears of my riding astride. It would be such a scandal."

"Mrs. Funderburk," Slocum said, "I doubt we'll run across any Boston society types out here. And your secret will be safe with us."

A quick smile dimpled her cheeks. Then she silently turned to help Elaine gather small twigs and dry sticks for the fire.

Slocum remembered his promise after handling the horse apple. He strode to a small pool, picked up a bit of sand, and scrubbed his hands. Elaine already had the fire laid and the coffeepot out when Slocum returned. He felt a bit guilty over Elaine's doing most of the work around camp, but the feeling passed. She would balk if she felt taken advantage of, and she brewed coffee a hell of a lot better than he did. Slocum's mouth watered when he remembered the horsemeat steaks and his gut rumbled at the recollection. But tonight, supper would be jerky, coffee, and a couple of leftover flat cornbread cakes. They could have had venison. An hour ago a young mule deer doe had stood less than a hundred yards off and watched them pass. Slocum didn't even consider shooting her. Most of the meat would have been wasted in this heat. Slocum wouldn't say it aloud, but she was such a handsome deer he couldn't have shot her anyway unless starvation was at hand. At the moment they had enough supplies to live on.

Darkness descended on the camp as they finished the last of the jerky and coffee. Elaine rinsed the pot and refilled it with water from a pool. In the morning, all they had to do was start the fire and toss in a few grounds. Slocum knew he could survive without his morning coffee, but he couldn't call himself real sociable without it.

"Mr. Slocum? Would it be all right if I bathed in the morning, when we're finished with the water in the pools?" Iris Funderburk scratched at her scalp.

Slocum nodded. "Just use one of the pools a few yards downstream," he said, "and do it early. We'll move out at first light. Be ready." He nodded toward the .38-40 in the scabbard of the saddle Iris Funderburk leaned against. "Take the rifle with you. Fire a shot if you run into trouble."

"Mr. Slocum, surely I won't need a gun." He could hear the inward shudder in her tone. "Perhaps just a scream would do instead?"

Slocum sighed. "Just take the damn gun."

"Mr. Slocum, you're getting snippy again," she scolded.

Slocum's temper boiled over. "Mrs. Funderburk, I am going to be snippy until Blue McCorley and his bunch are dead. I am going to be snippy until we get our horses back. I am going to be snippy until Elaine and I have you safely in Santa Fe and your money in our pockets. I am going to be snippy as long as there are men with big guns out there waiting to blow my guts all over the landscape." Slocum slowed for a breath, trying to regain his composure. "Now, I am going to be snippy once more tonight, Mrs. Funderburk. Let me explain something to you: Shut the hell up."

Iris Funderburk pouted at the rebuke but fell silent, staring off into the gathering blackness.

Elaine squatted beside Slocum, the bottle of Old Overholt in her hand. "I think we could both use a belt of this," she said. Slocum took a stiff drink and handed the bottle to Elaine. He glanced at Iris Funderburk. Her upper lip wrinkled, but she didn't say a word.

9

Slocum awoke with a start, his hand instinctively moving to the butt of the Colt beside his bedroll. He lay still, senses tuned to the sounds and smells of the thin gray first light of dawn as he tried to pinpoint what had awakened him. His gut twitched and the hairs on his forearms lifted in the familiar warning tingle.

Something was out there.

The thought flashed through Slocum's mind that McCorley's bunch might have doubled back. Just as abruptly, the thought faded. McCorley wouldn't chance leaving the horse herd under a light guard. The horses were too much money on the hoof. Maybe just a prowling coyote or bobcat—

The thin clink of steel on steel cut the thought short. It was the sound of a curb bit or bridle. And that meant men on horseback.

Slocum tossed his blanket aside and glanced toward Elaine's bedroll. She sat erect, the shotgun in her lap, head cocked, listening. *So she heard it, too,* Slocum thought. He strapped on his gun belt and stood. He caught Elaine's attention with a soft whisper and gestured toward the clump of junipers on the north edge of the camp. She nodded her understanding, came to her feet in a catlike motion, and disappeared into the dense shadows of the trees.

Slocum thumbed back the hammer of his Colt and glanced toward Iris Funderburk's bedroll.

It was empty. *Where the hell is that woman,* Slocum grumbled to himself.

"Slocum!"

Four horsemen had topped the low bluff at the west edge of the camp. All four had guns in their hands. The muzzles of two rifles and two handguns were trained on Slocum. He knew at a glance he probably was looking at his own death. Nobody could take down four men with guns already drawn.

"You killed my boy, Slocum," a man on a stocky buckskin said. "Shot him down like a dog."

Slocum bit back a curse. In his preoccupation with Blue McCorley, he had forgotten the showdown with the kid in Mobeetie. Slocum's mind raced, hoping to find a way to buy time. The sun would be up in a matter of moments; the four gunmen would be staring almost straight into it and Slocum would be in shadow. It was a thin chance, but better than he had now.

"Silas Calhoun?" Slocum could see a slight similarity in the build. The light in the clearing was brightening quickly.

"One and the same, Slocum."

"Your boy same as killed himself, Calhoun," Slocum said. "You talk to anybody in Mobeetie, you'll know he pushed me into it. I gave him every chance in the world to walk away."

"That don't mean shit to me, Slocum. You killed my boy. His ma set a lot of stock in young Wes."

Slocum lifted his left hand, palm out. "Wait a minute, Calhoun. Let's talk this over." His gaze flicked from Calhoun to the other riders. The two at Calhoun's left held rifles, the man on his right a handgun. They looked like men who knew how to use them. "There's no reason for you to get killed, too. Your boys might get some lead into me, Calhoun, but you'd never live to see me go down."

The first rays of sun silvered the gray in Calhoun's handle-bar mustache. Slocum could see him well now, except for the eyes still shaded by the wide brim of a weathered hat. Calhoun was wiry, bandy-legged, obviously a man who had spent long hours and hard weather on horseback. One of the tough breed, the type who set their minds to a chore and didn't quit coming until the job got done. He held a big Smith & Wesson New Russian Model .44 in his left hand. An ugly weapon, but accurate, and the slugs packed a hell of a wallop. Slocum knew that if he lived past Silas Calhoun, he'd have to take the man on the rancher's right next. It would take the men with rifles a second or two longer to aim, especially from horseback. Horses tended to get antsy when guns started going off. A man with a handgun could fire a shot and still control a nervous mount.

"Boss," the man with the pistol said, a touch of concern in his voice, "we been trackin' three people. Ain't but one here. Two empty bedrolls down there."

Calhoun snorted in disdain. "Hell, don't even worry about 'em, Pecos. It's this bastard here I want. I want to tie his guts on my saddle horn and drag the son of a bitch halfway to Tascosa." Calhoun's shoulder muscles tensed. "Take him, boys!"

Slocum twisted to his left and swung the Colt into line. He stroked the trigger, felt the weapon slam back against his palm. Calhoun jerked in the saddle, the impact of the slug throwing the rancher's shot off line. Lead burned past Slocum's shoulder. Slocum threw himself to the ground, thumbed back the hammer of the Colt as he rolled and came to his feet. A bullet thumped into the ground where he had stood. Slocum fired by instinct, heard the solid *whop* of lead against flesh. The slug hammered the man called Pecos back against the cantle of the saddle. Pecos dropped his pistol and slumped forward over the saddle horn.

Slocum crouched low and whirled toward the rifleman on his left as he thumbed the hammer—and found himself looking into the black hole in the muzzle of a Winchester. Slocum slipped the hammer, hoping for a quick unaimed hit. But instead of a muzzle blast and recoil he felt the dull metallic click as the hammer fell on a faulty primer. He braced himself for the bullet shock.

The slug never came.

It was as if a huge fist slammed into the rifleman, picked him up, and threw him from the saddle. The heavy cough of a big-bore shotgun sounded from the junipers. Slocum thumbed the hammer, dove to his left, rolled onto his belly, and tried to bring the Colt into line on the fourth man. He slipped the hammer. The hurried shot went wide. Slocum knew he would never have a chance to cock and fire again; the rifleman had him dead in his sights. Slocum could almost feel the gunman's sense of triumph.

The rifleman's head suddenly snapped back. He tumbled over his horse's rump as the sharp whipcrack of a Winchester muzzle blast rattled the clearing. Slocum glanced to his right and saw the gray haze of powder smoke hanging low over the wild plum thicket. He lay stunned and surprised for an instant. The shot could have come from only one source. Iris Funderburk.

The surprise saved Slocum's life—and almost killed him.

Silas Calhoun had pulled himself erect in the saddle. He rammed spurs to his horse. The animal jumped, landed halfway down the side of the bluff, scrambled for footing, slid to the bottom of the slope in a cloud of dust and rock fragments, and charged wild-eyed in a dead run at Slocum from less than thirty feet. Slocum rolled again and felt a sharp pain as the skin of his back peeled away on a stone. Smoke billowed from Calhoun's .44 as the horse sped past, a hoof almost brushing Slocum's gun arm. The slug ripped into the sand where Slocum had been a split second earlier. Slocum scrambled to his feet as Calhoun reined the horse into a tight turn and charged again. Slocum didn't think; he whipped the hat from his head and sailed it toward Calhoun's horse. The animal ducked by instinct and for a moment Slocum had a clear shot at Calhoun. He waited a fraction of a heartbeat to steady his aim and squeezed the trigger.

The slug hammered Calhoun in the side of the chest. Slocum knew it had torn through the man's heart and likely exploded a lung. The rancher's pistol dropped from numb fingers. He stayed in the saddle for ten yards. Then he slid from the horse's back. A boot hung up in a stirrup. The terrified horse bolted, running and kicking, its hooves slashing into the lifeless body bouncing along underneath its belly. The horse rounded a bend in the arroyo and disappeared from sight.

Slocum gasped air back into aching lungs as he lunged for his rifle, still in its saddle boot at the head of his bedroll. He holstered his handgun, racked a round into the chamber of the Winchester, and scrabbled up the steep bluff.

Pecos was still alive, but his will to fight was gone. He sat moaning in pain, his left hand pressed against his bloody shirt. Slocum's slug had taken him high, broken his collarbone, and ripped away a quarter-sized chunk of muscle between neck and shoulder. Slocum picked up Pecos's fallen handgun and went to check on the other two men.

It didn't take long. The rifleman hit by the shotgun blast had been almost cut in half by the double-ought buckshot charge. The man Iris Funderburk had shot had never known what hit him. The .38-40 slug had nailed him at the bridge of the nose and exited near the top of the man's skull. His hat lay nearby, blood and brain matter filling part of the crown.

The whole shoot-out had lasted less than two minutes.

Slocum returned to Pecos and squatted at the wounded man's side. Pain and shock glazed the man's brown eyes. He turned a blank stare toward Slocum.

Slocum studied the wound more closely. "You'll live, Pecos. But you won't stop hurting for a long time. I tried to tell Calhoun and he wouldn't listen, so now I'll tell you. I've got no quarrel with the Calhouns. It ends here. I'll get you patched up, catch the horses, and you'll take the bodies back. Then you'll make sure no more Calhouns try to take my trail. Agreed?"

Pecos nodded, his face twisted in a fresh blast of pain from the wrecked collarbone.

Slocum glanced around at the sound of a boot against sand. Elaine stood a few feet away, her jaw set, both barrels of the shotgun cocked. The cold, detached look in her eyes rustled the hairs at the nape of Slocum's neck. Elaine Storm had just blown a total stranger in half, and her expression showed no more concern than if she had shot a marauding coyote. Slocum wondered if the girl's mind was still off track from that day at the ranch and the night in McCorley's camp. *One thing's for damn sure,* he thought, *I'm glad she's on my side.*

Slocum nodded his thanks. "I owe you, Elaine. That jasper had me dead in his sights."

Elaine shrugged. "These men were in our way. I'm not through with you yet, Slocum. I can't take McCorley on alone." She lowered the hammers of the shotgun. "What now?"

"See what you can do for Pecos over there. I'm going to catch their horses."

Elaine stared at Slocum for a moment. She looked as if she might object, but then cradled the shotgun in the crook of an arm and strode toward the wounded man.

Iris Funderburk climbed to the rim of the bluff and stared at the battlefield, her violet eyes wide and face ash-white. The muzzle of the .38-40 Winchester jiggled in trembling hands.

She stared for a moment at the man she had shot, then noticed the blood-and-brain contents of the hat nearby. She shuddered, lowered the weapon, and turned away.

Slocum stepped to Iris Funderburk's side. "Are you all right, Mrs. Funderburk?"

She nodded. "I just—need a few moments—to regain my composure. That poor man—"

"Don't waste tears on him, Mrs. Funderburk. He would have done the same to me, and probably to you as well. He chose his road. It just turned rocky on him."

"Still, it's rather shattering to know that one has just taken a life."

Slocum nodded. "I know the feeling. You never really get used to it." He cocked a quizzical eyebrow at the auburn-haired woman. "I thought you said you hated guns."

"I said I hated them, Mr. Slocum. I never said I couldn't use one. My brother taught me. He was a superb marksman and a fine teacher. He was killed by a sniper during the war."

Slocum winced inwardly. It could have been his bullet that killed Iris Funderburk's brother. Stranger things had happened on those bloody battlefields, and Slocum had been a sniper for the Confederacy. "I'm sorry to hear that," he said, "but I'm glad he taught you well. You saved my life with that shot."

Iris Funderburk glanced at the Winchester in her hands. "I wasn't trying to shoot him in the head," she said. "I wanted to hit him in the shoulder, but this weapon shoots high and right—my God, listen to me! Here I've just killed a man and now I'm talking like a—a gunfighter!" She raised her hand to her mouth in a gesture of dismay.

Slocum stared at her for a moment. "You surprise me, Mrs. Funderburk," he said. "Not that I'm ungrateful to be alive, but I never expected you to use a weapon. Where were you when this all started?"

"I had just finished bathing and dressing—you told me to get my bath early, you remember—when that awful man called your name. I saw what was happening, and it dawned on me that I had a vested interest in seeing that you stayed alive." Her lips lifted in a wan smile. "I'm a woman of many surprises, Mr. Slocum." The smile faded as she stared again at the rifle in her hands. "I can only pray that I never need use this terrible instrument again."

Slocum nodded. "I understand, Mrs. Funderburk."

"Dammit, Slocum!" Elaine's call was sharp and angry. "Are you going to stand around and talk all day, or are we going after McCorley?"

Slocum sighed. "Give Elaine a hand with the wounded man, will you, please?" He turned to walk away.

"Mr. Slocum, you're bleeding!" There was alarm in Iris Funderburk's voice. "Are you shot?"

Slocum became aware of the sticky wetness of his shirt against the stinging abrasions on his back. "It's nothing to worry about. Lost a little skin on a rock down there."

"Please—let me attend to it—"

Slocum cut her off with a wave of the hand. "Later. Right now I've got work to do." He made his way back toward camp. As he walked he shucked the empties from his pistol, threw the dud cartridge away with a sharp curse, and wondered just how many men had died because of misfires like that one. It had damn near cost him his life. He saddled Jug and set out after the Calhoun men's horses.

Almost a half day had passed before Slocum stood and watched as the man called Pecos led three horses, each with a dead man tied across a saddle, over the eastern horizon.

Silas Calhoun's horse had been the hardest to catch. What was left of Calhoun was still hung up in the stirrup. It wasn't a pretty sight. Slocum had seen more than his share of dead men, but the mass of bloody meat that had been Silas Calhoun had left even Slocum a little queasy.

Slocum had taken the precaution of disabling the Calhoun bunch's guns before turning the grim pack train over to Pecos. Slocum had no use for more weapons. They already had more than enough firepower. He didn't think Pecos was feeling up to coming back after them, but a man who didn't take anything for granted tended to live a lot longer.

At Iris Funderburk's insistence, Slocum stripped off his shirt and let her tend the scrapes on his back. She clucked her tongue as she washed the dirt and blood free, then reached into the Gladstone bag. She brought out a small bottle of clear liquid.

"This may sting a little bit, Mr. Slocum," she said, "but we don't want any infection. Even a small injury can be dangerous."

Slocum winced as she dabbed liquid onto the raw scrapes. The sharp burning sensation soon began to fade. He became more conscious of her touch. Her fingers were warm and gentle. He felt the pressure of her breast against his shoulder. The firm point of her erect nipple traced a tantalizing path across his bare skin. Slocum felt a stir in his crotch and realized how long it had been since he had had a woman. Slocum idly wondered if the tit against his skin was an innocent mistake or an invitation. He decided it had to be an accident. Iris Funderburk didn't seem to approve of much of anything that was fun, and Slocum figured that included sex.

Still, he thought, while she might be a pain in the butt with her bluenose rantings and ravings, nobody could deny she was a damn fine-looking woman, built to make any grown man whimper. He pushed the thought aside. He had more than enough trouble on his hands as it was. Thanks to Silas Calhoun, McCorley had gained another half day.

"There," Iris Funderburk said as she finished work on Slocum's back. "That should take care of it for now. The injuries weren't severe enough to require stitches."

She stepped back. Slocum noticed for the first time that Elaine sat well off to the side, swabbing the powder residue from the barrels of the shotgun. She glanced toward the older woman, her face drawn into a scowl. It was the first emotion she had shown since the shoot-out with Calhoun. Slocum wondered for a moment what kind of bee Elaine had in her britches now, then mentally shrugged the question aside. She was probably just itching to get on the trail again like he was. He reached into his pack for a clean shirt. It was his last one.

"Saddle up, ladies," he said. "We're losing ground on McCorley by the minute."

Slocum pulled Jug to a stop in the stand of cottonwood and native elm trees that dominated Coldwater Spring Canyon. He grumbled a quiet curse. The scout of the campsite had taken an hour out of the fading day, and it told Slocum they had lost more ground. McCorley's bunch had pulled out better than two days ago.

He fought back the urge to ride out the night. It would accomplish nothing except to wear down their already tired horses, and he was now in unfamiliar country. All Slocum knew of the land from here almost into Santa Fe was that Death's Head Trail turned abruptly south onto the Staked Plains once again. There would be no sure water supply for seventy to a hundred miles over that treeless, desertlike country. He dismounted, waved his hat to let the women know to ride in, and let Jug drink from the stream. Slocum knelt and tasted the water. It was pure, almost sweet, and cold.

Overhead, swallows swooped and chittered as they made for their mud nests built onto the almost vertical face of a sandstone bluff twenty yards from the camp. Below the nesting grounds a steady stream of water the size of a man's wrist poured into a broad, deep pool. The steady sound of falling water had an almost instant calming effect on frayed nerves. Slocum understood now why this had been a popular spot for travelers from early Indian times to the present. The walls of the canyon were studded with aromatic cedars and junipers, even a few pecan and piñon pine trees planted by wayfarers and Mexican shepherds years ago. The grass was thick, green, and lush, and showed little evidence that fifty head of stolen horses had grazed here for a night and part of a day.

The headwaters of the spring fed several pools along the firm sand and pebbles of the creek bed. Some of the pools were deep enough to swallow a man on horseback. Others were shallower, ranging from a few inches to waist deep. Most were several yards across. Wild berry vines snaked into tangled thickets that harbored rabbit, quail, turkey, small rodents, and the creatures that preyed on them. Tracks at his feet told him that a mule deer family had passed this way only an hour ago, a big buck, two does, and two fawns. The tracks also spoke of shy pronghorn antelope drawn to the pure water from their normal range on the flats above the canyon. Across the stream a porcupine labored its way up the trunk of a dead cottonwood, unconcerned about attack. The prickly creature would settle in for the night in a comfortable fork in the dead limbs. A slight breeze swirled through the canyon, carrying the faint gabble and chatter of wild turkeys settling in for the night in a chosen tree.

Slocum stood in silence for several minutes, awed by the sheer beauty of the place. The first evening stars had appeared against the darkening sky. Within an hour or two the canyon would boast a roof ablaze with thousands of pinpoints of light. Then the canopy would fade as a fat, full moon rose red in the east, later to turn hard and white as it crossed the heavens, its facelike markings staring down at the wonders of the land beneath.

Slocum's fascination with Coldwater Spring was tempered by the realization that McCorley and his gang had been here.

The splash of hooves in water, jangle of bits, and creak of saddle leather interrupted Slocum's quick moment of solitary peace. The two women rode up beside him, Elaine leading the pack mule. The horses dropped their heads and drank, quenching the thirst of the long ride.

"My goodness," Iris Funderburk said, her voice so soft as to be a reverent whisper, "this is such a beautiful place, an oasis stuck in the middle of a barren desert. This will be our most wonderful camp yet."

"Speaking of which," Slocum said, "we better pitch camp before we run completely out of daylight. Elaine, would you mind getting a fire started? We haven't had a decent meal since Torrejo Peak." He stabbed a thumb toward the river. "I heard a bunch of turkeys settling in to roost just south of here. This time of year there should be some young ones, maybe half grown, in the flock. I could do with some fried turkey tonight."

Iris Funderburk's brows puckered in confusion. "How do you intend to capture one, Mr. Slocum? I've heard they're exceptionally shy birds."

Slocum smiled. "That's true in the daytime. At night, they're not very bright. When they've settled down to roost, you just sneak up under the tree—they always roost in a dead one—pick out the bird you want for supper, and shoot him." He turned to Elaine. "Loan me that .32."

Elaine reached behind her back and handed Slocum the derringer without speaking. Slocum broke the action and checked the loads, then stuck the double-barreled weapon in his hip pocket.

"Why not use Miss Storm's shotgun? It seems it would be more efficient."

Slocum chuckled. "Mrs. Funderburk, we only need one small turkey. That sawed-off scattergun would drop a whole tree full. Maybe the tree, too. Besides, it makes too much noise.

The small-caliber gun will do the job on the quiet, and it won't mess up too much meat."

Slocum leaned against his saddle, content, his belly full, and worried a sliver of turkey meat from between his teeth with a pick carved from a juniper branch.

He had managed a quick bath and a shave in the cold, clear waters of one of the canyon pools. He was, he mused, beginning to feel almost human again. He reached for his tobacco sack, thought *oh, the hell with it,* and pulled out his last remaining cigarillo. He lit the smoke with a twig from the dying fire and sucked it into his lungs, savoring the rich flavor of prime tobacco.

Slocum became aware he was being watched. He turned his head and saw Iris Funderburk's upper lip wrinkled in that irritating manner of hers.

"Something bothering you again, Mrs. Funderburk?"

"That awful habit of yours, Mr. Slocum." She sniffed in haughty disapproval. "Those cigars. Such foul-smelling things. I simply do not understand how a grown man can abuse his body so with those products of Satan's workshop."

Slocum half smiled to cover the flash of irritation that swept through his gut. He raised an eyebrow at her. "Mrs. Funderburk, Old Scratch puts out a fine line of goods. In fact"—he couldn't resist the urge to needle her just a bit— "I think I'll treat myself to another of my many vices."

He plucked the bottle of Old Overholt from the pack, took a hefty swallow, and released an exaggerated sigh of pleasure. He offered the bottle to Elaine, who sat beside her bedroll a few feet away. She shook her head.

Iris Funderburk tossed her hands skyward in disgust. "Mr. Slocum, you are completely incorrigible in your dedication to vices—tobacco, strong drink, taking the Lord's name in vain, carrying on with a girl barely more than half your age." She stood, her back ramrod straight. "I shall pray for you tonight, Mr. Slocum. You obviously need someone to appeal on your behalf to the Almighty."

"Thank you, Mrs. Funderburk." Slocum lifted the bottle in a mock toast and downed another swallow. "I expect an old sinner like me, a man with no sense of right and wrong, the morals of an alley cat, and no visible code of honor can use someone to speak for him with the Great Spirit."

Iris Funderburk sniffed in disdain and strode to her own equipment at the edge of the clearing. She rummaged in the Gladstone bag, hefted a bottle of Lady Lydia's Elixir for Women, and downed a hefty gulp.

Slocum decided to ignore Iris Funderburk. It was too nice a night to listen to any sermons from a bluenose temperance tigress. He glanced at Elaine. The girl gave no sign of having heard any of the conversation. It was as though the two other people in the camp had ceased to exist, their presence beyond the veil of the frown that twisted Elaine's features and emphasized the hard glitter in her eyes. She had not spoken since the end of the fight with Calhoun and his riders, answering Slocum's questions or instructions with silence or a simple grunt.

Slocum was growing more concerned about Elaine. He had never seen such a deep hate in such a young woman. It was like blood poisoning, spreading to kill the spirit and finally the person. Slocum shrugged, corked the whiskey, and leaned back against his saddle. Elaine would have to find her own way back from the twilight range she now rode.

Slocum closed his eyes, listening to the night sounds of the canyon. An owl called, its throaty hoot comforting in the cool night air. In the distance a coyote yelped, its voice cracking on the last long syllable of its wail. Slocum curbed the urge to tell Iris Funderburk that this was his church, a living, breathing, bleeding, hunting, feeding, and breeding example of the Creator's hand at work. "Ah, the hell with it," Slocum muttered. He felt his muscles go slack in complete relaxation and contentment.

10

Slocum had always been a light sleeper, and now his eyes popped open, senses fully alert in less than a heartbeat. His hand rested on the butt of the revolver at his hip as he cocked his head, listening for the sound that had jarred him awake.

He still leaned against his saddle, fully clothed. A glance at the sky told him almost two hours had passed since he had fallen asleep. The full moon overhead washed the campsite in a bright white light.

Slocum's breathing was slow and steady, his muscles relaxed and calm despite the tingle of hairs on his forearms and the back of his neck. He glanced toward Elaine's huddled form. She was curled in her blankets, her light snoring a small, rhythmic buzz. Iris Funderburk's blankets were empty.

Slocum came to his feet, his movements fluid and silent, as he pulled the revolver from its holster. A faint scuffle like the sound of a boot on sand drifted to his ears from the nearby creek. He hesitated for a moment, thinking of waking Elaine, then dismissed the idea. There was no need to alarm her yet; the noise was probably nothing. And a yell or gunshot would bring her awake, scattergun in hand, if need be. He crouched and strode silently from the campsite toward the tangle of berry vines along the creek, stalking the source of the sound.

He had eased his way for twenty yards along the edge of the dense berry thicket when the scuffle sounded again, nearer this time. Slocum placed his left hand over the backstrap of the .44-40 to muffle the distinctive four-click sound of the Colt being drawn to full cock and eared the hammer back.

The rustle came again, only a few feet away. Slocum raised the pistol, stepped through the thicket to the edge of the creek, and breathed a soft sigh of relief.

The intruder stared back at him from the trickle of water, eyes covered in a black mask, something clutched in small forepaws. The raccoon studied Slocum for a moment, seemed to decide the strange creature on two legs was no threat, then calmly went back to washing a morsel of food in the flowing waters of the spring-fed creek.

Slocum grinned at the creature in the comical mask, lowered the hammer of his handgun, and was about to return to camp when his acute hearing picked up a distinctly human sound a few yards down the creek. It was a soft humming sound, barely audible but carried to him on the gentle breeze. He slipped back into a crouch and worked his way with care toward the sound.

He rounded a sharp bend in the creek and stopped dead in his tracks, frozen by the unexpected sight before him.

Iris Funderburk stood at the edge of a small pool. Moonlight danced over her naked body. Damp hair tumbled about her shoulders. Drops of water caught and held the moonlight on her skin, highlighting full breasts thrust forward as she arched her back. Her nipples stood erect, ringed by a patch of dark pigment almost as big as a half dollar. The curve of her breasts flowed into a tapering rib cage, then to a narrow waist, on to broad but firm, high buttocks, then to long, smoothly muscled legs and slender ankles.

Slocum felt the breath whistle through his nostrils. The moonlit statue at the edge of the pool was the most jarringly voluptuous body he had ever seen. He felt the stir in his crotch. Iris Funderburk's soft, tuneless humming stopped. Slocum knew he should quietly slip back to camp unseen, but the sight of her full body nailed his feet in place as if an anvil lay across his boots. Water droplets sparkled on the dense vee of hair at the junction of firm thighs and flat stomach. A hint of hipbone emphasized her narrow waist and broad hips. Slocum stood mesmerized by the scene, unable and unwilling to move, as she bent forward, picked up a strip of cloth, and began to wipe the water from her body. The movement of the towel over her skin tightened the bulge in Slocum's crotch.

He tried and failed to tear his gaze away as she dried herself. The towel rubbed across her breasts, down her abdomen, and into the thick hair of her lower belly. He heard her soft moan as the cloth slipped between her legs. He had almost found the self-discipline to turn away when Iris Funderburk suddenly looked up, her gaze locked onto Slocum's face.

Christ, here it comes, Slocum thought; *she's going to light into me with a tongue-lashing like I've never had before. But, by God, it was worth it—*

Iris Funderburk smiled, her full lips slightly parted, white teeth flashing in the moon's rays. She straightened, squared her shoulders, and stood facing him. She made no attempt to cry out or to cover her nakedness with the towel.

She beckoned to Slocum to come closer. He holstered the Colt. His heart hammered against his ribs as he strode toward her. *This can't be,* he thought, a bit dazed; *not the bluenose; she probably just wants me to get close enough that she can scratch my eyes out.* But he couldn't stop his feet from moving.

He stopped within arm's length and stared into her eyes, unable to read the expression in the moonlight. "I'm sorry, I didn't intend—"

She reached out and placed a finger on his lips, the universal call for silence. She stepped closer. The scent of her filled Slocum's nostrils, the smell of scrubbed skin, of rose water, the heady, musky aroma of an aroused woman. She slid her hand behind his head, pulled his face to hers, and kissed him. Her lips parted and her tongue flicked against his, hungry and demanding. Her breath was warm and moist, with a faint taste of mint.

Slocum slid his right arm around her shoulder, held her close for a moment, savoring the heat of her body. The tightness in his Levi's was almost painful. He slipped his hand from her shoulder, beneath her arm, stroked her rib cage and cupped her full breast in his palm. She broke off the kiss and twisted to her left, making it easier for Slocum's hand to move. A small, throaty groan of pleasure formed in the back of her throat as his fingers stroked the curve of her breast and brushed her nipple.

Her right hand forced between their bodies and slipped down Slocum's chest to rest on his groin. She stroked the swelling there. Her breathing was rapid now, the movements of her hand eager. Slocum let his hand slip from her breast to stroke her waist, then drop past the distinct edge of hipbone to the outside of her thigh. She moaned again as he slipped his palm to the inside of her leg and moved his hand slowly upward. She parted her thighs as Slocum's fingers touched the soft thatch of silky hair where her legs met. She whimpered as his fingers stroked her; her back arched, she pushed her pelvis against his hand, and moments later a shudder rippled through her body. "Wait—wait," she whispered, her voice husky. She pulled away from Slocum, reached for a blanket she had brought from her bedroll, and spread it on the soft, level sand of the creek bed.

Slocum unbuckled his gun belt, lowered the rig to the ground, and reached for the buttons of his Levi's.

"Let me," Iris Funderburk whispered. She knelt on the blanket before him, unbuttoned his trousers with trembling fingers, and slid them past his knees. He felt her warm breath against his belly. Her hand stroked his testicles, touched the sheath of his erection. Slocum's breath caught in his throat as her lips touched the swollen head of his penis. She lowered her head, slid lips and tongue around his shaft. He felt the swelling grow more intense until a few seconds later he had to reach down and lift her chin before he passed the point of no return.

She lay back on the blanket, pulling Slocum down with her. He ran his tongue along the base of her throat, down the exquisite curve of lush breast, and tongued her nipple. She put a hand behind his head and arched her back, her hips grinding into him. Then she reached down with both hands, parted the damp hair between her legs, and guided him into her. Slocum lay still for a moment, lost in the heat and tightness of her. Then, gently, he began to move his hips.

Iris Funderburk's mouth opened in a moan of intense pleasure. She thrust her hips up to meet him, slowly at first, then gradually increasing the tempo. Her breath came in gasps now; she suddenly convulsed, ramming her hips up to him, driving him deep inside her, her muscles jerking in the sharp intensity of orgasm. Slocum felt her spasms against his shaft, throbbing, involuntarily stroking him, and then he exploded into her. Every muscle in his body went taut, his own pulsations answering her contractions. She held him tight, her chin rammed into his neck and shoulder, until their throbbings eased and finally faded.

They lay locked together, spent and silent, their breathing slowly returning to normal. Slocum felt the sweat where their skins touched, slick and moist despite the cool night air.

Neither noticed the small figure in black vest and trousers watching from the underbrush a few yards away.

Elaine Storm had awakened as Slocum slipped from the campsite. She followed, shotgun in hand, and now her gut churned as she watched the coupling of the man and woman.

A whirlwind of emotions boiled through Elaine—an aching sense of betrayal, a deepening of the loathing she felt toward the woman who now lay beneath Slocum, a deep, sharp pain like an ice pick stabbed into her heart. And, she had to admit, jealousy.

Elaine wasn't sure if her jealousy was for Iris Funderburk's seduction of Slocum, or for the woman's obvious and uninhibited joy in the act. The sight of the naked couple on the blanket by the creek ignited again the fires of pain and humiliation she had endured at the hands of Blue McCorley's bunch; the sex act now held nothing but revulsion for her. Worst of all, she felt abandoned by the only man who had shown her sincere kindness outside her own family.

Tears burned Elaine's eyes as she turned and silently made her way back toward camp. *That whore will lead him around by the balls from now on,* she thought bitterly, *and he won't give a tinker's damn about me.* She practically threw the shotgun to the ground, rolled into her blankets and curled into a ball. Moonlight glinted on the moisture on her cheeks.

On the blanket by the creek, Slocum sighed, raised himself on his elbows, and looked into Iris Funderburk's eyes. "My God, woman," he said, his voice husky, "I never expected anything like this from you."

Her laugh was soft, throaty. "As you and I both said, Mr. Slocum, I am a woman of some surprises."

"But I thought—I mean, of all the things you hate—"

She placed a finger on his lips. "Just because I don't condone strong drink, gambling, foul language, and tobacco, sir, does not mean I abhor things natural and good in the world." She kissed him lightly. "You'll remember, I said the human body was a temple. This is that temple's highest form of worship, Mr. Slocum." She smiled seductively. "Besides, it's been months since I've had the pleasure of a man, and you, sir, are one hell of a man. I haven't come with that much intensity in my life."

I can't say that I have either, Slocum thought; *I'm not sure my knees are ever going to work again.* He became aware that Iris Funderburk's hand had snaked between them, stroking his testicles. He felt the stir of a new erection. Her hips moved; she leaned back, eyes closed, and moaned softly. Slocum felt her contractions against his swelling shaft, the quickening thump of his own heartbeat.

"Did you pray for me tonight, Mrs. Funderburk?"

"Yes. And my prayers have been answered. Now, Mr. Slocum, will you for Christ's sake shut up? Don't say another word. Just do your duty."

Blue McCorley crouched atop a rocky ridge, the highest point in the rolling plains, and muttered a sharp curse as he studied the back trail through a pair of battered Army binoculars. He saw nothing.

Bill Duggan squatted at his side, a stem of grama grass clenched between his teeth. The wiry tracker's keen eyes swept the expanse of open range. Duggan didn't need any help from binoculars. There were those who said his eyesight was better than a hawk's.

"Where's that damn Turk? He's two days overdue," McCorley grumbled.

Duggan plucked the stem of grass from between his teeth and spat. "Can't say. Maybe his horse got crippled."

"Yeah. And maybe not." McCorley lowered the glasses. "Bill, we've lost four men since we hit that horse ranch. Doby with his throat cut. Arkansas and Smokey ain't showed since I sent 'em to Tascosa. Now Turk Cannon's late. I ain't buyin' that as coincidence."

"Still got that twitch in your gut, boss?"

"For damn sure, and it's gettin' worse." McCorley turned to survey his camp. It had been two days since the last good water. The stolen horses were gaunt, too thirsty to graze on the dry grass. Don Pedro Alexandro Corajos would sure as hell cut the price on gaunt horses.

The men were as antsy as the horses, maybe more so. They'd been four days without whiskey. Biscuits, beans, and flour were all they had left for grub, and the flour was nearly gone. McCorley had already had to step in and break up two fistfights and one near shoot-out. He knew he had to do something, and do it soon. They were still a day's ride from the nearest fresh water, two days from the San Miguel foothills in New Mexico, another day to the secluded canyon south of Glorieta Pass where they would deliver the stolen horses to Corajos. And Corajos wasn't due at the canyon until two days after McCorley.

"Bill," McCorley said, "Arkansas and Smokey were too damn dumb to pour piss out of a boot. I ain't surprised they didn't get back. But Turk Cannon wasn't no fool. His not comin' back does bother me some." McCorley pulled a tobacco twist from his pocket, gnawed off a chew, and offered the quid to the tracker. Duggan shook his head.

"I want you to saddle the best horse we got and circle our back trail." McCorley worried the chew a moment, then spat. "I got to know who's out there and how many. Don't go gettin' trigger happy. Just take a look-see and hightail it back. We'll be close by Puerto de Luna on the Pecos in two days. Meet up with us there."

Duggan rose to his feet in an easy, fluid motion. "Sure thing. See you at Puerto de Luna." He strode off toward the camp. McCorley watched him go. *Good man,* McCorley thought. *If I had a dozen like him I could take half the livestock in Texas and most of the banks to boot.*

McCorley turned his glass back to the rolling hills. He saw nothing but heat waves and an occasional dust devil spinning across the parched grasslands.

Slocum nudged Jug into a steady, ground-eating trot. He knew he was pushing the horses bard, but he was gaining on McCorley's bunch. After Coldwater Spring, he and the two women had ridden out the day and half the night, made a dry camp for four hours' rest, and were in the saddle again before dawn.

Slocum's gaze constantly scanned the landscape, searching the seemingly endless horizon for any sign of danger. They rode through dry, rolling plains broken only by an occasional cluster of spiny Spanish Dagger plants with their tall white blooms and scattered growths of needle-sharp cactus bushes. The grass had brittled under the blazing sun and lack of rain. It crunched under their horses' hooves.

The view from atop one ridge looked much like the view from any other. Slocum now understood how so many travelers had become hopelessly lost in the vast prairie. Landmarks were nonexistent and water almost as scarce. The signs told Slocum that at times torrents of rainwater scoured the now dry arroyos and shallow creeks that infrequently scarred the ocean of grass. Their quick pace combined with the blazing sun and ovenlike southwest wind had already taken its toll on canteens topped off at Coldwater Spring. He knew he had to find water at least by sundown tomorrow if he expected to keep up this pace.

He glanced at Elaine, riding behind and a couple of yards off to one side, pointedly keeping her distance from Iris Funderburk. Slocum was worried about Elaine. She hadn't spoken since the Coldwater Spring camp and she quickly turned away when their gazes happened to meet. As far as Slocum knew she hadn't looked Iris Funderburk in the eye throughout the long ride and the brief rest. It was as if Elaine had built some sort of wall around herself to keep the rest of the world out.

And Iris Funderburk had surprised Slocum again. She acted as if the session on the blanket had never happened. She still frowned whenever he rolled a cigarette, and her upper lip went into those vertical lines again last night when he had taken the last drink from the bottle of Old Overholt. He tried smiling at her, and the only response had been an expressionless stare. Maybe, he thought, she was feeling guilty about opening her legs to him. Maybe she was trying to keep up a consistent front for Elaine's benefit. Women, Slocum mused, were nothing but a series of maybes. He wondered idly what the Creator had in mind when he built women. It seemed to Slocum as if the Creator had, with a warped sense of humor, taken all the contradictions left over after building the world and stirred them together, shaped them into a form a man couldn't resist, stuck Adam's rib in the concoction, then chuckled at the world's first man and said, "Lots of luck, fella."

A faint moan reached Slocum's ears. He glanced again at Elaine. Her face was pale. She hunched over the saddle horn, an arm pressed against her stomach. Slocum reined Jug in, let the animal drop back alongside Elaine's mount.

"Are you all right, Elaine? Are you sick?"

Elaine righted herself in the saddle with an obvious effort. "I'm all right, Slocum," she said. Her tone was cold and tight. She rode at his side in silence for a hundred yards, her eyes locked on the distant horizon, ignoring his presence. Then she suddenly gasped in obvious pain and again leaned over her horse's neck.

"Elaine, what—"

She shook her head, handed the pack mule's lead rope to Slocum and reined her gray mustang toward a nearby cluster of tall cactus. He started to follow, but drew Jug to a stop as she glared at him and waved him back.

Iris Funderburk drew her mare alongside Slocum's big bay. "Something ailing Miss Storm?"

Slocum shrugged. "Damned if I know." He stepped from the saddle. "Might as well stretch your legs a bit, Mrs. Funderburk," he said. He offered a hand to help her dismount. She ignored it and swung to the ground, massaging her firm rump.

Elaine returned a few minutes later, leading the mustang. Her face was still pale, but there seemed to be a fresh light in her eyes; the cold set of her mouth had relaxed a bit.

"Elaine, what's the matter?" Slocum asked. "If you're sick, I've got to know—"

Elaine stared at him for a moment in silence, then half smiled. "If you must know, Slocum, it's good news for once. I'm not pregnant."

Iris Funderburk gasped in indignation. Slocum stood, confused, for several heartbeats. Finally, it dawned on him what Elaine meant. He had never even considered the possibility that the gang rape might have made her pregnant. *My God, what the girl must have been going through,* he thought. "Jesus, Elaine—I never thought about it. That is good news."

Iris Funderburk sniffed haughtily. "I should certainly think it's good news. For both of you." She turned her lip-creased frown on Elaine. "You should consider yourself lucky, young lady—and maybe this will teach you the perils of sleeping with a man twice your age—"

"Now, wait a minute," Slocum sputtered, "I never—"

"And you, sir, are a cad of the lowest order to take advantage of such a helpless young girl—"

"Goddammit, that's enough!" Pure rage rang in Elaine's outburst. She took a step toward Iris Funderburk, her chin thrust out defiantly. "You two-faced, sanctimonious, holier-than-thou bitch! I ought to turn this shotgun on you, you pompous whore! You don't know what the hell you're talking about! Slocum and I never shared any blanket!"

Slocum felt the first tickle of anger—and a hefty dose of raw fear—bubble in his gut. He was about to have to referee a cat fight for sure, and didn't have a ghost of an idea how to go about it. He stepped between the two women. "Now, Elaine, settle down."

"Settle down, my ass!" she snapped, her eyes glittering in anger and hurt. "I saw you and Miss Clean here humping like hogs in heat by that spring!"

Oh, shit, Slocum thought; *how in the hell am I supposed to get out of this one?*

"Miss Storm," Iris Funderburk's tone was icy, "Mr. Slocum and I are both adults, of the age of consent. You, of all people, have no right to call another woman a whore!"

"Ladies, listen—"

Both women ignored Slocum.

"At least, by God, I'm no adultress!" Elaine's voice trembled. She seemed to be on the verge of tears. Slocum couldn't tell if the tears were from rage or hurt. Or maybe both.

"There are things you are too young to understand, Miss Storm," Iris Funderburk said, drawing herself to her full height and staring past Slocum's shoulder at Elaine. "But it's obvious you consider yourself grown up in one respect!"

Elaine lunged toward Iris Funderburk, fist swinging; Slocum grabbed for her wrist, missed, and small, hard knuckles caught him on the bridge of the nose with a solid crack that threatened to make his eyes water. Iris Funderburk reached around Slocum, fingers curled into a hook aimed at Elaine's face. Slocum grabbed Elaine by the shirtfront with his right hand, put his left against Iris Funderburk's chest, and tried to hold the women apart at arm's length. It was like trying to keep two bobcats separated. Amid the yanking and squealing Slocum absorbed a fingernail scratch on a cheek, another on his forearm, and a solid whop alongside the head from Iris Funderburk's flailing arms.

"Goddammit, *enough*!" Slocum roared.

The bellow seemed to startle both women. They looked at Slocum as if he had suddenly sprouted a second head. "Settle down, both of you!" He glared hard into Elaine's face for several heartbeats. "You tell her, Elaine, or I will," Slocum snarled.

"Tell me what?"

"Shut up, Mrs. Funderburk. Elaine?"

Elaine shuddered visibly and drew a long breath. Slocum could tell she was trying to regain control of her rage. Finally, he trusted her enough to release his grip on her shirt. She turned away, her shoulders shaking.

Slocum turned to Iris Funderburk. "I never bedded this young woman, Mrs. Funderburk. She was gang-raped and brutalized by the men who killed her family. The men we're tracking right now. You know what they did to her aunt, the woman who was the same as a mother to her? They cut both her breasts off, skinned them out for tanning into tobacco pouches—*before* they killed her, as far as I could tell. They planned to sell Elaine into the whore stable of some Mexican when they were done with her."

Slocum saw Iris Funderburk's face go white in shock. "Oh, dear God," she muttered, her voice barely audible. "What a horrible, horrible thing—"

"I'm breaking a solemn promise to Elaine by telling you this," Slocum said. "She asked me never to mention it to anyone. But the three of us are in this mess together and I don't have the time to keep you two from going at each other's throats. I will insist, Mrs. Funderburk, that you keep Elaine's secret to yourself."

Elaine spun back to face Slocum, her face almost scarlet in fury. "You want secrets, Slocum? Ask this slut how she can rant and rave about the evils of demon rum while she stays oiled herself on that tonic she drinks. I tasted it, Slocum. The goddamn stuff's nearly half alcohol!"

Slocum raised an eyebrow at the auburn-haired woman. "Is that true, Mrs. Funderburk?"

"It's for medicinal purposes only," Iris Funderburk said defensively. "And, Miss Storm, as a woman myself, I know that a girl in your—your current condition—could benefit from a dose or two of Lady Lydia's."

"Bullshit," Elaine snapped. "If I want whiskey, by God I'll drink the real thing and sure as shit won't sneak around about it."

Slocum thought he could use a solid belt of Lady Lydia's himself at the moment. He sure as hell felt a case of the vapors coming on. He decided not to make an issue of the tonic at the moment; he had other, bigger problems. He knew he didn't owe Elaine any explanation for screwing Iris Funderburk. But if he didn't, why did he all of a sudden feel like the world's biggest asshole?

Slocum reached out, grasped Elaine gently by the shoulders, and looked her straight in the eye. "I'd like to talk with you about this, Elaine."

"You don't have to explain a damn thing to me, Slocum," Elaine said. "I don't want her pity. Or yours. I don't care if you fuck Iris Funderburk all the way to Santa Fe. Just don't waste so much time doing it that those bastards get away." She slapped a hand against the receiver of the shotgun. "Just get me close enough to kill Blue McCorley."

11

Blue McCorley sat behind a rough wood table in the lone cantina of Puerto de Luna, a half-empty bottle of tequila in a big fist, and sighed in contentment.

The horses were grazing along the banks of the Pecos a few miles outside the sleepy little adobe village, replacing the flesh lost in the long, dry drive across the Staked Plains. At dawn tomorrow, they would be on the last leg of the trip. By sundown they would be in San Miguel Canyon off Glorieta Pass, a day's ride from Santa Fe. Then another day's work and Blue McCorley would be a wealthy man.

He still had most of the money from the raid on the Storm place—a little more than seven hundred in gold, silver, and specie—and fifty head of prime horses worth a touch over two thousand on the hoof. His share of the take would keep a man in fine style down in Mexico for months. McCorley had always been partial to Mexicans. Especially Mexican whores. *Must be the chili peppers that puts the hots to 'em like that,* he thought. He chuckled aloud at his own joke.

McCorley lifted the bottle and downed two quick swallows. The tequila went down smooth and hit hard. It exploded like a buffalo gun in his belly. He wiped his lips, drew in a deep breath, and stretched his legs. It was a wonder what a good bottle of tequila would do to cut the edge off a man's nerves, he thought. The boys had even quit bitching, now that they had plenty of grub and whiskey. They'd had a chunk of good luck finding the drift line shack and just one old cowboy there to kick wandering stock back onto their home range. McCorley

115

shot him in the back. The shack yielded a side of bacon, a sack of flour, coffee, beans, and a gallon of homemade corn liquor. A gallon didn't go far among six men, but it took the edge off their tempers until they got some real whiskey in Puerto de Luna.

After the horses changed hands the boys would have all the liquor, grub, and women they wanted. McCorley idly wondered how many of his crew would head south to Mexico with him. Duke Willison, the thin man with the scarred face, and paunchy Able Conroe had already said they were game. McCorley would welcome their company. Both were hellers with handguns, good men to stick to. He wasn't sure about Frank Tyler, the one-eyed half-breed Cherokee. Tyler was an independent cuss. Nobody ever joshed Tyler. At least not twice. He'd as soon gut a man as breathe. Curly Hogue, six foot four and two hundred forty pounds, without a hair on his head, probably would come along. McCorley liked the big man who could always find something to laugh about. Hogue was good for a man's disposition.

McCorley freely admitted he wouldn't miss Arkansas and Smokey all that much. Those two were just plain ass-backward dumb. He could put their shares to better use, anway. But who in hell was the jasper that cut Doby's throat and stole the girl? And where was Turk Cannon? Turk wasn't too bright, but he was solid and dependable. Something must have gone wrong. Turk was way overdue. McCorley couldn't shake the feeling there was a connection there somewhere.

He hefted the bottle again. He was beginning to get a little down in the mouth, thinking about his losses. It wasn't good for his reputation to lose too many men. Good gunmen were a tad picky about who they worked with. McCorley swallowed another couple of ounces of tequila. The mellow heat in his belly smoothed out a few of his worry wrinkles. Sweat beaded his forehead and his cheeks were starting to feel numb. The potent liquor was beginning to hit him hard. He knew he would feel like shit in the morning, but right now he didn't care.

The door of the cantina swung open. Bill Duggan stepped into the dim light, whacked travel dust from his clothes, and looked around.

"Over here, Bill," McCorley called. He waved at the Mexican

behind the plank bar. *"Dos cervezas, por favor.* My friend here looks a touch on the dry side."

McCorley waited until Duggan slugged down the first beer and reached for the second. The little tracker looked like he'd been rode hard and put up wet, McCorley thought. This was one tired man.

"Find anything, Bill?"

Duggan swiped a grimy hand across his lips. "Yeah. Turk's dead. Shot all to pieces, back at the peak."

McCorley slammed a fist onto the tabletop, sending a beer bottle skittering. "Shit! Dammit, he was a good man. Who shot him?"

"Probably the three that's tracking us now, boss," Duggan said.

"Just three? That ain't much of a posse."

Duggan shrugged. "Maybe. Maybe not."

A sudden chill of apprehension clamped down on McCorley's gut. "Bill—is one of 'em Pat Garrett?"

The tracker swigged at his beer, then shook his head. "Nah. Thought one of 'em might of been, at first. Tall man, over six foot. But he ain't Garrett. Hell, I'd know Garrett's hide in a tanning factory. Old Pat got a slug into me once down by El Paso."

McCorley breathed a silent sigh of relief. Nobody with the sense God gave a goose wanted to tangle with Garrett. The man was poison on the trail and a worse dose than that with a handgun. "Any idea who it is?"

"Yep. One of 'em, anyway. The gent on that big-foot horse I tried to track after he stole the girl. One I first thought might be Garrett. Other two, I didn't get a close look at, but I don't recall seeing 'em before." Duggan paused for another pull at the beer bottle. "Kind of a funny bunch, though. One of 'em looks to be a young Mexican kid. Big hat like the Mexes wear. Black vest with silver studs and the like. Rides a gray mustang." Duggan drained the second beer and waved for another. "Somethin' sort of familiar about the Mex kid. Can't say what it is. Might have run across him somewheres. Anyhow, third one's medium height, wears a funny-lookin' hat with feathers in it. 'Peared to me that one was wearin' old Turk's clothes."

McCorley leaned back in his chair and scratched at the

week-old beard on his jaw. "Well, hell. Just three of 'em. We oughta be able to handle three." He chuckled. "Damn, there for a minute I thought it might be Garrett on our tail. We'd of been in a speck of trouble then."

Slocum knelt in the shadows of the pines and piñon trees at the lip of rugged San Miguel Canyon and studied the outlaw camp below.

At his side Elaine Storm lay belly-down in the pine needles, shotgun in hand, jaw set, eyes glittering in cold hate at the men on the canyon floor.

The secluded canyon was a narrow, winding gouge in the southern Rocky Mountains, opening on the northwest to Glorieta Pass and to the southeast on the broken badlands and rocky foothills of the Sangre de Cristo range.

A small stream fed by springs and snowmelt ambled along the canyon floor. It nurtured rich green grass and a profusion of greasewood and sage underbrush on its way to feed its fresh, clear waters into the upper Pecos River. The southeast end of the canyon was barely passable by a man on horseback, choked with rockslides and a dense tangle of fallen timber. The deadfall practically plugged one way out of the canyon, Slocum thought, but it might have its uses.

Only a mile or so away in Glorieta Pass, one of the crucial battles of the Civil War had been fought when Texas volunteers and Confederate soldiers tried and failed to cut through Union forces and lay claim to the western lands, especially the rich gold fields, and trade with California.

Now, Slocum was trying to devise his own battle plan.

It wasn't going to be easy. In addition to McCorley's remaining half dozen gunhands, four more men had ridden into the camp barely an hour ago. Slocum recognized the leader— Don Pedro Alexandro Corajos, one of the premier dealers in stolen horses on both sides of the Rio Grande. With Corajos were three tough-looking vaqueros, each carrying a brace of handguns, a rifle, and bandoliers heavy with ammunition across their chests.

The presence of the Mexicans complicated more than just the gun odds. Slocum knew he had to open this ball in a hurry before the horse buyers moved the herd out. He could only hope that Corajos would spend a few hours haggling over the price. Even traders in stolen horses liked to dicker. It was all part of the game.

Corajos squatted on his heels now, sharing a bottle with McCorley in front of the tent pitched on the north end of the campsite.

The stolen horses grazed along the side of the stream at the south end of the canyon, loosely herded by a tall, thin rider who slouched in the saddle, rolling a cigarette.

"The one watching the horses is called Duke," Elaine whispered. "The little man sitting by McCorley is Duggan. Duggan never touched me. Brought me water, in fact. But he was the one who shot Martinez."

Slocum nodded, connecting the faces with Elaine's descriptions. Sometimes it was best not to know the names of the men you had to kill. Other times, it made the job easier. Maybe even fun. This was one of those times.

Two McCorley men stood watch at the north canyon rim, one on each side. Elaine identified the big man on the west side as Curly Hogue, the one on the east as Conroe. A third man, dark-skinned, with a nose like a hawk's beak, had solitary guard duty above the deadfall to the south. He went by the name of Frank Tyler. Strange name for a half-breed, Slocum thought.

Slocum didn't recognize any of Corajos's riders. They looked like men who would fight, and they were an unknown quantity. But they weren't on Slocum's wanted list. If they stayed out of the scrap, fine. If not, he'd take them down without a second thought.

Ten tough men against one, Slocum thought; *I'm right back where I started.* Except that now he had a couple of allies—if he could keep Elaine Storm and Iris Funderburk from killing each other in the meantime.

"Well, Slocum? What now?" Impatience tinged Elaine's question.

Slocum studied the camp for a few more minutes. "I see a way. Let's Injun out of here for now."

He led the way back to the stand of piñons where Iris Funderburk waited, holding the horses. Slocum refined his overall campaign in his mind as he and Elaine strode side by side over a thick carpet of fallen needles and pinecones. A red squirrel chittered overhead, scolding the intruders.

Slocum knew the key to the whole operation was to take out Corajos before the horses changed hands. That wasn't any particular problem. The sticky part was to cut down the odds a bit and manage to stay alive in the process.

He had a few things in his favor. For one, outlaw gangs tended to function as a unit, like an Army patrol. Slocum worked best alone. Keep them confused, off balance, and he would have an edge. It was a thin edge, but at odds of ten to one, every little bit helped. For another, Slocum had a weapon the men in the camp didn't know about. A young girl with a heart full of hate and a handful of sawed-off shotgun. And finally, he had at least one night to work. The sun was low enough in the west that the outlaws likely wouldn't try to move the horses out before dawn.

As for Iris Funderburk, all Slocum could hope for was that she could stay out of the way, stand guard on their mounts and supplies, and keep her skin in one piece. There was no way to get her to Santa Fe before this chamber pot started running over. But there was a place she would be reasonably safe, a spot that also could give Slocum and Elaine a hidey-hole if the business with McCorley got too hot. A quarter mile back on the trail was a cave, its mouth hidden by dense underbrush. The cave was big enough for three people and the animals. The jumble of rocks and brush provided cover, and there was a good field of fire from the brush in front of the cave. It would make a good base of operations.

A half hour later, Slocum squatted on his heels on the sandy floor of the cave, a fine linen handkerchief from Iris Funderburk's Gladstone bag spread before him. Elaine waited patiently at his side as Slocum cut open four shotgun shells, poured the black powder into the center of the linen, and folded the corners with care. He tied off the ball with a firm knot. Then he used the point of his knife to trace a rough map of the outlaw's canyon hideout in the sand.

He glanced up at Iris Funderburk, who raised a questioning eyebrow. "Mrs. Funderburk, I want you to stay here with the horses. Elaine and I are going hunting. Most likely, all hell's going to break loose tonight. If we don't come back by sundown tomorrow, you're on your own. Saddle your mare and ride northwest along the river valley. You'll find people there who can direct you to Santa Fe."

Slocum turned to Elaine, hefting the linen-wrapped ball of black powder. "All right, Elaine, here's what we're going to do—"

The sun was a bare handspan above the western mountaintops when Slocum paused to catch his breath. His legs felt heavy from the long walk from the cave, but now he was in position on the northwest side of the outlaw camp. The first rule of a campaign was to flank the enemy, if possible. The second was to gain a position where the sun would be in the enemy's eyes, partially blinding him. The third was to ambush first, then engage. The fourth—the trickiest—was to get out of the scrap alive.

Slocum eased his way to the lip of the canyon and let his gaze sweep the rocky, tree-covered slope. It took him only a couple of minutes to spot the sentry. The man Elaine called Curly Hogue sat with his massive back against a pine tree, hat by his side, his bald head stark white in the fading light. He was less than fifty feet away. A Winchester rested across Hogue's lap. His handgun was still holstered. Smoke curled from a cigarette in his lips. He was, Slocum noted, one big son of a bitch, with shoulders the width of an ax handle and a neck like a tree trunk. Not a man to go up against in a fair fight.

Slocum didn't plan to fight fair.

He placed his rifle on the ground with care and slipped a tightly braided three-strand rawhide thong from beneath his belt. Ordinarily the supple, strong little rope served as a tie-down for range branding or an emergency hobble for a horse. Now it would have a different use. Slocum wrapped one end of the thong securely around each hand and began a slow, stealthy approach. Each silent, careful step brought him closer to the big man. Then he was behind the tree, the sentry still unaware of his presence. Slocum crossed his arms, forming a noose in the rawhide thong, and waited.

It was a short wait.

Curly Hogue leaned away from the tree and spat.

Slocum whipped the loop over Hogue's thick neck and yanked as hard as he could. Hogue's startled cry came out a choked grunt as the narrow thong cut deep into his neck. He thrashed and flailed his arms, clawed at the noose embedded in his flesh, and then in desperation hurled himself backward against Slocum, slamming him into a boulder, bucking his powerful back against Slocum's chest. Slocum felt the air rush from his lungs. He pulled harder and felt the slick rawhide cut into his own palms. The skin on his back slipped and parted against the rough stone. Slocum ignored the pain and increased the pressure on the noose. Red droplets formed along the deep crease as the thong cut deeper into Hogue's thick neck. Slocum found an opening, rammed a knee into the man's back, and yanked against the garrote with all the strength he could muster. The bald man shuddered, hands grabbing fitfully at the strangling rope, then went limp.

Slocum kept the pressure on for a full two minutes, his own breathing harsh and heavy from the exertion. His shoulder muscles ached and he felt as if his arms might fall off. Finally he released the tension. Hogue's body slumped forward, trousers stained as the sphincter muscle gave way to the slackness of death.

Slocum knelt on the big man's back, gasping air into strained lungs. The rawhide had cut through the arteries in Hogue's neck. Blood that had come in spurts slowed to a trickle. Slocum stood, legs trembling, and stared for a moment at the body. *Nasty way to die,* he thought, *but then, I guess there aren't any good ways.* Sweat stung the scrapes on Slocum's back and rawhide cuts on his hands. He released one end of the thong and tugged at the other. It was too deeply embedded in Hogue's neck to budge. Slocum left it there. *One down, nine to go,* he thought as he climbed back and retrieved his Winchester.

Slocum crept along the side of the canyon, keeping just below the rim, using the timber, boulders, and lengthening shadows for cover. A few minutes later he knelt between two big rocks overlooking the outlaw camp. He eased back the hammer of the Winchester and sighted toward the tent below. Corajos and McCorley still sat outside the tent, gesturing at each other between slugs from the bottle.

Slocum figured the range as a hair past two hundred yards, almost beyond the reach of the .44-40. He racked the rear sight elevation slide to its top notch and rested the forestock of the weapon across a nick in the boulder as he calculated the bullet drift in the slight breeze. Corajos's distant figure perched on the front blade sight of the Winchester, bracketed by the V notch in the rear sight.

Slocum elevated the sights another degree, took a deep breath, and exhaled slowly as he squeezed the trigger. The Winchester thumped against his shoulder as the whipcrack of the shot rang in his ears. For almost a second nothing happened. Then Corajos's body jerked under the impact of the slug. The Mexican slumped, grabbing at his side.

The sound of the muzzle blast reached the camp a split second after the impact of the slug; Corajos's vaqueros scattered, coffee cups flying as they reached for weapons and glanced about, trying to pinpoint the source of the unexpected rifle shot. McCorley came to his feet and dove behind the scant cover of a pile of saddles. Slocum levered three more quick rounds at the camp. The slugs kicked dirt and scattered embers from the fire, but hit nothing.

Slocum ducked behind the cover of the boulders, knowing the cloud of powder smoke would mark his position to the riflemen below. He thumbed cartridges into the Winchester as lead spanged off the rocks and thumped into trees. Then he sprinted from behind the boulders into the timber, ran fifty yards down the canyon, and skidded to a stop beside a lightning-struck piñon tree.

Three men ran from the camp toward the rocks where Slocum had been, rifles in hand. Slocum estimated the range, led one of the running men by three strides, and squeezed the trigger. The man stumbled and went down, rifle spinning away. The two others dove for what cover they could find. *Nine and eight down,* Slocum thought; *seven to go.* He ducked as a rifle slug ripped past his ear and cracked into the hillside behind him. Another thumped into the trunk of the tree.

Slocum chanced a glance toward the lower end of the canyon. The horse herd, spooked by the gunfire, milled about, keeping the wrangler busy heading off a stampede. In the distance Slocum saw the tall breed—Tyler, Elaine called him—sprint toward the camp. Slocum grunted in satisfaction. With the sentry drawn to the gunfire, Elaine would have a chance to plant the black powder fire bomb in the deadfall where the touch of a match would turn the dried timber into a ball of flame when the time was right. Everything was going according to plan.

One of the vaqueros had mounted and was spurring hard toward a narrow trail leading up the canyon side to Slocum's right. Slocum snapped a shot at the vaquero and missed. A slug ripped a splinter from the piñon tree and drove the fragment into the point of Slocum's shoulder. He winced at the sudden sharp pain. *Time to get out of here,* he told himself.

He fired two more unaimed rounds toward the gunmen below, then sprinted from the cover of the tree, bullets kicking dust and stone fragments at his heels. He reached the top of the ridge and raced to his left, sprinting south. He heard the sound of hoofbeats, a horse laboring up the steep trail, and thumbed fresh cartridges into the loading port of the Winchester as he ran, hoping to reach a firing point before the rider topped out and was able to maneuver.

Slocum suddenly skidded to a stop, barking a curse. A narrow, steep, pine-choked gorge sliced into the canyon wall before him. The heavy stand of pines had screened it from his view during his earlier scout of the camp. He heard the sound of pounding hooves only a few yards away. He had been too late; the vaquero had reached the lip of the canyon and now flanked him. Slocum was trapped on a narrow triangle of rocky outcrop. He slapped the rifle to his shoulder, whirled to take aim at the rider, and his boot slipped on a round stone. Pain lanced through his leg as his ankle twisted sharply. The ground came up, slammed into his side, knocked the rifle from his grasp. The earth and sky spun before his eyes as Slocum tumbled down the edge of the steep ravine. Then the light winked out as something thumped into the side of his head.

A hundred yards away across the narrow neck of the canyon, Elaine Storm watched from behind a clump of junipers in stunned disbelief and horror as Slocum's body tumbled down the steep ravine and landed in a shower of pebbles and small rocks. A few yards from Slocum, two men raced toward him, guns drawn. Elaine instinctively raised the shotgun and just as instinctively lowered it. The range was far too great for the scattergun. She felt her heart sink and almost cried out aloud as one of the men—the halfbreed called Tyler—pointed his pistol at the back of Slocum's head.

"No, Tyler!" the man with him yelled. "We need him alive!" Elaine recognized the wiry tracker named Duggan. "Dammit, man, think! There were two more with this one. We got to find out who they are and what they're going to do!"

Tyler scowled hard at Duggan for a moment, then grudgingly lowered his pistol. The two men bent, hauled the unconscious Slocum to his feet, and dragged him toward camp.

Elaine worked her way closer to the edge of the timber, staying across from the two men and their captive. She was able to keep out of sight and still stay within hearing distance as they dragged Slocum before Blue McCorley. Even in the fading light Elaine could see that McCorley was livid with rage. She saw Slocum shake his head weakly, as if to clear the cobwebs from the fall and try to get his feet back under him. At least he wasn't dead yet. Elaine cocked the shotgun and raised it. If McCorley gave the word to kill Slocum, she would cut loose both barrels. The range was still too great to kill, but the buckshot might draw their attention from Slocum for an instant. Maybe he would have his wits about him enough to grab a gun or make a break.

"Shoot the bastard!" McCorley raged, reaching for the gun at his belt. Elaine's finger tightened on the triggers.

"Wait!" The yell from the Mexican leader jarred through McCorley's hate. Elaine eased the tension from the triggers. Corajos limped to the group, blood flowing down his side and across his hip. He stopped with his face only inches from Slocum's, a tight sneer of triumph twisting his features. "This one does not deserve a quick and painless death." Corajos's voice was cold and tight. "We will wait. He will pay for shooting Don Pedro Alexandro Corajos. When the morning sun reaches the canyon floor tomorrow, this one will meet *el muerte de los caballos*—the death by the horses."

Elaine shuddered in revulsion and fear. She had heard of *el muerte de los caballos*. The unfortunate victim was tied to four ponies, one arm or leg to each horse, then the horses were whipped into a run. It was a gruesome death, one that left a man literally torn to pieces. She glanced at the faint salmon streaks of sunset above the canyon rim. She had until daylight to try to get Slocum free. But she would need help. And the only help available was Iris Funderburk. Elaine would rather make a pact with the devil than with the auburn-haired woman, but Old Scratch was never around when needed. Iris Funderburk would have to do.

Elaine worked her way quietly from the edge of the outlaw camp. When she was sure she would not be heard or followed, she broke into a run toward the cave. As she ran, her vision blurred by tears, she realized that for the first time since the hunt had started, there was something more important to her than Blue McCorley's death.

That something was Slocum's life.

A hard, high moon sat cold and distant above the canyon, its rays blackening the shadows of pine and piñon trees to the color of printer's ink. The light barely penetrated the mouth of the cave where Elaine paced, desperately forming and then rejecting one plan after another.

She cast a glance at Iris Funderburk, who sat with her elbows propped on her knees, chin cupped in a palm, her features dim in the weak light from a single candle. Iris Funderburk had not taken the news of Slocum's capture as Elaine expected. Instead of flying into a hand-wringing, helpless-female crying fit, she had listened calmly and paid close attention as Elaine described the layout of the outlaw camp. From time to time Iris Funderburk would bend over to study the map sketched into the cave floor by Slocum's knifepoint. Then the chin would go back onto the palm and the smooth brows wrinkle in thought.

The silence dragged on until Elaine thought she would scream from pure frustration. Finally, Iris Funderburk cleared her throat.

"Miss Storm," she said, "we can't just ride in and shoot it out with a group of accomplished gunmen. That would just get us killed—and Mr. Slocum, too."

Elaine clenched her fists. "At least he would die quickly, and like a man. Not like some—some *animal,* torn to bits between horses—"

Iris Funderburk raised a hand. "Hear me out, Miss Storm. There is one thing that might work. It could be worth a try." She bent over the map once more, touched a finger to the southeast end of the canyon where the deadfall lay. "Perhaps if we merely modify Mr. Slocum's original plan a bit. Can you still set off that powder and cause a fire to stampede the horses?"

Elaine nodded. "I can, but—"

"It wouldn't help much unless those outlaws are somehow distracted, would it?"

"What are you driving at, Mrs. Funderburk?"

"Mr. Slocum puts a great store in the element of surprise." The corners of Iris Funderburk's mouth lifted in a confident smile. "There is one way to distract those men, Miss Storm. By showing them the last thing they ever expect to see out here in the middle of nowhere. And I'm just enough of a brazen hussy to pull it off."

12

Slocum fought his way back to full consciousness and almost immediately regretted it. Every muscle, joint, and tendon in his body seemed to be afire with pain and the pounding in his head was like the clang of hammer on anvil.

He became aware of the bite of rawhide against his wrists and pulled against the bonds that held his hands behind him. The ties held firm. He was trussed up like a pig headed for the spit.

Bits and pieces of conversation drifted through his brain. Dawn. *El muerte de los caballos*. A hell of a messy way to go, he thought. But it wouldn't be that way. Slocum wasn't going quietly to be torn to shreds. They would have to loosen the ropes at least once, to lash him to the ponies. That split second would be enough to grab for a gun. With luck, he could take a couple with him before he was shot to pieces.

Slocum had long ago come to grips with the idea of his own mortality. He had no particular fear of death. It came to all, sooner or later. At least this way he knew when and where. The only question left now was the how of it.

He opened his eyes, blinked at the flickering lantern on a low table, and realized he was in McCorley's tent. He heard a cough and a moan nearby. Don Pedro Alexandro Corajos lay on a bedroll, a bloody rag pressed against his side. The Mexican's black eyes bored into Slocum's face.

"So the gunfighter awakes," Corajos said.

"Go to hell." Slocum's voice was a croak. His tongue felt

fuzzy, heavy with thirst, and there was the coppery taste of blood in his mouth.

At Corajos's side, Blue McCorley stared at Slocum, a grin of triumph baring stained and chipped teeth. McCorley rose ponderously to his feet, stepped in front of Slocum, and slammed a heavy fist into Slocum's jaw. The lantern seemed to spin for a moment. McCorley turned away and sat back down, rubbing his knuckles.

"You have killed me, amigo," Corajos said, his voice calm and matter-of-fact. "Your bullet has entered my side and torn my intestines. For that, at least, you owe me a name. And I will live long enough to see you die."

Slocum ignored McCorley. He stared unblinking into the Mexican's eyes. "My name is Slocum, Corajos."

"Ah, yes. I have heard of this name." Corajos sighed. "At least I was not killed by some peon with a hoe handle, but by a *pistolero* of some reputation." Corajos's eyes narrowed. "But how is it you know my name, Slocum?"

Slocum shrugged, setting off a new blast of pain from torn skin and strained muscles. "I saw you once in Sonora. You were running guns to the Indians at the time. I didn't know you'd turned to honest work like dealing in stolen livestock."

"Enough of this shit," McCorley snapped. "Who's riding with you, Slocum? And where are they?"

Slocum spat a glob of blood from between split lips. "Nobody riding with me, McCorley. They stayed behind at Puerto de Luna." Slocum didn't really expect McCorley to buy the lie, but if he did, at least the women would be safe. Most likely they had already left the cave, riding hard toward Santa Fe like he had told them to do if anything went wrong.

"You killed a bunch of my men and crippled a couple more," McCorley said. "I had my way about it, I'd take a knife, open up your guts, and stuff 'em down your throat. But maybe Don Corajos's idea is better." McCorley chuckled in genuine amusement. "Be sort of fun, seein' pieces of you scattered from hell to breakfast."

Slocum leveled a cold stare at McCorley. "You talk pretty damn tough when somebody can't fight back, Blue," he said.

McCorley started to his feet, his face livid with rage.

"Sit down, McCorley," Corajos barked. "Don't let him bait you into shooting him." The Mexican winced at a fresh stab of pain through his wrecked guts. "This one will not meet so easy a fate. My *segundo* will take your horses and pay you as would I. But if you shoot this Slocum, my man will shoot you. We have dealt with each other in the past, McCorley. You know that I am a man of my word."

McCorley sputtered, but sat.

Slocum didn't sleep that night. He did rest from time to time, between bouts of tugging against his bonds without success. But the struggles kept the blood flowing to his hands, kept the aching tingle alive. When the time came to make his move he didn't want to be caught with hands that wouldn't function.

The night seemed endless, yet sped past. Slocum understood now why men facing the hangman hated the clock that ticked away inside their heads, counting down their last moments on earth. The sides of the tent paled with the first light of the new day. Slocum watched the canvas lighten with few emotions other than a tinge of regret. Someone else would have to build the small ranch up in the Musselshell country. Slocum wouldn't be around to do it. But he wasn't going meekly to his execution. A couple, maybe more, of these horse thieves were going with him.

On the cot nearby, Corajos stirred and moaned. The Mexican had had a rough night. Slocum had seen gutshot men before. Corajos would have suffered the raging agonies of the damned but for the numbing effects of tequila. Three empty bottles lay beside Corajos's bunk and a fourth was within easy reach at his side.

"Eh, Slocum. You awake?" Corajos's voice sounded weak.

"I'm awake."

Corajos coughed and gasped aloud in pain. "Your last dawn, Slocum. A short time from now you knock on the gates of Hell."

"I'll hold them open for you, Corajos."

The Mexican half smiled. "You are a man of courage, Slocum. It is a pity to see an end such as this. For both of us. Perhaps, if we could have combined our talents, we would both be very wealthy men today." Corajos sighed. "Alas, it is not to be." He raised his voice. "McCorley!"

The tent flap swung open. McCorley's bearded face appeared in the passage. His eyes were bloodshot, contrasting with the blue-black stain on his cheek. McCorley was grinning. Slocum could tell at a glance the man had been punishing the bottle hard during the night. That was something else in Slocum's favor. He had vowed that the first man he would take—if he got the chance—was Blue McCorley. He owed that to Elaine, to the Storms.

"It will soon be time," Corajos said. "Have my *segundo* select four strong horses from the remuda. Then help me outside." He glanced at Slocum. "I wish to see if this man dies as bravely as he lives."

McCorley nodded and left. Slocum caught a glimpse of the brightening sky before the canvas closed behind the horse thief.

A half hour later, the gunman called Able Conroe stood at Slocum's right side, a revolver rammed into Slocum's ribs, and a bloody rag wrapped around a thigh. At Slocum's left the thin, scar-faced shooter called Willison stood, a hand clamped on Slocum's upper arm. His pistol was still in its holster. McCorley stood to one side, weaving slightly, the grin still twisting his face. Slocum's gaze caught the eye of a fourth man, the little tracker called Duggan. The wiry Duggan quickly glanced away. It was obvious he wanted no part of this little fandango.

At the side of the tent blankets shrouded two bodies, one much larger than the other. The big one would be Curly Hogue, the smaller one the vaquero Slocum had gotten a slug into in the fight on the hillside.

Corajos lay on the cot that had been carried from the tent. The Mexican's face was pale, the features twisted in agony. He swung his feet over the side of the cot and sat upright with an effort.

"It is time," Corajos said.

Corajos's *segundo*, a stocky man with a scraggly mustache, led four horses toward the captive. Rawhide riatas were tied securely to their necks and chests, the loose ends of the ropes dangling alongside. Slocum noted that one of the four was the Nez Percé gelding he had bought from Storm. The major had mentioned that the gelding was broken to ride. A fleeting hope flickered in Slocum's brain. If he could somehow manage to get to the horse—

"Tie him to the horses," Corajos said. *"El muerte de los caballos* begins."

Slocum felt a knife blade slip through the ropes binding his wrists. He flexed his fingers and awaited his opening.

The scarred outlaw at Slocum's side suddenly stiffened. "Jesus Christ—" The man's voice trailed away as his jaw dropped in astonishment.

Slocum looked in the direction of the man's gaze and almost swallowed his own tongue in surprise.

A little more than thirty yards from the camp Iris Funderburk rode from the timber. She was stark naked, her right leg draped casually over the saddle horn. The morning sun touched flecks of gold in her auburn hair and glowed on the skin of her full breasts. She carried her head high. Her right hand was out of sight on the mare's off side. She looked neither to right nor left, but rode as if the men in the camp did not exist. The mare moved at a leisurely fox-trot toward the camp. Slocum tore his eyes from the sight and glanced at the outlaws. Every man stood transfixed in disbelief and awe at the vision that rode toward them.

"Holy shit," Able Conroe muttered. "What in hell?"

Understanding hit Slocum like a sledgehammer. *God bless you, Iris Funderburk,* he thought. He willed his muscles to relax, felt the calm of pending combat spread through his body, and waited. She was within ten yards now.

At the edge of the deadfall in the southeast end of the canyon, Elaine Storm held her mustang under tight rein, the shotgun cocked and ready in the crook of her arm. Twenty feet away the half-breed named Tyler stared toward the naked figure on horseback in the camp. The breed was unaware of Elaine's presence.

Elaine heard the faint sputter of the makeshift fuse, then a whoosh as the black powder firebomb flared. The half-breed spun toward the sound, his hand slapping for the pistol at his belt. Elaine raised the shotgun. "Over here, Tyler!" she yelled.

The outlaw turned to face her, his eyes wide with surprise. Elaine triggered the left barrel. Frank Tyler's chest exploded in a red mist as the heavy wallop of the buckshot tumbled him backward. Elaine rammed spurs to the mustang, charging toward the herd of stolen horses. The crackle of flames in deadwood was distinct in her ears. Smoke billowed from the deadfall behind her, swirled down the canyon on the wind toward the camp. The horses milled for a moment, then Elaine was behind them. She whooped and fired the second barrel of the shotgun into the air. The horse herd stampeded, tearing toward the camp at a dead run. Elaine reined in, broke the action on the shotgun, and quickly reloaded.

The flat cough of the shotgun reports jarred through the outlaw camp. At Slocum's side, Able Conroe flinched, startled. The muzzle of Conroe's handgun dropped away from Slocum's ribs.

"Now, Slocum!"

Iris Funderburk's yell came as she threw her right leg back across the saddle. Steel glinted as her right hand came up. She slammed heels into the sorrel mare and charged into the confused, stunned riders. The spiteful crack of a .32 sent a slug into the man at Slocum's left. Slocum spun to his right, swept his forearm against the pistol in Conroe's hand and drove a doubled fist into the brige of the outlaw's nose. The man went down like a poleaxed steer.

The derringer spat again as outlaws scattered like quail. Willison grunted at the impact of the little slug. Slocum spun and drove an elbow into the back of the man's neck. The four horses with riatas bolted. Slocum lunged at the Nez Percé gelding as it raced past, grabbed a handful of mane, and swung aboard the spotted horse. He heard the buzz of a pistol slug past his ear, then the earth-shaking rumble of hooves. He glanced over his shoulder. The stolen horse herd bore down on the camp, the animals racing in blind panic, nostrils flared and eyes rolling. The first wave of the stampede thundered through the camp. The cot on which Corajos sat disappeared under the pounding hooves and dust.

Another wild shot from the camp whistled over Slocum's head. He leaned over the neck of his horse, urging the gelding to top speed. He pulled alongside Iris Funderburk's mare and flashed a grin at her. She reached into the saddle boot, pulled out the .38-40 Winchester, and handed it to Slocum.

"Elaine's back there!" she yelled.

The flat blast of the shotgun sounded again behind Slocum. He kneed the spotted gelding into a tight turn, cracked the action on the Winchester, and saw a cartridge in the chamber. He charged back toward the camp, trusting his Nez Percé pony to thread its way through the oncoming stampede. Thick smoke billowed though the canyon in the wake of the rampaging horses.

Through the smoke and dust he caught a glimpse of Elaine riding hard behind the horse herd. She was in the midst of the wrecked camp now, the barrel of her shotgun swinging toward a vaquero who was trying to bring his handgun into line. The shotgun roared. The vaquero went down.

Able Conroe had managed to regain his feet. His pistol swung toward Elaine. Slocum slapped a quick shot, heard the slug hammer home like the slap of a hand against a side of beef. Conroe pitched forward on his face.

Slocum again spun his horse as Elaine's gray mustang raced past. The leggy Nez Percé gelding had more speed than Slocum had realized. He caught up with Elaine's mustang within a few yards and waved toward the cover of the timber. Elaine yanked her horse toward the trees, Slocum alongside.

Slocum pulled his mount to a sliding stop, dismounted, and ducked behind the thick trunk of a tall pine. He squinted through the pall of dust and smoke toward the outlaw camp. The thin scar-faced man Iris Funderburk had shot stood on unsteady legs, pistol in hand, trying to find a target. Slocum pulled the Winchester's sights fine and squeezed the trigger. The scar-faced outlaw spun and fell, the side of his head blown away.

"Blue, wait!"

Slocum glanced in the direction of the cry and mouthed a curse as he levered a fresh round into the Winchester. Blue McCorley had managed to hold on to his horse and now was riding hard toward the far side of the canyon and the narrow trail to the top. Slocum aimed and fired, thought he saw McCorley wince, and emptied the .38-40 at the fleeing horseman. The range was too great. Slocum snorted in disgust as McCorley topped the far side of the canyon rim and disappeared.

The wiry man named Duggan stood alone in the carnage of what had been a cozy outlaw camp, handgun dangling in his fist as he stared toward the canyon rim. Slocum tossed the useless Winchester aside. "Dammit, I should have saved at least one shot," he scolded himself.

"Here."

Slocum turned to Elaine. She had dismounted and now stood

behind a nearby tree. She had Slocum's spare Colt from his bedroll in her hand. She tossed it to him. Slocum caught it, drew the hammer to half cock and spun the cylinder. It was fully loaded.

"Stay here, Elaine," Slocum said. "You've taken enough chances for one day." He stepped from behind the tree and strode toward the tracker. Duggan stood, shoulders slumped, staring toward the spot where McCorley had disappeared. He was unaware of Slocum's approach.

Slocum stopped fifty feet from the tracker, cocked the Colt, and called, "Duggan!"

Duggan whirled around. He stared at Slocum for a moment, making no effort to lift his handgun. "I don't know who you are, hombre," Duggan said, "but I got no quarrel with you. This whole thing was Blue's idea."

Slocum's gaze was steady, his voice calm. "Doesn't matter, Duggan. You rode with McCorley. His gang killed two friends of mine and raped a young girl."

Duggan raised his left hand, palm out, in supplication. "I swear to you I never laid a hand on that girl." Sweat poured from beneath Duggan's hatband, trickled down his face, and left white streaks through the dust and grime.

Slocum shrugged. "You picked your pack to run with, Duggan. Now you've got to pay the wolfer. Quit whining. You're getting a better chance than Ed and Eva Storm got."

Duggan's eyes narrowed. "Listen, hombre. There's a lot of money in this camp. The Mex was carrying a bundle. I know where it's at. I'll show you. Just let me get a horse and you keep the cash."

Slocum studied the tracker's face. There was no surprise or fear in the man's eyes now, only a cold, calculating glint. Slocum nodded.

Duggan sighed and turned away. Slocum kept a close watch on the back of Duggan's head. If you couldn't see a man's eyes, watch the head anyway; where the head went, the body had to follow.

Duggan took three steps. Then his head moved. Slocum lifted his Colt as Duggan spun, threw his handgun up, and fired. The tracker's hurried shot went wild. Slocum took a split second to be sure of his aim and squeezed the trigger. The .44 slug hammered Duggan back a step. Slocum took his time, let the weapon's recoil roll the hammer back beneath his thumb. He cocked the Colt, aimed, and fired again. The impact knocked Duggan off his feet, spun him facedown into the dirt. Slocum took careful aim and shot Duggan in the back of the head. The echoes of the last shot rumbled down San Miguel Canyon, bounced along the steep walls, and faded. Slocum glanced over his shoulder at the sound of hoofbeats.

Elaine rode into the wreckage of the camp, leading Slocum's Nez Percé gelding, shotgun cocked and resting in the crook of her left arm.

Slocum worked the ejector rod, kicked the spent shells from the Colt, and reloaded. "It's over, Elaine."

"It isn't over yet." Elaine's tone was hard and cold. "McCorley got away. I want him, Slocum."

"We'll get him, Elaine. Sooner or later. Where's Mrs. Funderburk?"

Elaine shrugged. "Probably waiting for you to find her before she has to get dressed."

Slocum stared at the girl for a moment, then sighed and turned away. "Well, let's see what we can find here. Then we'll gather the horses. They won't run far."

Elaine dismounted and walked at Slocum's side as they prowled the camp. Finally, Slocum lowered the hammer of the Peacemaker and slipped it inside his belt. He wouldn't need it here.

Corajos's crumpled body lay beside the overturned cot. His head had been pounded to jelly by the hooves of stampeding horses. Able Conroe and the scarred Duke Willison lay dead where Slocum had shot them. He found the body of Corajos's *segundo* a few yards from the tent, his ribs blown away by a charge of buckshot. The second vaquero lay on his back, sightless eyes fixed on the morning sky. His chest was crushed, a bloody hoofprint still visible in the middle of his shirt.

Slocum searched the wreckage of the tent, found his holster and gun belt, and finally his other Colt and Winchester. The weapons were dusty but undamaged. He strapped on the gun belt and holstered the weapon Elaine had brought. He'd have to clean the other guns later.

"I count eight dead down here," Slocum said.

"Nine." Elaine's voice was flat, expressionless. "I cut that breed in half with this shotgun up by the deadfall."

Slocum stared at Elaine for a moment. The enormity of what they had done had just dawned on him. One man and two women had gone up against ten gunmen and nine of the rustlers lay dead. This wisp of a girl at his side, her face streaked by dust, dirt, and black powder stains, clothes reeking of woodsmoke and horse sweat, had personally killed at least two men here. Another in Tascosa, a fourth on Death's Head Trail. And Iris Funderburk, the bluenose high-society reformer from Boston, now had one outright kill and part of another in her purse. *These two,* Slocum thought, *may just be the most dangerous posse I've ever ridden with.*

Elaine's expression showed no remorse, no queasiness over the bodies huddled in the camp clearing. She seemed calm and relaxed, but rage still burned in her eyes.

Slocum strode to the mangled body of Don Pedro Alexandro Corajos, knelt, and ran a hand over the once-fine cloth now covered in gore and dirt. His fingers touched something hard and lumpy. He ripped away Corajos's vest and shirt and stripped the money belt from his waist. The belt was stained by blood and ooze. Slocum's rifle shot had nicked the belt before ripping into Corajos's side. Slocum lifted several flaps on the pockets of the money belt. Each pocket was stuffed with gold and silver of both Mexican and American coinage. Slocum estimated there was more than two thousand dollars in the belt, a more than considerable fortune. He smiled at Elaine.

"We got your money back, with interest," he said, holding the coin-laden belt aloft.

"It doesn't matter, Slocum." Elaine made no move to take the money. She climbed back into the saddle, lowered the hammers of the shotgun, and slung the weapon over her back. "There's only one thing that will pay me back in full," she said, "and that's when I hold Blue McCorley's bloody balls in my hand. Let's go, Slocum. We've got horses to gather."

Iris Funderburk met Slocum and Elaine at the northwest end of the canyon. She was fully clothed and led the pack mule. Her face was flushed, her teeth glistened in a wide smile, and the glitter of excitement danced in violet eyes.

"Mrs. Funderburk, are you all right?" Slocum asked.

She nodded. "My tits are going to be sore as hell from all that bouncing around, and my ass feels like it's been dragged over sandstone," she said, "but I've never felt so—so *alive*—in my entire life."

"My, my, Mrs. Funderburk," Elaine said, sarcasm heavy in her voice, "such language from a woman of society."

Slocum glanced at Elaine but bit back the urge to scold her. "Ladies," he said, "I owe you two my life. That's something I won't forget. How in the world did you come up with that idea?"

"We merely expanded on your tactics a bit, Mr. Slocum," Iris Funderburk said. "You mentioned once that surprise was the major element in winning a conflict. We figured that the spectacle of a nude woman on horseback might be a sufficient diversion."

Elaine snorted. "And you damn well enjoyed it, I'll bet."

Slocum saw the quick flare of hurt in Iris Funderburk's eyes. "Miss Storm," she said, "there's a great deal about me that you don't know. But I'm getting a little tired of this incessant bitchiness of yours."

Slocum sat silent in the saddle, wondering what a man could say. Here two women had just joined forces to keep him from being solidly dead, and they were still bristling at each other like two strange dogs. Slocum raised a hand. "Ladies, please. Call a truce until we get the horses rounded up. That will take the rest of the morning. Then we still have a long ride until we reach Santa Fe. I'd appreciate it if our last night's camp together doesn't end in bloodshed."

13

Iris Funderburk pulled the blanket tighter across her shoulders against the night chill of the New Mexico high country and stared thoughtfully into the cheerful blaze of the campfire.

The horse roundup had gone well. They had lost only one, a bay mare that had stepped in a hole and broken a leg during the stampede. Now they were within a half day's easy ride to Santa Fe and home.

She sat pensively and studied the scowling face of Elaine Storm, seated across the fire on her blanket roll. Slocum prowled the valley where the horse herd was being held for the night, keeping an eye out for trouble. He would ride what the Westerners called "nighthawk" until the stars read midnight. Then it would be Elaine's turn.

Iris Funderburk felt somewhat slighted that Slocum and Elaine split the guard duty, but she accepted the fact that she was not as well tuned to the ways of western horses and the many threats that lurked in the darkness, from men to mountain lions.

She had come to realize she hated to see the adventure end. For the first time in her adult life she had felt alive, vibrant, even useful. That would end in Santa Fe. She would again trade freedom for the stuffy comfort of wealth and society. She doubted that she would ever be able to again view the lords and ladies of wealth and power with the same respect. She had grown accustomed to the feel of the wind in her hair, even the supple grace of a horse between her knees. She would miss the sudden surge of emotion in time of crisis or danger, the tingling jolt when the senses sharpened until the veins of a single leaf or the texture of a small stone stood in sharp relief.

Most of all she would miss the man called Slocum.

Iris Funderburk knew she did not love Slocum. She had lived long enough now to know that she could never love a man, at least not in the spiritual sense of the word. She had respect for Slocum—and no small amount of lust. The man with the green eyes, raven hair, and trim, lithe body of a mountain cat was a magnificent lover. She would dream of Slocum, form his face in her mind, feel the memory of his touch in her moments of solitary need when her fingers traced their way down her belly as she lay alone in her bed. It would be a memory that would not soon fade.

She knew also that she would miss Elaine Storm. The young woman with her strikingly lovely face and blooming figure reminded Iris of her own youth. Elaine had an air of detached competence and cold self-reliance about her, but Iris saw the vulnerability, the pain, the gentle nature that lay beneath the hate and bitterness that clouded Elaine's eyes. Elaine was a young woman who should be able to feel the depths of love as well as hate. And shame. No girl could endure what she had gone through and still maintain her sense of dignity and self-worth. Once tarnished, the lamp was stained until finally someone found it and polished it back to its original luster. Iris could only hope that Elaine would someday allow someone to get close enough to polish that lamp.

Iris Funderburk suddenly became aware of the reason for the need she felt at this moment. She wanted Elaine Storm's respect, or at least her understanding, more than she needed or wanted the fawnings and false posturings of the rich ladies of the social circles she soon would rejoin. It was no different in Santa Fe than it had been in Boston, she mused. People were people no matter what the geography. The haves looked down upon the have-nots, felt superior, and were reassured. Those who had wealth and power were the users of the world, chewing up bodies and souls and lives for their own pleasure and advancement. *My God,* she thought, *I've missed so much in life.* She shook the thought away. She had chosen her path and made her decision, and at times—as now—she had to pay her dues.

She cleared her throat.

Elaine Storm glanced at her, forehead wrinkled in a frown.

"Miss Storm, may I speak with you about—some private matters?"

Elaine shrugged. "Go ahead."

"I know that you don't especially care for me, and I certainly can't blame you." Iris Funderburk's voice was soft and sincere, the words forming small puffs of steam in the crisp mountain air. "I gave you every reason to dislike me. I came into your life, even so briefly, without an invitation. I insulted you, spoke without thinking, derided you, jumped to erroneous conclusions, misjudged you in many respects. I apologize for that and beg your forgiveness." She paused for breath. "I expect you will be delighted to be rid of me."

Elaine stared at her thoughtfully for a moment. "I suppose I will be," she finally said.

"Miss Storm, you were right about me. I am a two-faced hypocrite of the worst order." Iris reached into a saddle bag beside her, took out a bottle of Lady Lydia's Elixir, and downed a couple of swallows. The liquid warmed her inside. "I don't dare hope for your friendship. But I would hate to part knowing you would remember me with loathing. I'm not sure where to start, Miss Storm."

Iris Funderburk leaned against the saddle which served now as a chair and later would be her pillow, probably for the last time, and stared at the stars overhead.

"I came from a dirt-poor family," she said. "My father was a miner in the Pennsylvania coal fields. Mother died when I was a young child, Father on my fifteenth birthday. He died of lung rot from a lifetime of working in the mines." She took another swig of Lady Lydia's. It seemed to loosen her tongue, make her confession easier.

"Shortly after my father died, I made a solemn vow that I would never know hunger or want again in my life. My only surviving relative was my older brother, who was then a West Point cadet. I was left in the charge of a maiden aunt. We didn't get along. So I left that home, determined to better myself. I won't bore you with the details. I managed to get a decent education, a rare thing for a girl, especially one from my social class. I was a late bloomer, as they say, rather plain until my eighteenth year. Then one day I discovered that I had become attractive to men."

Iris Funderburk paused for breath, glanced at Elaine, wondering if the girl was actually listening.

"Soon after that," Iris continued, "I started looking for a man. Not necessarily a man I could love, but a man with money. A lot of it. I found him."

"Your husband?" Elaine's tone was polite, even curious.

"Yes. Charles Y. Funderburk. Born to money and with a talent for making even more. We were married when I was twenty-three and on the verge of becoming an old maid. From that day on, I've known no material wants. But I traded something very special for those creature comforts money could buy, Miss Storm."

"You don't love your husband?"

Iris Funderburk shook her head. "No. And Charles doesn't love me. It is a marriage of convenience for us both. Charles's talent lies in acquisitions. He buys things."

"Including you?"

"At first, yes. Charles needed an attractive wife to enhance his image. Later he discovered I had a rather keen business sense of my own, but it's terribly difficult for people to accept or deal with a woman in business unless she makes hats or bakes pies or runs a laundry." Iris sighed. "That's the tragedy of America today. I've known a number of women who would be valuable assets to the operation of certain large companies."

Iris leaned toward the fire, the bottle of Lady Lydia's still in her hand. "We became a team, Charles and I. My talent lies in analyzing the future of certain business ventures. To that end, Miss Storm, I've been the complete hypocrite you pronounce me to be. I am now, and have been for several years, living a lie each day."

Elaine's brow wrinkled in obvious confusion. "I don't understand."

Iris Funderburk smiled. "Miss Storm, I'm a scout, like for the Army. But instead of hunting Indians, I hunt investment opportunity. What better way to gain access to remote towns and gather information than to stage a crusade against the evils of drink, of smoking, of the vices of men? The wives of powerful and influential men have access to a great deal of information about what the future of a town or a business holds. And they don't feel threatened by a bluenose temperance fanatic who shows absolutely no interest in their husbands. They invite me into their homes and tea parties and brag on their husband's accomplishments and boast about their plans, and I listen."

She lifted the bottle and took another small nip. "Besides, it is socially acceptable in Boston society circles for a woman to be active in the temperance movement. The Boston Biddies, we're called."

She shook her head, a wry smile on her lips. "It's good business for Charles to have such a wife. My travels through the West as a Boston Biddy already have pointed out numerous areas where fortunes are to be made. Soon, Charles will decide to expand his Virginia tobacco holdings and acquire a major distillery in Kentucky. He will purchase large blocks of stock in three railroads—the Atchison, Topeka and Santa Fe, the Fort Worth and Denver, and the Central, Burlington and Quincy lines. We will diversify into ranching—and please promise you won't ever tell Mr. Slocum this—into the production of barbed wire. I am convinced the days of the open range are doomed. There's a brand new fortune to be made in barbed wire."

Elaine winced. "Uncle Ed hated the idea of barbed wire," she said. "The devil's thread, he called it." Elaine stared at Iris Funderburk curiously. "Why are you telling me this?"

"Because I don't want you to hate me. And I trust you to keep my secret, as I will keep yours." Iris capped the Lady Lydia's bottle and replaced it in her bag. "I feel I owe you an explanation for one other thing, Miss Storm," she said. "Charles has two mistresses—money and power. There's little room in his life for another woman. We haven't slept together, in the earthy usage of the phrase, in months. I am not, as you may think, a loose woman. But on occasion, the woman animal in me breaks its tethers. I am not especially proud of that, but I make no apology for it. There are some men, a few—"

"Like Slocum." Elaine's tone turned tart.

"Yes. Like Mr. Slocum." Iris sighed. "I'm sorry you had to see that, Miss Storm. I'm sure it must have hurt you deeply—"

"Why should it? The sight of two people rutting around on a blanket doesn't mean a damn thing to me."

"I think it does, Miss Storm. I think Mr. Slocum means more to you than you care to admit. I know the horrible experience you went through. I see how you still flinch at Mr. Slocum's touch. It's a terrible thing you must bear. Not just the painful memory of being raped, but the torture of not knowing whether you can ever share a man's bed."

Iris Funderburk leaned forward and added another small stick to the fire. "My dear, you're a beautiful young woman. I hope you can overcome that horrid experience and eventually find the love you deserve with some understanding young man. What I'm trying to say, in my own awkward way, is that one wasted life—my own—is enough. Miss Storm, I honestly *will* pray that you find the strength to come to grips with what has happened to you."

Silence fell on the camp for several moments. Finally, Elaine spoke.

"And what of the men I killed, Mrs. Funderburk? Isn't the taking of a life the most terrible of sins?"

Iris Funderburk chuckled softly. "Don't worry about that, my dear. Those bastards deserved killing." She sighed and stretched. "Thank you for listening to my confession. I feel much better now. Perhaps we should get some sleep? You must relieve Mr. Slocum on watch at midnight, and morning will come quite soon enough for me. It has been a rather tiring day." She smoothed her bedroll and slid between the blankets.

"One last question, Mrs. Funderburk?"

"Certainly."

"Why Santa Fe? Couldn't your business be handled in Boston just as easily?"

Iris Funderburk reached beneath her bedroll, extracted a small stick and tossed it aside. "Santa Fe is the major center of trade between Saint Louis and San Francisco. It is the center of the expanding West, so to speak. The unofficial capital of the last part of the United States to be settled. The last outpost of the next generation of money." She sighed. "That makes it attractive to Charles. As for me, I simply like the city. It's beautiful, the climate is magnificent, and there are fewer Boston Biddies like myself about."

"I see. Good night, Mrs. Funderburk."

"Good night, Miss Storm."

Elaine sat and stared into the fire, brows bunched in thought, as the stars wheeled overhead.

Santa Fe dozed in post-noon siesta as Slocum led the procession into the outskirts of the sun-washed adobe of the ancient town.

Santa Fe nestled in a basin high in the Sangre de Cristo range. It was one of Slocum's favorite towns, and he made it a point to visit the city when he was within traveling distance. The climate was almost perfect, especially in late spring and early summer. The sun broiled down during the day, but at night the temperature fell rapidly.

The city had housed conquistadores, padres, Pueblo and Hopi Indians, Mexican soldiers, Anglos, and travelers of all races and destinations. Over the years it had seen its share of bloodshed, uprising, and brutal repression. Now, it was a welcome oasis on a long trail. Slocum was seeing it for the first time from the end of Death's Head Trail.

He twisted in the saddle and glanced toward the back of the horse herd. The animals were strung out along the wide thoroughfare between dun-colored adobe homes and businesses. Iris Funderburk and Elaine Storm rode side by side behind the horses. And they were talking, frequently laughing. Slocum shook his head in wonder and confusion. Yesterday they had been ready to tear each other's eyes out; now they rode like old friends, smiling and chatting. *Anyone who thinks the Chinese are hard to figure out,* Slocum thought, *has never spent much time around women.*

He dismissed the puzzle from his mind as the public stables came into view.

A one-eyed hostler of apparent mixed Indian and Mexican descent leaned against a corral gatepost, his remaining eye fixed on the approaching horse herd.

"Afternoon," Slocum said, touching his hat brim in greeting. "We need a place to put some horses up for a couple of days, maybe three."

The hostler switched a cud of tobacco to the other cheek and spat. "Can't help you, friend. Ain't got room for that many animals."

Slocum stared for a moment past the corrals toward a rail-fenced meadow beyond. It enclosed the better part of a hundred acres, the grass summer-scorched but stirrup deep. "How about there? We don't need stalls, just a holding pasture. I've got the money."

The one-eyed man shook his head. "Nope. Savin' that grass. Reckon you'll just have to move on, feller."

Slocum felt his temper stir in his gut. He was about to deliver an ultimatum to the hostler when hoofbeats sounded at his side. He glanced at Iris Funderburk.

"What's the problem here?" she asked.

"This jasper wants to board them horses and I ain't got the room or the inclination, lady."

"I would suggest you find the room, Mr. Dade. And the inclination. Immediately." Iris Funderburk's tone was icy and menacing.

The hostler glanced at her, then his one good eye went wide in surprise. "Mrs. Funderburk! I swear, I didn't recognize you. I didn't know these was your horses."

"Except for the mare I'm riding, they aren't, Mr. Dade. But they belong to friends of mine."

The hostler swept the hat from his head. "Sure 'nuff, Mrs. Funderburk. Why, I reckon we got plenty room for friends of yours." He scuttled away to lower the rails of a gate to the pasture. Slocum reined his spotted Nez Percé aside as the bay gelding Jug led the trail-wise horses through the gate into the meadow beyond.

Slocum glanced at Iris Funderburk, an eyebrow raised.

"Sometimes money and power can be of use, Mr. Slocum," she muttered, flashing a slight smile. She turned to the hostler. "Mr. Dade, you will keep these mounts until my friends come for them. You will charge our regular rate. If you try to cheat my friends, my husband will be in need of a new hostler within the day."

Dade swallowed, twisted his hat in his hands, and nodded furiously. "Yes, ma'am, Mrs. Funderburk. Whatever you say." He turned to replace the gate rails as the last of the horses entered the pasture.

"You own this place, Mrs. Funderburk?" Slocum asked.

"My husband does. It doesn't make as much money as some of his other holdings, but it produces a steady income. Rather profitable over the course of a year, in fact." She swung down and handed the reins of her mare to Dade. "Take care of this animal, and my friends' horses as well, Mr. Dade."

Slocum and Elaine waved the hostler away. "We'll see to our own horses," Slocum said. "Long-time habit of mine, Mr. Dade. Just point us to the grain and curry combs."

Iris Funderburk waited patiently until Slocum and Elaine had cared for the horses, stowed their gear, and shouldered saddlebags. Slocum's bag was heavy with gold.

"Come along," Iris Funderburk said. "My home is only a couple of blocks away. We've plenty of room for you both there. We even have running water and bath tubs inside the hacienda." She brushed at a dusty sleeve. "I don't know about you two, but I could certainly use a good hot bath."

Slocum stood on the balcony outside his second-floor bedroom, twirled one of Charles Funderburk's fine Havana cigars between his fingers, and breathed deep of the cool New Mexico mountain air.

Iris Funderburk's arrival had set off a small but lively and genuinely happy celebration among the half dozen or more servants in the sprawling mansion. But when she was told that her husband was in San Francisco on business and wouldn't be back for at least a week, she had merely nodded and smiled. *A curious woman,* Slocum thought; *there's a hell of a lot more to her than meets the eye, and that's plenty to begin with.*

She had already paid Slocum the four hundred dollars for his "escort service," scoffing at Slocum's reluctance to accept the money after she and Elaine had pulled his hair out of the fire at the outlaw camp. "A deal, Mr. Slocum, is a deal," she said firmly. That money and most of the gold from the outlaw horse buyer now rested in a safe in the crowded office off the main dining room. Slocum had blown a few dollars on new clothes for himself and Elaine.

Elaine had balked at buying a dress, but finally had agreed on a pale yellow silk shirt, midnight blue vaquero pants and vest, new boots, and a hat.

Slocum had indulged himself. He now wore a black silk suit, white shirt with string tie, and new boots of a fine soft cowhide. A new silver-belly Stetson hung on a peg inside the door of his room. When it came time to point the horses back toward

Mobeetie, he would be back in his worn trail garb. Until then, Slocum planned to live a little.

And it looked like the Funderburk mansion might be just the kind of place to do that very thing, he mused. He was freshly shaved and bathed and his new hand-tooled belt creaked beneath a stuffed belly. He couldn't remember the last time he had sat at such a heavy table. Roast beef, pork smoked over a wood fire, quail baked in a rich wine sauce, wild rice and refried beans with a spicy but not scorching salsa, soft and buttery tortillas, strong, rich coffee, and an after-dinner brandy had punished him to the point of feeling almost decadent.

The sprawling, thick-walled adobe home seemed more like a huge hotel than a residence. It had at least seventeen rooms, all luxuriously equipped, and it seemed to Slocum that there was a servant of some sort at every doorway. Baskets of fresh fruit, cheese, and wine waited beside his bed. Downstairs, Charles Funderburk's liquor cabinet held the finest Kentucky bourbons, tequila, rum, even imported vodka, gin, and a half dozen varieties of brandy.

The mansion had a presence of its own. It stood like a fortress only three blocks from the Governor's Palace. Its thick adobe had seen the passage of more than two hundred years of history. Iris Funderburk had said, half jokingly, that ghosts sometimes prowled the rooms. Slocum didn't believe in ghosts, but it seemed he could feel the presence of the Texans once held prisoner here after the ill-fated Santa Fe Expedition in the days of the Republic of Texas. In the courtyard behind the main house an adobe wall pocked by bullets stood in testament to the expedition members who had been executed by Mexican firing squads. Maybe, Slocum mused, the spirits of those men did linger amid the fragrant blooms of flowers in that courtyard.

Slocum dragged at the cigar, savored the full-bodied flavor of fine tobacco on his tongue, and sighed in contentment. *A man could get comfortable damn fast in a place like this,* he thought.

There was only one thing that kept him alert and cautious. A piece of business yet unfinished. Blue McCorley.

Slocum knew McCorley was somewhere in Santa Fe. He didn't know how he knew, but McCorley was here. Slocum could feel the man's presence.

Slocum again ran through his mind what he knew, firsthand and by campfire yarns, of Blue McCorley. The onetime Jayhawker from the state known as Bloody Kansas had a reputation as a dangerous man, one without mercy. Yet, McCorley had turned tail and run when the fighting broke out in the canyon. McCorley still had the money from the raid on the Storm ranch, enough to keep a man in fine style for a time in Mexico.

Slocum didn't believe for a minute McCorley had ridden south. He had been humiliated, beaten by one man and two women. McCorley wasn't the type of man who could stand that. It pointed out his own weakness, and no man faced his weaknesses well—especially a man who lived by the gun. No, McCorley wouldn't run. He was here, in Santa Fe, looking for his own brand of vengeance. It wouldn't come in a face-to-face showdown. Slocum was certain McCorley didn't have the guts for that. It would come in an ambush from an alley or the window of a building. A man who ran from a straight-up fight was the most dangerous enemy in the world.

Slocum had already put out the word in Santa Fe that he sought the man with the blue-black mark on his face. He knew his best chance was to find McCorley before McCorley found him.

Slocum stubbed out the cigar and dropped it into a brass ashtray that rested in a niche on the balcony rail. It would be wise, Slocum reminded himself, to watch his back until he found out where McCorley was.

He listened for a moment to the sounds of Santa Fe at night. It was a town noted for its fiestas, cantinas, and bawdy houses. Not a wide-open, hell-for-leather town like Tascosa or Dodge or Deadwood, but a place where a man could find anything he wanted as long as he went about it the right way and in the proper part of town. The Santa Fe constabulary frowned on rowdy behavior in the better parts of town, and it was an accepted fact on the frontier that the local lockup was not a place of creature comforts.

In the distance he heard the cheerful wail of a cornet accompanied by lively guitars and frequent high-pitched yelps of celebration. For a moment, Slocum was tempted to join the distant fiesta. The Mexicans might have some faults, he thought, but one thing couldn't be denied. They sure as hell knew how to enjoy life. The impulse to join the fun passed.

Slocum took one last deep breath of the fresh, clean air, then stepped back into his room.

He knew there would be no celebration for him until Blue McCorley was facedown in a pile of horse manure somewhere.

14

Blue McCorley slumped in his chair at a drink-stained table in a cantina on Santa Fe's south side, a half-empty bottle of tequila and a greasy glass before him, and cursed steadily beneath his breath.

There were few drinkers in the cantina this night. Most of the regulars were at the fandango a block away, where the liquor was cheaper and better and the women were free. The smattering of cantina customers made it a point to stay well away from the gringo with the blue mark on his face. One did not kick a snarling dog, and this one looked ready to snap off a leg or an arm.

McCorley poured another three fingers of tequila into his glass and swirled the clear liquid. He grunted in disgust. For three American dollars a bottle, at least the tequila should have the golden tint that meant quality. McCorley raised the glass and downed half the contents. He winced as the fiery liquid burned its way down his gullet.

He thumped the glass back on the table. *Damn that son of a bitch Slocum,* he thought; *two months of planning and work shot to hell. Bastard even had the balls to bring those horses into Santa Fe—my horses, goddammit. I worked for 'em. He'll by God pay for that.*

McCorley became aware of a presence at his side. He turned to snap at the arrival, but the bitter words died unspoken on his tongue. A young Mexican girl stood there, looking down at him, the nipples of oversized breasts showing through the thin white peasant blouse she wore. Her face was painted and rather plain, her waist ran a bit to the thick side, and McCorley suspected she would have a few pones of fat on heavy thighs. Still, he hadn't had a woman since that little brunette virgin. The memory of the girl, the tightness of her, stirred in McCorley's groin.

"Mister, you look lonely," the Mexican girl said in a border Spanish dialect. "Perhaps you would buy a girl a drink?" She winked at McCorley. It was supposed to be flirtatious, McCorley guessed, but the gesture came across as bored and without much enthusiasm. But she *did* have big tits. He shrugged. "Sure, why not?" he replied in Spanish. "Have a seat, honey."

He waved for another glass as the girl sat beside him, pressing her thigh into his and brushing an ample breast against his forearm. McCorley became more interested. She smelled like he might not be her first customer of the day, and that increased the pulse of his desire. Sometimes a hot, sloppy piece was the best of all. He waited patiently as she sipped at the drink, tried not to flinch at the bite of cheap liquor, and smiled at him.

"I like you," she said. "You look like you could do a girl some good. There are rooms in the back, where we could be alone."

McCorley cocked an eyebrow. "How much?"

"Five American dollars." The girl forced a leering smile. "I give you anything you enjoy, my friend."

McCorley suddenly grinned and put his arm around the girl's shoulders, letting his fingertips rest on the swell of her upper breast. "Sure, why not." The price might be too high for the quality of the merchandise, he thought, but he still had plenty. Better than seven hundred dollars left from the raid on the Mobeetie ranch. No reason a man couldn't enjoy himself for an hour or so.

He pushed back his chair and started to stand, then froze as someone called his name. The flash of tension faded as quickly as it struck. The voice held a distinct Mexican accent. He turned to face a middle-aged Mexican peasant dressed in little more than rags. The man's face had a hangdog look to it.

"I'm McCorley."

"There is a man who seeks information about you," the peon said, twisting a stained and battered hat in his hands. "I thought perhaps you might find this to be of value."

McCorley fixed a cold, steady stare on the Mexican's face. He saw no sign of deceit there, only a frightened hope. McCorley nodded. "It might be, my friend," he said. "Who is this man?"

"He goes by the name of Slocum," the peon said. "He brought this afternoon a large herd of horses into Santa Fe—"

"I know that," McCorley interrupted. "The damned horses are mine. This Slocum—is he tall? Dark hair, green eyes? Carries a pistol crossdraw on his left hip?"

"Yes." The Mexican nodded vigorously. "He is the one. He has said that someone who could tell him of your whereabouts would be well rewarded."

McCorley felt a tug on his sleeve. "Come on, honey," the whore whined, "I want to show you—"

McCorley held back the urge to drive a fist into her painted face. He forced a smile. "Be patient, little sister," he said. "I will make it worth your while." The glimmer of a plan took shape in McCorley's mind. "This Slocum. Does he have a message for me?"

"No, sir. He just wants to know where to find you."

McCorley rubbed a hand through his unwashed beard. *The bastard could be playing right into my hands,* he thought; *work this right, Slocum'll walk dead into my sights and never know what hit him.* He waved the peon into a chair. "Something to drink, my friend?" he asked.

"Mr. McCorley, I haven't eaten since yesterday. I was hoping—"

"Done, friend." McCorley waved at the bartender. "You have food here?" The barkeep nodded. "Good. Give this man here all he can eat and a couple of beers if he wants 'em." McCorley fished in a shirt pocket, found a gold coin, and handed it to the barkeep. "Don't try to cheat him on the grub, friend, or I will personally stuff your balls into your own meat grinder and make you eat them as seasoning on your greasy chili."

The whore started to rise. McCorley clamped her into the chair with a powerful fist. "Keep your pants on, Chiquita, until I tell you to take them off," he snapped. He turned to the peon. "Here is what I want you to do, my friend. I am going into the back room with this young woman here. I will be gone maybe an hour, maybe an hour and a half. In that time, eat and drink your fill. Then I want you to take a message to this

Slocum." McCorley pulled a five-dollar gold piece from his pocket. "This will be yours when I come back. I want you to tell Slocum that I can be found just down the street here, at the *fandango*. Agreed?"

The Mexican nodded eagerly. "I will do as you say."

McCorley stood for a moment staring out a nearby window, studying the street. *I've got Slocum by the nuts now,* he thought. *When the bastard walks past this building toward the party, I'll pop one between his shoulder blades.*

Blue McCorley chuckled aloud. He hadn't felt this good in days. He slipped a hand under the whore's arm. "Come on, baby," he said, "let's see if you can show me some tricks I don't already know."

Slocum lay nude on the soft, down-filled mattress, letting the cool breeze from the open window caress his skin. He knew that before morning the breeze would turn downright chilly, making him reach for the blanket folded with care at the foot of the bed. Outside the window a night bird sang, its crisp, bell-like notes seeming to harmonize with the distant music of the *fandago*.

Slocum stretched and flexed his muscles, enjoying the feel of the clean, crisp linen sheet beneath his back. It had been a long time since he had slept indoors on a real mattress; so long, in fact, that it even seemed a bit strange. He wasn't sleepy, but it didn't matter. His muscles were relaxed, resting from the exertions of the past few days. Sleep would come when it came, and not before.

His clothes were draped over the rack Iris Funderburk called a butler tree near the bed. A bottle of fine Tennessee sour mash shared space on the small table at his bedside with a water pitcher, a basket of fruit, and his holstered handgun. *Just about everything a man needs, right at hand,* he thought. *This would be real easy to get used to—* He started at the slight click of a doorknob turning. His hand was on the butt of the pistol before he realized the sound had come not from the front door of his room, but a side door along one wall.

The portal swung open. Iris Funderburk stood in the doorway, her hair down, the light from a kerosene lantern behind her outlining the lush contours of her body beneath a filmy white gown. She stood with one hip slightly cocked, a statue frozen in an instant of time. The light behind her emphasized the contours of long, smoothly muscular legs, outlined the swell of the side of an unfettered breast, stroked her narrow waist and full hips.

"Mr. Slocum?" Her voice was soft, husky. "Are you awake? May I come in?"

"Please do," Slocum said. He felt the stirring begin in his crotch. He lay on his side and stared at her without embarrassment, aware of his awakening response.

She strode toward his bed, leaving the door ajar behind her. "I like to see what I'm doing, Mr. Slocum," she said. There was a husky catch in her breath. She was breathing deeply, her breasts rising and falling with each expansion of her rib cage. She reached to her throat, tugged at a slip of satin, and shrugged her shoulders. The filmy gown slipped to the floor. She stood at the side of the bed for a moment. Slocum reached out, stroked her waist, let his hand slide to the firm muscle of her buttocks and pulled her closer.

He raised his head from the pillow and kissed her softly on the stomach. His tongue flicked out, stroked her skin, and he felt her shudder as his lips touched the thick mat of hair between her legs. She moaned softly, arched her back, and spread her legs, opening herself to his tongue. In a few moments she moaned again, thrust her pelvis against his face, and her muscles went into a spasm. She slipped her hands behind his head, pressed his face to her, her hips pushing her moist muskiness more firmly against his tongue.

Gradually the muscular contractions faded. She eased her grip on his hair and leaned over him. "My God, Mr. Slocum," she gasped, "I don't know how you do it, but it seems all I have to do is get near you and I start to come." She gently pushed him back onto the bed and came into his arms, her nipples brushing against his chest, her hand reaching down to stroke him. She lowered her lips to his and kissed him, gently at first, then with a growing urgency. Her tongue flicked against his. Her breath grew shallow, rapid, and finally she pulled away with a soft moan from deep in her throat.

She knelt above him as he raised his head, let his tongue trace the outline of her left breast, then circle her erect, firm nipple. She cradled his head for a moment, then gently pushed him back against the pillow, still straddling him, her knees alongside his ribs. She stroked his erection, then gently guided him into her and slowly lowered herself onto him.

Iris Funderburk sat astride Slocum for several long moments, not moving her body, contracting and relaxing her interior muscles. Slocum felt the wet heat swell him even more. She began to move her hips, a faint rocking motion at first, then up and down, the tempo increasing with each thrust. Slocum lifted his hips to meet her, the timing of the thrusts instinctive, until he thought he was going to burst apart in her. He managed to hold back a few moments longer. Her entire body tensed; she gasped aloud, her contractions strengthened and throbbed against him, and he could no longer hold back. The explosion from his scrotum wracked his entire body. He felt his deep, pulsing throbs empty into her. Seconds later another spasm jerked at her muscles. Her breathing all but stopped, small explosions of air puffing from between parted lips. Then she shuddered once more and collapsed on Slocum's chest.

Slocum gently stroked the side of her neck as his own pulses subsided. He felt the sticky wetness against his crotch hair and knew it was a mixture of both their juices. Sweat slicked Iris Funderburk's breast and belly despite the cool breeze as she lay in his arms. Slocum stroked her cheek and was surprised to feel the wetness of tears there.

"Something wrong?" he whispered.

"God, no," she said, still gasping for breath. "Nothing has ever been more right." She reached up and dabbed at her damp cheeks. "Mr. Slocum, you are a wonder. I've never come with that much intensity. I never cried before, never." She drew her head back until she could smile at him. "God, if I could only keep you a prisoner here forever—" Her voice trailed away.

After a few moments she lifted herself from his body and rolled onto her back beside him on the bed.

Slocum lay spent, exhilirated and exhausted. His knees were rubbery. He chuckled softly.

"Something amusing?"

He reached out a hand and stroked her hair tenderly. "It would never work out, Mrs. Funderburk. You'd have me dead of exhaustion within a week."

"Maybe," she said with a teasing smile, "but can you think of a better way to go?"

Slocum couldn't.

She snuggled her cheek against his chest for a long time. The pale lamplight from the adjoining bedroom cast a golden glow over her skin. Her fingers traced the angry white scar on his belly, touched the puckered skin of the bullet wound on his chest.

"Mr. Slocum," she said, "it appears that you've made some people unhappy at one time or another."

"You might say that." Slocum's voice was calm, his mood languid. "The scratch on the belly's courtesy of a half-breed down in Soccorro. He's not with us any longer. The hole in the chest is from my days with Quantrill. I didn't like the way they sacked Lawrence up in Kansas, killing just for the hell of it. I took a bullet for my sudden attack of conscience. Quantrill was not a nice man." Slocum sighed. "That bullet hole still bothers me at times. But the fact I couldn't stop the Lawrence massacre bothers me more."

"One man against a gang of cutthroats? Why should you feel responsible for that?"

Slocum ran a lazy finger along her cheekbone. "Most of what I did in the war was just a job. I did what I was told, like any other soldier. Before it was over I got sick of the killing, but I kept on doing it." He winced at the memory. "Maybe Quantrill was necessary. He was ruthless and a cutthroat, sure enough. I stopped trying to figure out where he fit in the war the day I finally decided I wasn't going to die from the Lawrence bullet."

Iris Funderburk gazed into Slocum's face, the expression in her eyes quizzical. "I don't understand you at all, Mr. Slocum. You're a gentle man, fantastic in bed, with a soft spot for orphans and strays and other helpless creatures. Yet you think little of killing. You're most complex, my friend."

Slocum was silent for a moment. "I don't take killing lightly, Mrs. Funderburk. I had enough of that during the war. Since then I've tried to avoid trouble. Take a human life and you can't put it back. But I don't believe I ever killed a man who didn't deserve it or who didn't push me into it. At least since the war." He kissed her lightly on the forehead. "And you calling me a complicated person is a fine example of the pot calling the kettle black—"

Slocum suddenly jerked upright at the sound of a tap on the door. He reached across Iris Funderburk's body and swept the pistol from the table. He cocked the weapon as the knock sounded again.

"Mr. Slocum?" The voice from outside was a woman's.

"Who is it?"

Iris Funderburk reached out a hand and pushed Slocum's gun hand aside. "Come in, Carmelita," she called.

The door swung partly open and Iris Funderburk's maid peered into the room. If she was shocked by the sight of her mistress in bed with a strange man, it didn't show.

"There is a man to see you, Mr. Slocum. He says it is important. About a man with a blue scar on his face."

"Thank you, Carmelita," Iris Funderburk said. "Mr. Slocum will be down in a moment."

The door closed. Slocum swung his feet over the bed, holstered the Colt, and reached for his clothes. "What will your maid think, catching us like this?"

Iris Funderburk shrugged. "She will think nothing of it. And she will say nothing. She is very loyal, a good friend, and she knows I don't chase just any pair of pants that happen by, Mr. Slocum. Forget that. What are you going to do about Blue McCorley?"

"That depends on what the man downstairs has to say, Mrs. Funderburk." Slocum tucked in his shirt, buckled his belt, and pulled on his boots. He reached for the gun belt on the table. "Most likely, I'll kill him. Or he'll kill me." He strapped on the gun belt and reached for his hat.

"Mr. Slocum?"

Slocum turned to the nude woman on the bed. "Yes?"

"If it comes down to it, kill that dirty egg-sucking son of a bitch."

Slocum touched his hat brim in salute. "You have my word, Mrs. Funderburk, that I will do precisely that." He turned and strode through the door.

Slocum walked down the narrow, hard-packed street, the sounds of the *fandango* growing in his ears. His gaze moved constantly back and forth, alert to any sign of danger. His suit coat was swept back, the tail tucked beneath his belt, leaving the grips of the Colt exposed for a quick draw. Light from lanterns and fireplaces glowed gold in windows of homes and businesses. The light gave a warm, festive mood to the street. Two short blocks ahead, strings of lanterns marked the site of the *fan-dango*, illuminating the dancers and musicians but darkening the shadows in alleyways between buildings.

The fiesta was unfolding in the Plaza de Carretas, known to the Anglos as the wagon yard, the main center of trade in southern Santa Fe. Behind the colorful, swirling costumes of the dancers two dozen freight wagons were parked, their hulks dark and formidable beyond the reach of the light from the festival lanterns.

Now and again Slocum met or passed a cluster of people or a solitary couple strolling toward the lure of lively music ahead or going home, danced out. He scanned the faces as he walked. Blue McCorley was not among them. Some of the men and a few of the women staggered on legs turned unsteady by too much liquor. The heavy pedestrian traffic worried Slocum. A slug once fired didn't care if it hit a combatant or an innocent bystander. More people had been killed by accident than on purpose in gunfights.

Slocum's muscles were loose and relaxed, but something was working on his head and in his gut. It just didn't *feel* right. He stepped into a darkened alley, leaned against the adobe, and drew a deep breath. He ran the conversation with the messenger through his mind again and again. The man in the peon's clothing had spoken in a rapid-fire dialect, the mixture of Spanish and Indian tongue of the mestizo half-breed. Slocum managed Spanish fairly well, but the Yaqui Indian words were all but beyond his grasp. And the peon had crossed himself after delivering the message and accepting the gold coin from Slocum. That in itself was curious.

Slocum went back over the conversation in his mind, word for word, grappling with the translation, the strange lingo, the context in which the words were spoken. He felt his back stiffen as a phrase from the message suddenly took shape. The peon had not said that McCorley was *attending* the *fandango*; he had said that McCorley *awaited* Slocum at the *fandango*. Slocum relaxed, a wry smile lifting the corners of his lips. The difference in those two words was as wide as the Grand Canyon when a man was about to deal with a back-shooter.

Slocum stepped from the shadows and continued his slow walk down the Sur de Camino. A block from the swirl of dancers, he ducked into a narrow alley to his left, worked his way silently through the litter of trash, and turned back onto the street that paralleled the Sur de Camino. He strode cautiously along the narrow street as he tried to put himself in McCorley's boots. The man would be expecting Slocum to come walking down Sur de Camino, studying the crowd of dancers for sight of his prey. It would be an easy step, then, to hide in the shadows of an alley or deeply recessed doorway, wait until Slocum was within point-blank range, and pull a trigger.

Slocum conceded his reasoning was a gamble, but it was a damn sight better hand than he had expected to be dealt. If he guessed wrong, it would cost him nothing but time. If he guessed right, it evened the odds.

Slocum slowed as he neared the mouth of a narrow alley leading toward Sur de Camino. He glanced around the corner. At the front of the alley, just inside the shadows cast by the lanterns, a familiar figure crouched, back turned toward Slocum. Light glinted from metal in the man's hand. *McCorley, you son of a bitch*, Slocum thought, *I can be just as sneaky as you—and now your ass is mine.* He slipped the Colt from its holster and slowly eared the hammer to full cock. He flattened himself against the rough adobe and crept silently to within thirty feet of the big man at the mouth of the alley. Slocum lifted the pistol.

"McCorley!" he called.

Blue McCorley's big body jerked in surprise at the sound of his name. Then he whirled, quick for a man of his size. The muzzle of his pistol swung toward Slocum.

Slocum took his time; handgun work in the dark was part reflex, part deliberation. His finger started to squeeze the slack from the trigger—and Slocum barked a curse. Two women in Mexican costumes had stepped into the street behind McCorley at the instant Slocum was about to fire.

Slocum released the trigger and flung himself flat against the adobe wall. Fire blossomed from McCorley's handgun. The slug ripped into the adobe three feet from Slocum's head. Fragments of the building material peppered his cheek.

"Get out of the way!" Slocum yelled in Spanish. The women only stood and stared, open-mouthed, frozen in fear at the sound of the gunshot.

McCorley fired again as Slocum pushed away from the wall and threw his body into the dirt of the alley floor. McCorley's bullet slammed into the adobe where Slocum had stood. Slocum came to one knee and leveled the Colt, and cursed in disgust and rage as McCorley spun away, dashed between the two women, and sprinted toward the wagon yard.

Slocum held his fire. There were too many innocent bystanders about to chance a shot. He scrambled to his feet, ran to the street, and pushed his way through the crowd of confused and now frightened dancers. Slocum heard the screams of the women, the startled yelps of men, the sudden silence from the bandstand as the music stopped. Then he broke free of the milling crowd, darted into the shadow of a big Studebaker freight wagon, and flattened himself against the thick oak sideboards. *Dammit, Slocum,* he scolded himself, *why didn't you just shoot the bastard in the back when you had the chance?*

Slocum crouched, slipped beneath the big freight wagon, and waited, straining his senses for a sound or a glimpse of movement in the near-blackness of the wagon yard. The light from the *fandango* lanterns barely penetrated the darkness. Slocum mentally cursed the racket from the dancers, tried to block it from his senses. He saw and heard nothing except the excited babble of the crowd.

"McCorley!" Slocum yelled. "You're such a stud horse gunfighter, haul yourself out here and let's see how big your balls are!"

Only silence greeted the challenge. Slocum eased his way from beneath the freight wagon and stood. His heart skipped a beat as a faint sound reached his ears—the metallic click of a loading gate as it snapped shut on a revolver cylinder. McCorley was nearby. A sound like that wouldn't carry far.

Still, Slocum waited, his breathing steady, muscles loose. The best hunters let the game come to them. The seconds dragged on. Slocum became unaware of the passage of time. Time meant nothing to a cougar waiting to pounce. Then he heard a small scuff of boot against sand at his back and the ratcheting click of a hammer drawn to full cock. Slocum spun and crouched, the muzzle of his Colt swinging into line at the hulking body in the shadows.

McCorley rushed the shot. Slocum felt the air crack beside his head and heard the solid whack of lead into the oak planking of a wagon. He let the heavy Peacemaker settle in his hand and squeezed the trigger. The .44 slug tore into McCorley's gut. McCorley staggered a half step, tried to bring his pistol into line. Slocum thumbed the hammer and fired again. The impact of soft lead hammered McCorley back against the tailgate of a wagon. Slocum cocked the pistol again, then watched as McCorley's handgun slipped from his grip. McCorley slowly slid down the tailgate of the wagon. He sat bent over, an arm clasped across his belly.

Slocum walked cautiously toward the downed man, kicked McCorley's handgun away, and stared at the bearded outlaw.

"You son of a bitch," McCorley gasped, his eyes glazed in shock and disbelief in the pale light from distant lanterns. "I'm—I'm gutshot."

"I know, McCorley," Slocum said. "I intended it that way. I'm going to sit here and enjoy watching you die. I'm sure Ed and Eva Storm are watching, too. And the young girl you and your bunch raped. It's over, McCorley."

McCorley's eyes suddenly widened, the shock glaze fading to fear. Slocum realized with a start that McCorley was not looking at him, but at something off to his left.

"It's not over yet, Slocum."

The voice from the shadows hit Slocum an almost physical blow. He turned to see Elaine Storm standing six feet away, the sawed-off shotgun at her shoulder and the hammers eared back.

"Elaine, he's as good as dead now," Slocum said. "Let it go."

Elaine shook her head. "That's not enough, Slocum. I want more than that from this—this *animal*."

The muzzle blast of the shotgun jarred Slocum; fire flashed from the end of the sawed-off barrel. Blue McCorley's crotch disappeared in a spray of bloody mist and dirt. The outlaw screamed. His head dropped and he stared at the mangled flesh between his legs.

"How's it feel, Blue?" Elaine's tone was calm, her voice relaxed. "Does it hurt a little? Well, you hurt me, damn your soul. Now it's my turn." She leveled the shotgun. "I've got a barrel left, Blue."

"Elaine, no!"

Slocum's cry was smothered by the throaty roar of the shotgun. The charge took Blue McCorley in the chest, slammed him back halfway beneath the wagon. McCorley's boots cribbed at the sand, then stilled.

"Now it's over," Elaine said. She stood looking at the mass of mangled flesh that had been Blue McCorley. She didn't resist when Slocum reached for the smoothbore.

15

Slocum snugged the cinch tight on the Nez Percé gelding and stood for a moment, surveying the city of Santa Fe for perhaps the last time. When he rode away from a town, he never knew if the trail would lead him there again some day.

Santa Fe had barely begun to stir in the early light of dawn. Its winding streets and adobe buildings were almost deserted. The day's business had not yet begun and the previous night's transactions in the saloons and bordellos had been concluded hours ago.

The New Mexico authorities had been most understanding about the death of Blue McCorley. It seemed to Slocum they had been downright delighted about it. He hadn't felt it necessary to tell them Elaine Storm had seen him leave the Funderburk hacienda and followed to help send McCorley off to his promised land of fire and brimstone. She had been through enough without having to face questions best left unasked.

The authorities had been almost equally philosophical about the sudden end of Don Pedro Alexandro Corajos and his band. The don would not long be mourned, except by those who would have to find a new buyer for stolen horses. The only loss, the lawmen shrugged, was that since parties unknown had killed the don, the three hundred dollar reward on his head must go unclaimed. But it was perhaps for the best, they pointed out, for that person or persons would not then have to wait out any kind of investigation, and the local jail was not a pleasant place to pass the time. Slocum knew where the reward money would wind up—in the pockets of the local authorities. He didn't object. He liked money, but he didn't like it that much.

He and Elaine were free to go.

Slocum toed the stirrup and swung aboard the gelding. The spotted horse snorted and humped its back, toyed with the idea of pitching for the pure hell of it on a cool morning, but soon settled down under the firm hand on the reins.

Slocum touched the brim of his hat to Iris Funderburk. She sat on the seat of a shiny black buggy trimmed in gold paint and pulled by an equally shiny black mare. She gazed at him, her violet eyes misty.

"Mr. Slocum, thank you—for everything. And if you're ever in Santa Fe again—" Her voice trailed away, the invitation unfinished.

"I'll make it my first order of business to stop by, Mrs. Funderburk. You can count on that." He reined the spotted horse toward the holding pasture where Elaine herded the horses toward the open road and the long ride back to the ranch near Mobeetie.

Slocum still didn't know what had gone on between Elaine and Iris Funderburk the day after the fight with McCorley, but the two had huddled behind closed doors for several hours. Elaine's eyes were red-rimmed when she came out, but the tears she must have shed were long gone.

The most puzzling part of the whole thing was that Elaine Storm and Iris Funderburk suddenly were on a first name basis and treating each other like sisters. Women, Slocum mused, would forever remain a mystery.

"Slocum," Elaine had said, "I want to take the horses back home to the ranch. I've decided that's where my future lies. Uncle Ed gave his life to that place, and I owe it to him and Aunt Eva to see their dream through." Then she smiled. "Besides," she added almost as an afterthought, "I like horses. Will you help me drive them home? Then stay, at least for a while, and help me get the ranch back in shape?"

Slocum couldn't come up with a reason why not. Except Iris Funderburk, and Slocum had the feeling he'd shared her bed for the last time. Elaine did need help, and Slocum sure as hell didn't intend to turn her over to some stranger. He'd invested too much of himself in the girl to see her come to harm now.

At least she wouldn't be hurting for money. Slocum had fondled Corajos's gold, more money than he'd ever seen at one time in his life. Then he surprised himself. He gave the whole poke to Elaine, along with a little more than seven hundred dollars that remained of the money stolen from the Storm Ranch. Slocum had to wash Blue McCorley's blood from almost every coin he'd taken from what was left of the outlaw's body.

He'd handed Elaine a lot of money, but Slocum himself was far from destitute. He had Iris Funderburk's five hundred dollars "escort" money and a bill of sale signed by Elaine for three good Nez Percé ponies. Elaine had even paid him back the twenty-four dollars and change spent for supplies back in Tascosa. He had a full canteen, a solid, comfortable saddle, two Colt revolvers, a good Winchester Model 76, a stout bay half-Morgan gelding to pack his belongings, two bottles of fine liquor, and a pocket full of Havana cigars. By Slocum's standards, he was a rich man.

What the hell else could a man possibly want?

He took the point as the horses moved out at a quick trot, as if they knew they were headed home. Slocum tossed one last glance over his shoulder and saw the shiny black buggy make a turn in the street toward the adobe mansion a couple of blocks away.

There was one thing that still bothered him a bit, he had to admit. He still didn't know who the hell Iris Funderburk *really* was.

At sundown of the fourth day out of Santa Fe, Slocum lay back against his bedroll and studied the first burst of stars overhead. He was a contented man, his belly full, freshly bathed and shaved in the deep, cool spring that nourished the grass in the long, narrow box canyon along the Canadian River.

The mouth of the canyon was only forty feet wide. Slocum had rigged his and Elaine's lariats together to form a makeshift single-strand fence. The horses would respect it, even if they got the urge to roam before dawn. For the first time since Santa Fe he and Elaine would not have to share nighthawk duty. By sundown tomorrow, they would be at the ranch.

Slocum lifted a bottle from his saddle bags and sipped at the smooth bourbon. He sighed and reached for a cigar, wondering if Mr. Charles Funderburk would miss the whiskey and smokes. He fired the cigar with a twig from the fire and squinted through the smoke at Elaine. She sat with her forearms crossed over drawn-up knees, staring thoughtfully at the flames. Her dark skin shone from a fresh scrubbing in the cool water. Her hair was still damp. It tended toward ringlets when wet. That made her look even younger, Slocum thought.

She hadn't talked a lot since Santa Fe, but for the first time since the raid on the Storm ranch she seemed outwardly relaxed. The bitterness was gone from the deep blue, gold-flecked eyes. Slocum couldn't help but feel something was still bothering her, like an itch that wouldn't go away. He worried that the experiences she had been through could have knocked something off center like a wobbly wheel on a buggy, deep inside her mind.

"Something bothering you, Elaine?" he asked.

She lifted her gaze to his, her expression solemn. "Just thinking," she said, "about a lot of things." She sighed. "Slocum, I'm going to need help running the ranch. It's more than I can handle on my own. I plan to use part of this money to buy another section or two. Iris thinks it would be good business to expand the cattle end of the operation. I need a partner, or at least a range boss. Would you be interested?"

Slocum hesitated. It was the best offer he'd had since the Rocky Mountains were just pimples on the prairie. But finally he shook his head in sincere regret. "Thanks for asking, Elaine, but I'm not the kind of man you need for the job," he said. "I know me too well. You'd wake up some morning, the bunkhouse would be empty, and there'd be a set of horse tracks heading toward the mountains. It's tempting as hell, but I guess I'm just not ready to settle down yet."

Elaine nodded. "I understand."

"I'll stick with you until we can find somebody more reliable to help out, though." He dragged at the cigar and exhaled a cloud of blue-gray smoke. "There's another thing you haven't figured on, Elaine. I'm a man with something of a reputation. With a gun. I've made enemies. Some day, some hotshot gunslinger with more guts than sense would happen along. Or maybe some jasper with a grudge. They might be faster or luckier. You've already lost a family. I don't think you would want to lose a friend, too."

Elaine nodded and fell silent for a long time. Slocum listened to the night sounds of the camp. Horses snorted the day's dust from nostrils and ripped at the lush grass along the spring and the small creek it fed. The water rippled over smooth stones as it flowed past their camp. A dying breeze stirred the leaves of cottonwood trees, the soft rustle adding a musical note that reminded Slocum of aspens in the Rockies. In the distance an owl hooted twice and fell silent, apparently waiting for an answer. Faint rustling sounds in the grass marked the prowlings of cottontails, field mice, and other small night creatures.

Slocum felt completely relaxed and content for the first time in what seemed to be weeks. This was a good camp. Good camps were rare on the trails he rode.

"Slocum?" Elaine's voice was soft, with a slight hint of shyness.

"Yes?"

"I had a long talk with Iris Funderburk." Elaine sighed, tilted her head back, and stared at the growing blanket of stars overhead. "She isn't at all what she seems to be."

Slocum chuckled. "I had that much figured out."

"I came to understand a lot of things about her, and even more about myself." Elaine lowered her face until her gaze met Slocum's. "I owe you an apology. For saying all those bitchy things after I saw you and Iris—"

"You don't owe me any apology, Elaine," Slocum interrupted, the heat of embarrassment rising in his cheeks. "I'm the one who should apologize."

Elaine raised a hand. "Let me finish, please. I was jealous, Slocum. Jealous of you and Iris, and what the two of you had together. I see now that it was more than just jealousy. It was anger and envy. After what McCorley and his gang did to me, I don't know if I can ever stand a man's touch again."

Slocum ran a finger along his jawbone, trying to think of something to say. He couldn't come up with anything that wouldn't sound phony.

Elaine stood, picked up her bedroll and carried it to Slocum's side. She looked down at him, tiny lights of fear and apprehension dancing in deep blue eyes. She knelt, loosened the straps of the canvas ground sheet and rolled out her blankets.

"Slocum, I've got to know." Her fingers moved to the top button of her shirt and flipped it open.

Slocum's jaw went slack in surprise as the realization of what she intended finally hit him. A second button parted, revealing the valley between the smooth white swell of firm, high breasts.

"Elaine, wait," Slocum said. He heard the note of near-panic in his own voice, felt the contraction in his throat. "I'm not the right man for this—"

She leaned toward him and placed a slender finger on his lips. "I think you are the right man, Slocum. The right man to repair damaged goods. You can pretend I'm Iris if you'd like." She moved her hand away from his lips, back to the buttons.

"Elaine, it's not you, for God's sake. It's just that I'm not sure what I should do. I couldn't stand to cause you any more hurt."

She blinked against the moisture pooled in her lower lids. "Dammit, Slocum, help me. This—this isn't the easiest thing I've ever done."

Slocum watched in tongue-tied fascination as the last button parted. Elaine shrugged free of the shirt. Light from the campfire traced flickering golden streaks across the smooth contours of perfectly formed breasts, highlighted the dark circles around her nipples. Slocum felt an involuntary stirring in his groin. He had forgotten that Elaine Storm was a woman. He had seen her too long as a girl dressed in boy's clothes.

"Elaine, are you sure—absolutely sure—you want to go through with this?" Slocum suddenly realized he was stalling; for the first time in his adult life, he was afraid of failure. Not of his own physical failure, but of failing the young woman who knelt before him. It was one hell of a big responsibility, one he had never faced before.

"I'm sure, Slocum." Elaine lay back on the blanket, unbuttoned her vaquero pants, stripped them past her hips, and tossed the clothing aside. Her hand instinctively moved to cover the dark triangle of hair at the junction of firm young thighs. Slocum saw in her eyes the effort it took her to move the hand away and expose her crotch to his view. "Please, Slocum," she said, her voice barely a whisper, "don't be angry with me if I—if I can't—"

Slocum reached out, let his fingers gently trace the side of her temple, the curve of jawline, the side of her neck. She winced at his touch, her muscles contracting under his fingers. He continued to lightly stroke her skin until he felt her slowly begin to relax. Then he eased his palm onto the side of her shoulder; she tensed again, but this time her muscles softened more quickly. Slocum slid his hand down to cup her breast, making it a point to keep his fingers away from her tender nipples. He took his time until she again relaxed and was breathing normally.

Slocum brushed the palm of his hand over her left nipple, the touch as light as the stroke of a feather. He heard Elaine's sharp intake of breath. The nipple came erect. He leaned over her, let his lips brush her neck and shoulder, then the swell of her breast, and at length stroked his tongue around the nipple itself. He let his hand slide down her waist to her hip; she stiffened again, her body and mind momentarily rejecting his touch. Slocum moved his hand away.

"No—please," Elaine whispered, her eyes closed. "Don't stop now—help me through—"

Slocum touched his finger to her lips. "I'm with you, Elaine. I just don't want to rush it, to hurt you. Just keep your eyes closed and concentrate on how things feel. If something I do bothers you, say so and I'll stop."

His hand drifted back to her hip, stroked the outside of her thigh, then the inside of her knee. He left it there until he was sure she wouldn't tense up again. His fingers caressed the inside of her thigh, moved slowly higher, until his hand brushed against the dark pubic hair. He kept his hand there a long time, letting the warmth of his palm and softness of his touch soak the tension from her.

Elaine's breathing deepened. Slocum slowly slipped his fingers between her legs and stroked her lightly. He dropped his cheek to her chest and heard her heartbeat quicken. He couldn't be sure if it was from fear or excitement. He felt moisture flow beneath his fingers and knew that at least Elaine was responding to his touch.

"Now, Slocum," she whispered, her voice husky. "Do it now."

Slocum quickly shucked off his clothes and lowered his body onto her. She tensed again, arms at her sides, hands balled into fists. Again he waited until she relaxed, his erection resting against her thigh. *Easy now, Slocum,* he thought; *keep a rein on yourself; this isn't some town whore under you.*

Elaine's thighs parted. Slocum reached down, opened her, and carefully, slowly entered her, trying not to cause her pain or panic. He left his hand at her crotch, his index finger gently stroking the swollen nub of her clitoris. He felt Elaine's heart begin to throb against his chest. Her fists unclenched and her arms came up around his neck, pulled him closer. Her thighs opened wider. Her heels drew up. She pushed her pelvis against his. He heard her soft moan. He withdrew partially, then again eased back into her. Her hips lifted to meet his stroke. Slocum slowly picked up the rhythm. Elaine's hips moved, awkwardly at first, then finding and matching his tempo. Her moans were more audible now. Slocum recognized the soft groans as expressions of growing passion, not of fear or pain. He felt himself swelling inside her. *God, not now,* he thought, *she's not there yet.* He increased the friction of his finger at the upper folds of her slit.

Elaine's breath grew rapid and harsh in his ears. She gasped aloud, then suddenly cried out as a convulsion seized her body. Her arms clamped across Slocum's back as she hunched hard against him, forcing him deep inside. Her cheek pressed against his shoulder, her body jerking involuntarily in the throes of her orgasm. Slocum felt the tight knot as his balls contracted and he could no longer hold back. He gushed into her, riding the crest of release; this time it wasn't an intensity near the edge of pain, but deep, warm spasms of tenderness, of sharing. It was a sensation Slocum hadn't felt before.

They stayed locked together for a long time, sweat slicking the contact of their skin, muscles gone loose and spent in release. Elaine shuddered one last time, then kissed him softly on the lips. Tears flowed down her cheeks. Her eyes sparkled in wonder, relief, and a newfound happiness. Slocum became aware that he was resting most of his weight on Elaine. He grudgingly pushed himself up on his elbows, felt the trailing wetness of sticky fluid as he withdrew, limp. He rolled onto his side and gazed tenderly into her eyes. He raised a hand and gently brushed the tears from her face. There seemed to be a fresh glow in the skin of the small body beside him.

Elaine leaned her head against his shoulder.

"Thank you, Slocum," she said, "for being so patient, so

gentle. And for giving me back something I was afraid I might have lost forever." She sighed, contented. "I'm not afraid anymore."

Slocum held her tenderly, unable to think of anything appropriate to say. He suddenly became aware that for the first time in years, he had felt something more than the release of physical need. He wondered at the sensation he had so briefly touched. Slocum found it hard to even phrase the word in his mind. But if what he felt hadn't been love, he thought, then it must be damn close to it.

Elaine suddenly chuckled, deep in her throat.

"Something turn your giggle box over, girl?" Slocum asked.

"I just realized something. A rite of passage, I guess, like a girl's first period. I've actually had an honest-to-God, man-to-woman orgasm. And I don't feel used, or dirty, or shamed." She sighed again. There was a light in her eyes that Slocum had never seen before. "Slocum, do you realize what you've just given me?"

Slocum thought he had; after all, he'd been there. But he shook his head.

"You've given me back my future," Elaine said, her voice soft, still touched by the wonder of it all, "and you've helped me come to terms with the past. I'll be all right now, Slocum. I know now that I can be a woman." She kissed him softly on the lips. "I'll always be grateful for that—and for everything else you've done for me."

Slocum returned her kiss, then forced a solemn frown onto his face. "I suppose you realize," he said, "that you've just ruined our relationship forever."

Alarm flared in Elaine's eyes. "What did I do wrong?"

Slocum finally let his smile break through. "Not a thing. You just reminded me that you're not my little sister after all."

Elaine grinned impishly at him. "I never saw it that way at all, Slocum. Now, will you please move your sweaty body? You've done your repair work."

Slocum sat up and reached for a cigar. He felt better than he had in a long time. He lit the smoke and reached for the bottle of sour mash.

"Slocum, can I ask you a question?"

"Sure."

"When we—we were—well, were you thinking about Iris Funderburk?"

"Who?" Slocum asked.

Slocum leaned against the blast furnace heat of the strong southwest wind and sucked at a skinned knuckle. Building corrals had never been his favorite chore. But the holding pens on Elaine's newly acquired north section had to be finished before the shipment of new Hereford bulls arrived. Slocum agreed with Elaine's plan to upgrade the herd, but he still fretted and frumped over the necessity of building a place to hold them until it was time to scatter the bulls among the breeding cows.

He wiped the sweat from his face with a shirt sleeve. It didn't help much. The sleeve was as soggy as his face. He was down to the last four rails, cottonwood logs trimmed and snaked from the grove along a creek over a mile away. Then the corral would be finished.

Jug stood hipshot and half asleep, idly switching his tail at the flies that pestered his lathered bay hide. Dragging the logs from the grove had been the big gelding's job, and he had done it well. Slocum had looped the reins loosely over a low brace on the new windmill that chunked and rattled as it spat a steady stream of clear, cool water into the long wooden trough inside the holding pen.

Buying the section of grassland, the windmill, and expanding the ES Ranch's cattle operation had taken a solid bite out of the seed money the horse thieves had provided for Elaine's operating capital.

But Elaine kept surprising Slocum. She had already locked up handshake deals to supply saddle horses to two adjoining ranches, and among ranchers a handshake was a contract signed in blood. He got his biggest surprise after she returned from two weeks of travel with a contract to furnish beef to Fort Worth and Denver construction crews when the rails pushed into the Texas Panhandle. He asked how she knew which railroad would be moving into the Panhandle, and she just smiled and said, "Iris told me."

Slocum sighed in weary satisfaction. Elaine would make out fine, if they could just locate a good, reliable hand to help her out. Slocum was already getting that familiar high country itch again. He and Elaine had talked to a dozen would-be range bosses and rejected all of them for one reason or another.

Slocum flexed his shoulder muscles and bent to lift one of the rails into place, but straightened abruptly as a rider topped the low ridge a hundred yards away. Slocum's hand instinctively went to the Peacemaker at his belt, but he let the hand drop as the rider neared.

The horseman was young, barely in his twenties. His face was smooth, clean-shaven, browned by wind and sun, and he sat the big buckskin gelding like a man accustomed to long hours in the saddle. He carried a rifle in a saddle boot, a handgun in a worn holster riding high at the belt, and a hemp rope was coiled below the saddle horn. He wore rough, sturdy range clothes that showed wear and frequent washing, and a sweat-stained Stetson that had seen its share of rain and wind.

The horseman reined up twenty feet from Slocum. The young man's brown eyes were framed by crow's foot laugh lines when he smiled, showing teeth that were white and even.

"Afternoon," the rider said. "Looks like you could use a hand there."

Slocum nodded. "Be obliged," he said.

The young man dismounted, ground hitched the buckskin, and reached for one end of a waiting pole. He lifted it with an ease that belied the slender body. Slocum crouched and hefted the other end. Within minutes the final poles were secure, lashed in place by green rawhide that would be strong as iron when it dried in the heat.

The rider brushed the cottonwood bark and dirt from his palms and turned to Slocum. "Tad Davis," he said, offering a hand. His grip was firm, the hands callused. Slocum knew this youngster was no stranger to work.

"Slocum. Thanks for the help."

"De nada," Davis said.

Slocum reached for a bottle, took a swallow, and offered it to Davis. The young man shook his head. "Don't drink that much, but thanks anyway." He raised an eyebrow at Slocum.

"I hear there's a rancher out here looking for a hand. The ES outfit. Know where it is?"

"You're standing on part of it, Davis," Slocum said. "Hunting work, are you?"

Davis nodded. "With the right outfit. You the owner?"

"No. Just helping out for a spell." Slocum studied the young man carefully. He liked Tad Davis, and Slocum knew how to read men. It was something a man learned if he wanted to stay alive in the places Slocum had been. "Anything in particular you're looking for, Tad?"

"Some place where the work's honest. A place where maybe I could take part of my pay in young heifer calves." He sighed. "I plan to have my own place some day, Mr. Slocum, and I figure I better start now."

"Mind working for a woman?"

"Not if she knows her business."

Slocum grinned. "This one does, Tad. Little slip of a thing, not much bigger than a minute. But don't let that fool you. She could tackle a bear with a pocket knife and have the varmint skinned before the critter knew she was around. She's at the ranch house now, topping out a couple of broncs. Want to meet her?"

Tad Davis chuckled. "After that description, I'd hate to miss her," he said.

Slocum pulled the cinch tight on the Nez Percé gelding and checked his stock and tack. The young spotted stud and mare stood patiently at halter, linked to Jug by lead ropes. The big bay gelding was dozing again, ears flopped like a mule, unconcerned about the weight of the pack on his broad back.

Slocum turned to Elaine Storm. She stood at his side, Tad Davis waiting a few yards away. Slocum knew she was in good hands now. Two weeks of watching Davis work told Slocum he was not only a top hand with horses and cattle, but a good man, a gentle and patient man, as well. And it didn't take a genius to tell that Elaine and Tad had hit it off. The looks that passed between them told Slocum that the day would come soon when those two were more than boss and employee. Slocum wouldn't be surprised if there were some little Davises on the ground in a few years. Slocum was a bit surprised he wasn't jealous of Tad Davis. It made a big difference when you liked a man, he supposed.

"Slocum, do you have to go?" Tears pooled in Elaine's eyes.

"It's getting crowded here now, Elaine. You don't need me. I've got the horses that I came for, and more. I'd be just a reminder to you of the bad times. You'll have a good life. And if you recall, I told you I'd be moving on some day. That day's here."

She came into his arms and buried her face in his chest. He held her for a long time, fighting the lump in his throat.

"Slocum, thank you." Elaine's tone was soft, sincere. "For everything."

He ran his fingers along her cheek for one last time. "It was my pleasure, Miss Storm." He pulled away and swung aboard the spotted gelding before he changed his mind about leaving. He picked up the slack in the reins.

"Slocum?"

"Yes?"

"Will you come back and see us sometime?"

"Bet on it, Elaine."

Slocum touched his heels to the Nez Percé gelding. The horse snorted and moved out at an easy trot. Slocum looked back from the top of the ridge. Elaine and Tad stood side by side, each with an arm around the other's waist. Slocum raised a hand in a final wave. Elaine and Tad waved back.

Slocum pointed the spotted horse toward the northwest.

The Rockies should be nice this time of year, he thought.

Fury knew something was wrong long before he saw the wagon train spread out, unmoving, across the plains in front of him.

From miles away, he had noticed the cloud of dust kicked up by the hooves of the mules and oxen pulling the wagons. Then he had seen that tan-colored pall stop and gradually be blown away by the ceaseless prairie wind.

It was the middle of the afternoon, much too early for a wagon train to be stopping for the day. Now, as Fury topped a small, grass-covered ridge and saw the motionless wagons about half a mile away, he wondered just what kind of damn fool was in charge of the train.

Stopping out in the open without even forming into a circle was like issuing an invitation to the Sioux, the Cheyenne, or the Pawnee. War parties roamed these plains all the time just looking for a situation as tempting as this one.

Fury reined in, leaned forward in his saddle, and thought about it. Nothing said he had to go help those pilgrims. They might not even want his help.

But from the looks of things, they needed his help, whether they wanted it or not.

He heeled the rangy lineback dun into a trot toward the wagons. As he approached, he saw figures scurrying back and forth around the canvas-topped vehicles. Looked sort of like an anthill after you stomp it.

Fury pulled the dun to a stop about twenty feet from the

lead wagon. Near it a man was stretched out on the ground with so many men and women gathered around him that Fury could only catch a glimpse of him through the crowd. When some of the men turned to look at him, Fury said, "Howdy. Thought it looked like you were having trouble."

"Damn right, mister," one of the pilgrims snapped. "And if you're of a mind to give us more, I'd advise against it."

Fury crossed his hands on the saddlehorn and shifted in the saddle, easing his tired muscles. "I'm not looking to cause trouble for anybody," he said mildly.

He supposed he might appear a little threatening to a bunch of immigrants who until now had never been any farther west than the Mississippi. Several days had passed since his face had known the touch of the razor, and his rough-hewn features could be a little intimidating even without the beard stubble. Besides that, he was well armed with a Colt's Third Model Dragoon pistol holstered on his right hip, a Bowie knife sheathed on his left, and a Sharps carbine in the saddleboot under his right thigh. And he had the look of a man who knew how to use all three weapons.

A husky, broad-shouldered six-footer, John Fury's height was apparent even on horseback. He wore a broad-brimmed, flat-crowned black hat, a blue work shirt, and fringed buckskin pants that were tucked into high-topped black boots. As he swung down from the saddle, a man's voice, husky with strain, called out, "Who's that? Who are you?"

The crowd parted, and Fury got a better look at the figure on the ground. It was obvious that he was the one who had spoken. There was blood on the man's face, and from the twisted look of him as he lay on the ground, he was busted up badly inside.

Fury let the dun's reins trail on the ground, confident that the horse wouldn't go anywhere. He walked over to the injured man and crouched beside him. "Name's John Fury," he said.

The man's breath hissed between his teeth, whether in pain or surprise Fury couldn't have said. "Fury? I heard of you."

Fury just nodded. Quite a few people reacted that way when they heard his name.

"I'm . . . Leander Crofton. Wagonmaster of . . . this here train." The man struggled to speak. He appeared to be in his fifties and had a short, grizzled beard and the leathery skin of a man who had spent nearly his whole life outdoors. His pale blue eyes were narrowed in a permanent squint.

"What happened to you?" Fury asked.

"It was a terrible accident—" began one of the men standing nearby, but he fell silent when Fury cast a hard glance at him. Fury had asked Crofton, and that was who he looked toward for the answer.

Crofton smiled a little, even though it cost him an effort. "Pulled a damn fool stunt," he said. "Horse nearly stepped on a rattler, and I let it rear up and get away from me. Never figured the critter'd spook so easy." The wagonmaster paused to draw a breath. The air rattled in his throat and chest. "Tossed me off and stomped all over me. Not the first time I been stepped on by a horse, but then a couple of the oxen pullin' the lead wagon got me, too, 'fore the driver could get 'em stopped."

"God forgive me, I . . . I am so sorry." The words came in a tortured voice from a small man with dark curly hair and a beard. He was looking down at Crofton with lines of misery etched onto his face.

"Wasn't your fault, Leo," Crofton said. "Just . . . bad luck."

Fury had seen men before who had been trampled by horses. Crofton was in a bad way, and Fury could tell by the look in the man's eyes that Crofton was well aware of it. The wagonmaster's chances were pretty slim.

"Mind if I look you over?" Fury asked. Maybe he could do something to make Crofton's passing a little easier, anyway.

One of the other men spoke before Crofton had a chance to answer. "Are you a doctor, sir?" he asked.

Fury glanced up at him, saw a slender, middle-aged man with iron-gray hair. "No, but I've patched up quite a few hurt men in my time."

"Well, I am a doctor," the gray-haired man said. "And I'd appreciate it if you wouldn't try to move or examine Mr. Crofton. I've already done that, and I've given him some laudanum to ease the pain."

Fury nodded. He had been about to suggest a shot of whiskey, but the laudanum would probably work better.

Crofton's voice was already slower and more drowsy from the drug as he said, "Fury . . ."

"Right here."

"I got to be sure about something . . . You said your name was . . . John Fury."

"That's right."

"The same John Fury who . . . rode with Fremont and Kit Carson?"

"I know them," Fury said simply.

"And had a run-in with Cougar Johnson in Santa Fe?"

"Yes."

"Traded slugs with Hemp Collier in San Antone last year?"

"He started the fight, didn't give me much choice but to finish it."

"Thought so." Crofton's hand lifted and clutched weakly at Fury's sleeve. "You got to . . . make me a promise."

Fury didn't like the sound of that. Promises made to dying men usually led to a hell of a lot of trouble.

Crofton went on, "You got to give me . . . your word . . . that you'll take these folks through . . . to where they're goin'."

"I'm no wagonmaster," Fury said.

"You know the frontier," Crofton insisted. Anger gave him strength, made him rally enough to lift his head from the ground and glare at Fury. "You can get 'em through. I know you can."

"Don't excite him," warned the gray-haired doctor.

"Why the hell not?" Fury snapped, glancing up at the physician. He noticed now that the man had his arm around the shoulders of a pretty red-headed girl in her teens, probably his daughter. He went on, "What harm's it going to do?"

The girl exclaimed, "Oh! How can you be so . . . so callous?"

Crofton said, "Fury's just bein' practical, Carrie. He knows we got to . . . got to hash this out now. Only chance we'll get." He looked at Fury again. "I can't make you promise, but it . . . it'd sure set my mind at ease while I'm passin' over if I knew you'd take care of these folks."

Fury sighed. It was rare for him to promise anything to anybody. Giving your word was a quick way of getting in over your head in somebody else's problems. But Crofton was dying, and even though they had never crossed paths before, Fury recognized in the old man a fellow Westerner.

"All right," he said.

A little shudder ran through Crofton's battered body, and

he rested his head back against the grassy ground. "Thanks," he said, the word gusting out of him along with a ragged breath.

"Where are you headed?" Fury figured the immigrants could tell him, but he wanted to hear the destination from Crofton.

"Colorado Territory . . . Folks figure to start 'em a town . . . somewhere on the South Platte. Won't be hard for you to find . . . a good place."

No, it wouldn't, Fury thought. No wagon train journey could be called easy, but at least this one wouldn't have to deal with crossing mountains, just prairie.

Prairie filled with savages and outlaws, that was all.

A grim smile plucked at Fury's mouth as that thought crossed his mind. "Anything else you need to tell me?" he asked Crofton.

The wagonmaster shook his head and let his eyelids slide closed. "Nope. Figger I'll rest a spell now. We can talk again later."

"Sure," Fury said softly, knowing that in all likelihood, Leander Crofton would never wake up from this rest.

Less than a minute later, Crofton coughed suddenly, a wracking sound. His head twisted to the side, and blood welled for a few seconds from the corner of his mouth. Fury heard some of the women in the crowd cry out and turn away, and he suspected some of the men did, too.

"Well, that's all," he said, straightening easily from his kneeling position beside Crofton's body. He looked at the doctor. The red-headed teenager had her face pressed to the front of her father's shirt and her shoulders were shaking with sobs. She wasn't the only one crying, and even the ones who were dry-eyed still looked plenty grim.

"We'll have a funeral service as soon as a grave is dug," said the doctor. "Then I suppose we'll be moving on. You should know, Mr. . . . Fury, was it? You should know that none of us will hold you to that promise you made to Mr. Crofton."

Fury shrugged. "Didn't ask if you intended to or not. I'm the one who made the promise. Reckon I'll keep it."

He saw surprise on some of the faces watching him. All of these travelers had probably figured him for some sort of drifter. Well, that was fair enough. Drifting was what he did best.

But that didn't mean he was a man who ignored promises. He had given his word, and there was no way he could back out now.

He met the startled stare of the doctor and went on, "Who's the captain here? You?"

"No, I . . . You see, we hadn't gotten around to electing a captain yet. We only left Independence a couple of weeks ago, and we were all happy with the leadership of Mr. Crofton. We didn't see the need to select a captain."

Crofton should have insisted on it, Fury thought with a grimace. You never could tell when trouble would pop up. Crofton's body lying on the ground was grisly proof of that.

Fury looked around at the crowd. From the number of people standing there, he figured most of the wagons in the train were at least represented in this gathering. Lifting his voice, he said, "You all heard what Crofton asked me to do. I gave him my word I'd take over this wagon train and get it on through to Colorado Territory. Anybody got any objection to that?"

His gaze moved over the faces of the men and women who were standing and looking silently back at him. The silence was awkward and heavy. No one was objecting, but Fury could tell they weren't too happy with this unexpected turn of events.

Well, he thought, when he had rolled out of his soogans that morning, he hadn't expected to be in charge of a wagon train full of strangers before the day was over.

The gray-haired doctor was the first one to find his voice. "We can't speak for everyone on the train, Mr. Fury," he said. "But I don't know you, sir, and I have some reservations about turning over the welfare of my daughter and myself to a total stranger."

Several others in the crowd nodded in agreement with the sentiment expressed by the physician.

"Crofton knew me."

"He knew you have a reputation as some sort of gunman!"

Fury took a deep breath and wished to hell he had come along after Crofton was already dead. Then he wouldn't be saddled with a pledge to take care of these people.

"I'm not wanted by the law," he said. "That's more than a lot of men out here on the frontier can say, especially those who have been here for as long as I have. Like I said, I'm not looking to cause trouble. I was riding along and minding my own business when I came across you people. There's too many of you for me to fight. You want to start out toward Colorado on your own, I can't stop you. But you're going to have to learn a hell of a lot in a hurry."

"What do you mean by that?"

Fury smiled grimly. "For one thing, if you stop spread out like this, you're making a target of yourselves for every Indian in these parts who wants a few fresh scalps for his lodge." He looked pointedly at the long red hair of the doctor's daughter. Carrie—that was what Crofton had called her, Fury remembered.

Her father paled a little, and another man said, "I didn't think there was any Indians this far east." Other murmurs of concern came from the crowd.

Fury knew he had gotten through to them. But before any of them had a chance to say that he should honor his promise to Crofton and take over, the sound of hoofbeats made him turn quickly.

A man was riding hard toward the wagon train from the west, leaning over the neck of his horse and urging it on to greater speed. The brim of his hat was blown back by the wind of his passage, and Fury saw anxious, dark brown features underneath it. The newcomer galloped up to the crowd gathered next to the lead wagon, hauled his lathered mount to a halt, and dropped lithely from the saddle. His eyes went wide with shock when he saw Crofton's body on the ground, and then his gaze flicked to Fury.

"You son of a bitch!" he howled.

And his hand darted toward the gun holstered on his hip.

JAKE LOGAN
TODAY'S HOTTEST ACTION WESTERN!